RON DUBAS

Wildflowers Beyond the Road

First published by Ronald Dubas 2022

Copyright © 2022 by Ron Dubas

All rights reserved. No part of this publication may be reproduced, stored or transmitted in any form or by any means, electronic, mechanical, photocopying, recording, scanning, or otherwise without written permission from the publisher. It is illegal to copy this book, post it to a website, or distribute it by any other means without permission.

This novel is entirely a work of fiction. The names, characters and incidents portrayed in it are the work of the author's imagination. Any resemblance to actual persons, living or dead, events or localities is entirely coincidental.

Ron Dubas asserts the moral right to be identified as the author of this work.

First edition

ISBN: 979-8-9853311-0-3

Editing by Lauren Bonk
Cover art by Amy Jacobson

Printed in the United States by Morris Publishing®
3212 East Highway 30
Kearney, NE 68847
1-800-650-7888

FOREWORD

A goal of mine in writing this novel, was to share what it takes emotionally, physically, spiritually, and financially to be a farmer rancher when faced with the life-changing challenge of a serious, extended drought.

I dedicate the parts on the farm in this story to my grandparents who lived through the drought and depression of the 1930s. One family lost their farm because of the financial crisis; the other did not own the farm they lived on, and struggled to feed their large family.

As a young couple, my parents did not raise a crop during the drought of 1954-1956. They raised chickens to sell eggs and milked a small herd of cows by hand for a weekly milk and cream check. My dad also worked construction to make ends meet.

In the drought from 2000-2005, on our farm, we lowered our cattle herd because of a shortage of feed. We direct-marketed meat from our farm during this time. I drove a truck for two of the winters during this drought, and my wife cleaned homes to add income to the family.

I have admiration for the generations that farmed this land before me. They built a heritage by having faith in Our Heavenly Father. How fortunate I am that they passed down their faith, beliefs, determination, and a work ethic that I am thankful for.

I would like to thank my wife, Annette, who supported me through this project. Never once did she question the *why* or my ability to finish this novel. Annette has a true story of her own, moving from Omaha to small town rural Nebraska at age sixteen. She has now been a partner on our farm and ranch for 45 years. Annette, I am proud of all your accomplishments!

To our family friend, Sue, who proofread two of the rough drafts. Your corrections and opinions are valued by not only myself, but also my editor.

The first time I met my editor, Lauren Bonk, I handed her 300 pages of handwritten manuscript. You can only imagine the task that Lauren embarked upon. Even though I am twice Lauren's age, the insight of two generations working together turned out well. Lauren, thank you for helping me through this journey.

— Ron Dubas, 2021

CHAPTER 1

It felt like the twenty-mile-per-hour wind would peel the skin off his body.

The stifling, heavy air resembled the Sahara of Africa, not central Nebraska. It was August, and it had been hot and dry all summer. The wind was sapping the life out of the pitiful looking stalks of corn around him. Every step of his feet kicked up dust for the wind to carry away.

The heat and wind combined with the lack of rain drained the life out of everything, including himself. It was so hot that even the little sweat that his body produced was dried by the wind immediately. His mouth was dry; all that existed was the gritty, bitter taste of dust.

He wondered if he and the land were going through the same happenings of the dust bowl of the 1930s. He had heard the details of the dirty thirties and its depression from his grandparents.

"This must be what hell is like," he figured, muttering.

He knew that, had there been good rain over the previous two months, this corn would be standing eight or nine feet tall with a couple of nice plump ears on each stalk. Swearing, his fists struck out at the puny dried-up stalks no more than four feet tall.

"Damnit!" Strength spent, he fell to his knees in the dust and let the tears fall. Tears stored up from years of disappointment, tears which, as a man, he was forbidden to express. But he knew he wasn't the only man falling to his knees during this drought.

He had been as proud as any man. He always carried his six-foot muscular frame *like a man should*, doing what men were supposed to do: work hard, and don't let anything or anyone get the better of you.

But this drought had come close. He felt beaten physically and emotionally. His two-hundred-pound-body wasn't worth much under these conditions. Trying to make his way back to his pickup, he stumbled. He stumbled under the weight of what had happened to the land, to his livelihood, and to himself. To what he had once believed was his ability to deal with *anything*.

It was ironic, he thought, that his tired legs felt as if they were trying to drag his feet through sopping wet, relentless mud.

By the time he reached the pickup, his strength had finally run out. He barely managed to slump in the driver's seat, realizing he had never felt so alone. The land that he loved was under siege. Mother Nature was torturing both him and that precious land.

"God, what am I going to do? *There's no crop!* There's just no crop!" Defeated, he rested his head, and soon began to doze.

He dreamed that it was raining big, beautiful drops from heaven. It was that perfect kind of rain, the kind where each drop finds its way into the soil. In awe, he stepped out of the truck to stand in the downpour, feeling new energy from this soaking rain.

The air smelled of sweet, fresh clover. There was a clap of thunder, a cracking catalyst unleashing an even heavier downpour. After a few glorious, soaking minutes, he noticed a rainbow forming in the sky. It seemed to stretch from where he stood to only a short distance away; the other end close enough that he could make out a woman standing at its base.

She had no wings, but he was sure she was an angel.

With a bright glow surrounding her, she turned toward him, smiling. With glittering blue eyes, she spoke with a sweet voice as if she was right in front of him and whispered, "Have faith. All will be what is to be."

He awakened with a jolt.

It hurt to open his eyes, and it took every bit of his strength to sit upright in the pickup's seat. Lying there, exposed to the hot sun,

CHAPTER 1

had left him drenched in sweat. With dust blowing into the open window, he found himself caked from head to toe in a thin layer of muck. His dream of rain faded in a hurry, and he was brought back to reality and the disaster of a wilting cornfield surrounding him. As he looked across the field, the waves of heat rose up in another hopeless reminder of failure.

He tried to blink away his sorrow over the crops, reminding himself, "I've put as much work and care into this crop as I have any other in the past twenty-five years."

He needed to find some peace during this drought, so he did his best to turn all his fears and worry over to God.

With everything else around him lifeless and spent, that was the only answer he knew.

The quick bark of his dog, Tellie, interrupted the dusty silence. She was looking up at him from outside the pickup. He opened the door and let her jump onto his lap, licking his hands and nuzzling close to him, trying to comfort him.

He was glad to know she was the only living creature who had witnessed his breakdown. It was just him, Tellie, and the unforgiving heat.

CHAPTER 2

As the summer reached its scorching peak, Leah's anger reached its own point of feverish rage.

Rage toward her abusive husband, rage that pushed her into dragging all his belongings out to the driveway near the stinking, half-full trash cans. The front and garage doors had been continuously open for at least two hours, leaving the lagging air conditioner with the hapless task of trying to cool the house.

She barely noticed the heat. Her temper was hot enough.

She vented her anger through her work, and was grateful — just this once — for the absence of her son. She was cussing like a sailor, and while she had to admit that it felt good, she wouldn't have wanted him to see her like that.

She had the locks changed on all the doors that morning, and when she had cleared the house of her soon-to-be-ex's things, she called him to let him know where his stuff sat. "You'd better pick it all up before 6:00 am unless you want to go find it in the dump."

Smashing the "end call" button, she could feel the rage turning into something else. She practically fell onto the couch, covered in sweat. She was drained: her mind, her body, her heart. She gave in, and closed her eyes.

In her sleep, she dreamed that the doorbell had rung. She hurried to answer the door while straightening her blouse and running fingers through her hair. She suddenly found herself face-to-face with a very handsome man, a wonderful smile on his face. She had

CHAPTER 2

the sensation of the air around her cooling to a wisp of a breeze. The man extended his hand toward her, presenting flowers of a variety she had not seen before. His voice was as gentle as any she had heard as he told her, "These are for you."

Her surprise at all of this overwhelmed her senses. "No, you must be mistaken…" she murmured, but he handed her the flowers as he turned away. "No mistake, ma'am."

She closed the door, feeling uplifted and free. The feeling carved a huge smile on her face as she wondered, "Flowers? Who would send *me* flowers?"

This question was on her mind as she woke from her nap, savoring the dream. Soon, though, the reality of her life and the heat, both suffocating, quickly erased any memory of the dream, the handsome man, and the flowers. The decision Leah had made was starting to feel very real; she had never felt so alone. For now, it was her and the silence.

Her thoughts wandered to her son, Nick, hoping that he was enjoying his fishing trip with his uncle. Nick was the only good thing to come out of her marriage. The house felt lonely, and heavy with pain.

Leah had learned to control her feelings, and tried to demand resistance to her emotions. But she had no energy to fight any longer. It began with the burning of tears in her eyes, then changed to sobbing so fierce that her whole body was shaking.

This was no dream. This was a nightmare.

CHAPTER 3: FIVE YEARS LATER

Joseph Paul Dreul was his legal name.

He had been named after his two grandfathers, Joseph being his maternal grandfather and Paul being his dad's father's name. Immediately after his birth everyone started calling him J.P. No one knows who started the abbreviation, but it stayed with everyone except for his mother, Kate, who always called him Joseph. That name marked a special relationship between the two of them.

J.P. had lived on the farm his whole life. He learned what hard work was at an early age. At age five, his responsibility had been the chickens: watering, feeding, collecting eggs, and closing them in every night so some predator wouldn't steal them a way. When he turned six, his list of tasks grew with the feeding and watering of the sows and baby pigs in the barn. With each year, new jobs piled on. By age eight, he could milk the family's pet cow and sweep hay with a small Ford tractor during the summer haying season. Being the oldest of six, he was also responsible for watching over his siblings.

As he reflected on it now, J.P. could see that he'd been working his whole life… not that this was any different from the other kids he knew. He had known from a young age that he wanted to be a farmer-rancher.

Now, at forty-eight, he was getting tired. He wanted a break. From what he could tell, nothing had turned out right for him. He was in a loveless marriage, an extended drought, and he had run out of energy. Physically, emotionally, and spiritually.

CHAPTER 3: FIVE YEARS LATER

J.P.'s son Daniel was born to be a farmer, following J.P. around like a shadow as soon as he learned to walk. When he turned five, he didn't believe he needed to go to school. Only after J.P. promised that he could help around the farm when he got home each day, did Daniel finally agree to kindergarten. He was a natural mechanic at an early age. If a bicycle had a squeak, he'd roll up his little sleeves and strip it down to try to find the problem. Eventually he progressed to remodeling go-karts, then to vehicles, then finally to majoring in mechanics at a tech school.

It had always been their dream that Daniel would become J.P.'s partner on the farm and ranch. When Daniel graduated with a degree in Ag Mechanics, the farm was in its sixth year of drought. Together, they decided that as long as the drought had its stranglehold on the land, one of them would find employment off of the farm. Daniel's youthful energy, maturity beyond his years and the love that he showed toward his father was a comfort. With J.P.'s recent feelings of burnout, he wondered if it should be *him* to find a job elsewhere. Daniel and J.P.'s dream was not yet complete, but their focus was on the future.

There were many factors rolled together, all touched and complicated by this drought. They were so intertwined that at times J.P. couldn't separate them enough to figure out how to deal with a single one. Claire had gotten her first and only job off the farm with an insurance company six years ago. She caught on to the job so quickly that she was soon promoted to a position that called for a great deal of travel. Gone for weeks at a time, Claire became financially independent almost immediately — a new lifestyle that she enjoyed immensely. He shouldn't have been surprised; Claire wasn't from Frankton originally. She was an only child, moved from Omaha to this small town by her parents when she was a junior in high school — too young to appreciate the move and old enough to feel resentful about it. With long, dark hair and eyes the color of melted chocolate chips, she was a sight to behold. They had chosen each other and, whether it was carefree youth or a grudging resignation to her life in Frankton, it had clearly been the wrong decision for both of them. With her new job taking her away from home, it was obvious that she had gotten what she wanted — financial independence. She wasn't shy about flaunting that, either, especially to J.P. as the drought began to threaten the farm's finances. He could still hear their last big fight in the back of his mind, could see the ugly scene unfolding like an old film reel in his memory.

Claire had been pacing in the kitchen, repeatedly running her fingers through her hair. J.P. watched, silently, from the table, until she finally stopped at the counter and polished off the glass of amber liquid that was resting on the formica. She shuddered at the burn, and exhaled loudly. "J.P., what are we going to do?"

Knowing from experience that she had a lot more to say, he simply shook his head.

"This is the third year. The *third year* of this damned drought. The farm payments are piling up. You're miserable, and don't even try to deny it. I sure as hell know I am."

"Now, Claire —"

"How do you plan to make these payments? Praying, huh?" Her voice started taking a tone that he'd heard before, and it was a tone that made his blood itch in his veins. With an ugly sneer, she added, "Maybe if you just *pray a little harder* money will rain down from heaven. Is that your plan?"

She knew exactly which line to cross to get a rise out of him. "Claire, please!" J.P. stood up abruptly, slamming both hands flat on the dining table. "Just settle down!"

They stared at each other for what felt like an eternity before Claire let slip a dark, quiet chuckle. "That's your answer to everything. Settle down." She grabbed the top few papers off of the haphazard pile in front of J.P. and threw them on the floor. "Screw you, J.P. I hate this damned farm. We give and give, and all it does is take. It's like a frickin' black hole, just waiting to drag us into oblivion."

CHAPTER 3: FIVE YEARS LATER

J.P. tried to untense his shoulders, and sat back down in the chair. "I know it's challenging, Claire. I get it. But we've always managed to make things work." He reached forward and placed his hand on hers. "We can *still* make things work." He tried to add some warmth to his voice, to let her know he wasn't just talking about the farm.

She ripped her hand away from him like she'd been bitten by a rattlesnake. *"Challenging!"* Claire screamed. "Running a marathon is challenging, J.P. This? This is impossible." Again, her voice had changed. The poison had suddenly leached out of it, leaving only a hollow echo of anger. "I'm out of energy, J.P." Tears filled her eyes as she ripped her car keys off the hook by the door. "I can't take it anymore."

He hadn't seen her since.

At first J.P. was lonely, but then as time went on he realized it was only a physical absence. The two had been emotionally separated for years. It seemed to J.P. there was no true bond, even from the start of their marriage. So, adjusting to her being *physically* gone came rather easily. Actually, it was more difficult to adjust to her being at home for any length of time. For the first year, J.P. had slept in the basement when Claire was back. Her visits were fewer and further apart, and eventually she stopped coming to the farm altogether, simply staying at her parents' in town.

As J.P. and Claire's relationship faltered the last five years, J.P. and Daniel became increasingly closer. It was J.P. who had always been there for Daniel through his teenage years, and now Daniel wanted to be there for his dad. He wanted to be back on the farm. If J.P. was going to get a job, it wasn't going to be local. He loved the farm, but he was ready for a change. J.P. started watching the big city newspaper classifieds for jobs that might catch his fancy. He noticed the ad that stated "Vehicle oil change, tire repair, and brake installation. George's Service Station." This job was in the city, 130 miles from the farm.

J.P. immediately showed Daniel the ad. "What do you think?" he asked, a little nervous. "Think I should go in for an interview?"

Surprised but pleased, Daniel chuckled. "Sure, Dad. I've got to admit, though, I thought it'd be me who found a job off the farm."

Daniel was a young man wiser than his years. He had been concerned for his dad, especially when he was off to college. The two of them almost never talked about Claire, and he could tell the marriage was taking its toll.

J.P. called for an appointment to interview for the job, setting it for April 18th. The time was to be eight o'clock in the evening, which worked out well for both men. There would be no one else at the station after closing time to disturb them, and J.P. could get a day's work done before leaving.

When April 18th came around, J.P. could feel the nervousness in his stomach. Excited, too, his steps were quick as he worked throughout the day. Before he left, he made sure to slide a pack of Rolaids into his shirt pocket. For as long as he could remember, his nervous energy was always paired with a fiery, nagging heartburn. He knew he should probably talk to his longtime doctor about it, but just couldn't quite bring himself to make the call.

As J.P. drove toward the city, his thoughts and feelings raced from one end of the scale to the other. He was sad about the idea of leaving the farm; he hadn't worked anywhere else in his life. Other than his own dad, he'd never had a real boss before. There was a deep, tugging feeling in his soul, telling him it was the start of an adventure, an exploration, possibly a search. The question was: for what or whom?

CHAPTER 4

George had grown up in this gas station, much like J.P. had grown up on the farm.

George's dad had built the station in 1948 after returning from WWII. George learned the know-how of the station at an early age by washing windshields, checking air in tires, and pumping gas. The only time George was away from the station were the two years he served his country in the Marines. 1965 and 1966. He was in Vietnam for fifteen months and had never told anyone what he went through. Only he and his nightmares remembered. Other than his understanding wife, George let very few people into his personal circle.

Because of the heavy turnover of personnel during Vietnam, George had quickly advanced to the rank of squad leader and had the responsibility of leading men into battle. He had learned some eye-opening things about the very nature of men, and had acquired a good instinct when choosing who to trust... and who not to.

Over the years, George had many different men help him in the garage. Some had been to mechanical school. Some were good, some even lasting five years on the job. Truth be told, though, most of the guys didn't last more than a few days. Some without common sense, others without a healthy work ethic, many without either. For the past several months he had been going it alone — except for his bookkeeper who took care of the office. But, as much as he hated to admit it, he was now over sixty. He needed someone else to help carry the load of the labor in the garage.

George was anxious to meet this guy from the farm. He was older than most applicants for the job, and had to be coming with hands-on experience with tools. Well, this is at least how George usually envisioned what farmers were like. He also knew that the drought had been causing ongoing hardship in quite a few areas in central Nebraska. Surely, if this guy ran his own farm and equipment, he could do oil changes, fix tires, and take care of brake replacements.

George anxiously watched J.P. pull up to the station, but his well-kept pickup and firm handshake quickly dispelled any fears he had. This fellow knew how to work. He knew it was early, but he was pretty sure this was a man he could trust.

After a few minutes of introduction and chatting about the drought that affected the farm, George asked J.P. about himself.

"Sir, I'll be real honest with you. I've never had a job off my farm. Born, raised, and still working."

"Well, now," George smiled, "that's actually nice to hear."

"I'm the fourth generation on my dad's side to farm that land, and hopefully my son Daniel's on track to be the fifth."

"A son? Are you married?"

Reluctantly, J.P. explained the details of his estranged marriage. Determined to keep the mood positive, however, he added, "I'm positive I can handle everything you listed in the job description, George. All I need is a chance to learn your routine."

J.P.'s open and honest nature touched George, and he opened up. He told J.P. about his dad building the station after his return from WWII. How he had virtually grown up in the station. He chuckled, "Hell, I can remember fixing my first bicycle tire here."

J.P. and George had been so busy talking since he had walked in that J.P. took a moment and looked around the station. George noticed J.P.'s interest and said, "Let me show you around."

As J.P. looked and walked around the station, he was taken aback. The service station was perfectly preserved; it was as if they had stepped back in time. Everything was as it was in 1948. All of the product signs were metal. The four overhead doors were narrow,

CHAPTER 4

and the office was glass-enclosed with a small opening that stated "CUSTOMER SERVICE." J.P. was in awe of how unique it all was. George told him that the majority of his business came from loyal, long-time customers, with few new people stopping in. "Because we're on 27th street, we get a lot of gas-only customers who need directions to the stadium or capitol. Most people ask how to get to the football stadium and the Capitol building with questions about parking." J.P. smiled knowingly and George chuckled, pleased to have found a kindred spirit.

"Normal working hours are 7:30 to 5:00 with a half-hour dinner. Tuesdays I'll either order tacos from a restaurant down the street, or Martha will bring in a casserole. You also usually get a short break in the morning and afternoon." He adjusted the collar on his work shirt and continued, "And if you want more work, you can come in on some Saturday mornings." George paused, hopefully giving his prospective hire a moment to think, then asked, "What do you think? Are you interested in the job?"

"Yes, sir!" J.P. answered quickly, and with a smile. "I do have a request, though. If we have a harvest this fall, I would like at least a week off to return home."

George nodded, "If things work out that long we should be able to work around that."

With a long handshake, it was decided. "When can you start?"

"How about a week from today?"

"That's just fine. I'm looking forward to it. Besides me, the only other person here's a gal named Leah. She's my bookkeeper. Has been since she was a teenager."

J.P. thought he was saving time by meeting George in the evening, because he planned on going back home that night. He hadn't planned on getting the job this quickly. Now he needed to find a place to live in just one week. With a newspaper under his arm and a key to a last-minute motel room, J.P. set out to find himself a house. While he knew he wasn't interested in an apartment, he also wasn't too worried about finding the perfect place. He had already made up his mind: this was going to be just a house. *Home* was on the farm.

That night he had a difficult time falling asleep. Repeatedly, he asked himself, "What are you doing here?" and, "How are you going to leave the farm?"

Daniel was the only one who knew about his city job. He hadn't discussed it with his parents, for a few reasons. He knew his dad would only think of it as a crazy thing to do. His mom would be supportive but sentimental. His wife, Claire, was a mere fleeting thought; J.P. didn't care what her take was on this decision. He tossed and turned, at times sweating and the next minute shivering cold.

J.P. thought he was totally alone in the city, but he knew what to do. Finally giving up the fight, he got on his knees next to the bed and talked to his God.

CHAPTER 5

The next morning, he called about the houses he'd found in the classifieds. He could look at one of them at 9:30. It turned out to be small but furnished; just what he needed. It was only about 20 percent of the space of his farm house, but he reminded himself that this house was just a house. J.P. decided on the spot to rent the little place. He gave the woman showing the house a down payment and filled out a background form for her so she could be sure she was getting a reliable renter.

As he was looking through the classified ads again in the jobs section, another advertisement jumped out at him. "*Needed, part-time groundskeeper.*" It was at a local golf course, which sounded pleasant enough. J.P. drove out to the course and smiled. It was beautiful, a different beauty than that of the farm. The manager told him that the job was mowing the rough on the course in the early mornings.

"If it's alright with you, I'd like to start at 4:00 or 5:00 in the morning. That'd get me to my other job in plenty of time."

"So long as the work is done and done well, that's just fine with me. And don't forget, employees get one free round of golf a week. Just let the clubhouse know."

J.P. laughed to himself. He wasn't a golf nut — in fact he hadn't golfed more than a dozen times in his life — but it seemed like a good deal. It came to him that with these two paying jobs he still would work fewer hours a week than he would at the farm.

As J.P. drove home, his mind was spinning with the decisions he had made in less than twenty-four hours. Yesterday at this time, he was busy doing what needed doing around the farm. Now he had two new jobs and a house rented in a city he'd never lived in before. His thoughts were full of wonder and excitement for the future, but there was anxiousness as well. He had one more task at hand: telling his family.

After getting back to the farm, J.P. did his daily chores: feeding cattle in the yards and checking the herd for newborn calves. Then he popped a rolaid, and drove three miles to his parents' place to talk to them about his upcoming move.

That conversation went about as he expected.

Herb, his dad, got mad, of course. Totally against the idea of his leaving the farm, he called J.P. "A damned fool!" and stormed out the door. A minute later, he spun the tires of his old red pickup and peeled out of the driveway. That was the same anger that J.P. had been putting up with from Herb his whole life. If he were being honest, he'd admit he was rather relieved his dad was gone so he could have a heart-to-heart talk with his mom.

J.P. and Kate sat down and sipped on a cup of coffee.

"I'm not leaving the farm, Mom, I'm just going to do something different for a while."

J.P. was surprised when his mother answered, "I understand, Joseph."

That was the way it was between the two of them: similar thoughts and almost always on the same page. He continued quickly telling Kate about his jobs and the little house he had rented. He didn't stay long, since he had many things to do the rest of the week. Before he left, J.P. and Kate gave each other a hug.

As he left the drive, she watched from the kitchen window. She was not saddened by Joseph's decision; in fact, she was truly relieved. The six years of drought had put a strain on everyone in the area. Many people had searched for jobs off of the farm, so it

CHAPTER 5

wasn't a huge surprise. Kate knew Joseph's situation with Claire was yet another burden he was carrying. He never spoke of his feelings about his marriage, but she knew the drought and Claire were taking their toll. The smiles came less often, the brightness in his eyes was less common, and she could tell the spring in his step was buried under all the weight on his shoulders. Kate believed it was good that Daniel — with youth and energy — was back on the farm, so Joseph could find the things that had been taken from him, whether he realized they were gone or not.

For the next week, J.P. and Daniel worked overtime getting the crops planted and cattle moved to pasture for the summer. As J.P. began to adjust to the idea that he was leaving the farm, he started to see the things around him differently. He knew he was going to miss working with Daniel every day. They had grown closer since he had returned to the farm and J.P. could see how college had matured his son. He was going to miss the daily visits with his mother and her home-cooked meals.

Taking an extra moment to watch Daniel head across the field with the planter, he savored the fresh smell of soil turned over in the field. He took extra time to appreciate his cattle, lovingly watching the new cow-calf pairs. He noticed how the cow cared for her calf by licking it, cleaning and building the bond between them. He chuckled at the calves nursing off their mothers, with foam forming around their mouths from the plentiful milk. He found that he was almost jealous of the calves lying flat on the ground, taking in as much sun as possible. And with comfort, he noted that the grass was getting a better start this year; it was a darker shade of green from the healthy snows this past winter.

As J.P. was checking fences for breaks, he looked for the wildflowers that were just breaking through the soil. It was one sure sign that the soil was warming; an important factor in the timing of planting crops. J.P. made sure to pet his two dogs more than normal. He would never take them to the city. Their carefree lifestyle belonged on the farm, with open fields and plenty of room to run.

He watched the squirrels on the tree where he had placed a feeder, and smiled at the wild game who shared his farm. Rooster pheasants on the road, showing off their beautiful colors and crowing; trying to win the favor of any hens in the area. It was mating season.

Packing for the move was difficult. J.P. was leaving more than just the farm; he was leaving a way of life that can only be understood if you've lived it for a lifetime. A farmer comes to understand that his most important partner is Mother Nature. She is the most unpredictable of partners, but when she shows a farmer her favor she's most generous. He'd lived within five miles of this farm for the whole forty-eight years of his life. His roots ran deep and his faith in God was strong. Both were planted nearly one hundred years ago by his great grandparents who had settled two miles from J.P.'s farm.

J.P. had thought long and hard about the move, and finally decided that leaving was not a sign of failure. It was just a... kind of sabbatical in order to experience a part of life he had never known; what life off the farm was like. Over the years, J.P. seldom left the farm for the night, and if he did it was never for more than one. Filling a duffle bag wasn't going to do the job for this move. He found an old suitcase and stuffed it with clothes, followed by two garbage bags and two paper bags. For appliances, he loaded a microwave, crockpot, and a charcoal grill. J.P. didn't plan on leaving for the city until he absolutely had to: the Sunday evening before his first day on the job.

The week went faster than J.P. had hoped. Many a time he'd find his head in a tizzy about leaving the farm. Then he would tell himself that he'd be back the next weekend.

Everything would survive and be fine.

Kate had made sure that J.P. would stop for Sunday evening supper before he left. There was the usual family gathering every Sunday afternoon at his parents.' Some would play cards, others played checkers or dominoes. Several of his nieces and nephews

CHAPTER 5

were expressing their feelings about his moving by hugging him or putting their hand on his shoulder, looking to see how he was playing his cards. After having an early supper, J.P. knew it was time for him to leave for the city. Even though everyone knew that they would see him again next weekend and most weekends after that, they all still acted as if he was leaving and never coming back.

His son, Daniel, was last to give him a big hug at the pickup door. His son was taking this harder the J.P. would have guessed, and he shared Daniel's feelings. They had always had a bond. As J.P. drove out of the farmyard, he and Daniel knew exactly what each other was feeling.

Arriving at his house in the city at dusk, J.P. fumbled some with the key and lock. He opened every window in the little house to freshen it. The thought occurred to him that there might not actually *be fresh air* in the city.

As he made trips back and forth from the Dodge to the house while unloading, he noticed the bare spots in the lawn on both sides of the door. J.P. thought it would be a good place to plant some flowers. He started two lists: 1) Things He Forgot From Home and 2) What He Needed From the Store.

His cell phone rang. It was his mom, wanting to know if he had made the trip safely. He gave her the details of his little house and the progress of his unpacking. He smiled to himself as he hung up.

He could tell that his family was not about to let him go.

CHAPTER 6

George always arrived at the station by 7:30, and this morning he found his new employee waiting for him.

He gave J.P. another quick tour of the shop and a rundown on how he liked to handle things. J.P. set to work immediately, making himself familiar with his work area and putting a little cleaning touch on some of the tools. J.P. wasn't the kind of man who waited around for someone to tell him what needed to be done. He liked to keep busy.

He wasn't doing it to impress anyone; it was his way, but George was impressed anyway. He wasn't in the shop more than ten minutes when the first customer pulled in needing an oil change. J.P. was too busy to notice when the only other employee, Leah, arrived.

George had told Leah about J.P. after their first meeting, about how the drought had driven him to seek a job in the city. He also mentioned a son, Daniel, who would be running the farm.

"He made an awfully good first impression, Leah. He seems genuine in just about everything he does."

Leah nodded, but in her head, she thought, "Yeah, right!"

Over the years, the station had seen so many guys come and go that Leah was more than a little jaded. She figured J.P. to be some *plow boy*.

Upon meeting J.P. that morning she knew she could react one of two ways: she could be cordial and pleasant... or she could choose her normal response, which was to simply ignore the man.

CHAPTER 6

When George introduced them, Leah made no eye contact with J.P., just a glance in his direction and an expressionless "Hello." She wondered to herself about how long J.P. would last on this job. Leah had been working at the station for thirty years and had seen nearly one hundred guys come and go.

J.P. had planned on a "Hello," with a smile and a probable handshake with Leah, which was the norm for him. Immediately, J.P. knew Leah had no intention of warmth.

As he turned around to return to work, Leah lifted her eyes from her desk and absentmindedly fixed her gaze on the line of his broad shoulders. Her interest in J.P.'s physique surprised her. Since her divorce five years ago, she hadn't met a single man who raised any interest for her. In fact, she had begun to think that she would spend the rest of her life alone — not finding any one man appealing to her. One thing that shined her interest was that J.P. was near her age.

As J.P. reached the door of the office he glanced back, and Leah's eyes were locked on him. When their eyes met Leah quickly looked away.

J.P. stood there for a few seconds, but there was no furthering of the introduction. J.P.'s first thought "Does she ignore everyone? Is it just me?" Even though she appeared unfriendly, J.P. had noticed something special about her appearance, and realized that it was her eyes. They were an illuminating blue: pretty in color, but hard and cold at the moment. Her eyes were framed by blonde hair that was showing a few strands of white.

He knew he should get back to work, but as J.P. took a few more steps toward the shop area, he stopped again and glanced at Leah. She was busy at her desk as if nothing out-of-the-ordinary had taken place. He didn't take their introduction as an insult, and thought "Maybe she had something else on her mind... maybe she's just timid." He tried not to make judgement of her coolness toward him, but he did believe there was a story in those distant, pretty eyes. Resisting the urge to reach for his pack of Rolaids out of habit, J.P. returned to his job and wondered if he would ever know the full story.

Leah and her family were neighbors and friends with George and his wife, Martha. They had no children of their own and had always adored Leah. As a child, she was irresistible with her blue eyes, blonde hair, and full cheeks. At age fifteen, Leah had started helping around the station with the job of tidying up the office and the customer counter. It expanded to answering the telephone and taking messages and, as time went on, Leah could write up customer charge tickets at the service counter for work to be done. She had a knack for numbers and enjoyed her job. By her senior year in high school, Leah was keeping the account books for George's Service station.

George enjoyed having Leah around. He knew her background and character; she was someone he could trust. When she completed high school, he promised her, "If you go to community college and get your degree in accounting, you can have this job as long as you want." This added to George's desire to keep the station open — Leah had kept her end of the deal and he wanted to keep his. Leah had now been there for thirty years, and had expanded her bookkeeping services to other small businesses.

Nineteen years earlier, Leah had fallen for a man ten years older than she. Heath, with his coal black hair and an ever-trimmed beard. He had been her only official boyfriend and, besides the occasional date, her only romance. After fifteen years of cold, frustrating marriage she felt suffocated under the weight of loneliness. From the very beginning, Heath had been controlling and mentally abusive. Leah shut down emotionally; she wasn't the same person George had come to know. Gone was the Leah of the past, with the twinkle in her eyes and a warm, lovely smile.

Any physical contact with her husband became out of the question. There was no touching, no hugs, and certainly no sex. Eventually, she even avoided looking at him.

The only love at this point in her life was her son, Nick. Now seventeen years old, he was a well-rounded and likeable boy, despite his dad. He was a fine student in school and a real social butterfly.

CHAPTER 6

Nick was involved in many school and neighborhood activities, but he was always there for his mother. They were a team.

Leah decided that she'd had enough of that life. Heath had a good job and always had money... but that was the problem. It was *his* money and he did what he wanted with it, which usually meant drinking too much at the bar and playing pool — with *his* money on the line. If he won, he came home arrogant and if he lost, he came home angry.

The abuse always started with words: lazy, ungrateful, *the biggest mistake of his life*. If Leah showed defiance, he'd grab her by the shoulders and shake her until he left bruises... until the last time. The last time, he slapped her across the face in a fit of rage. She barely remembered how it all happened, but she knew it was time to stand up for herself and her son. She called her brother, who raced over. After twenty minutes of arguing and physical intimidation, Heath had decided he'd "...had enough of this interrogation!" and stormed out.

As soon as he left, she began to pack away all his belongings and anything that reminded her of him. She placed the boxes by the garbage, and called that morning to get the locks changed.

She finally called him one dreary morning and said, "All your crap is in boxes and sitting by the mailbox. Unless you want to kiss them goodbye on garbage day you'd probably better come collect." Taken off guard by her aggressiveness, he mumbled some kind of response but she hung up before trying to really listen. She didn't see him pick up his stuff, but it was gone later that morning.

She didn't see or hear from Heath at all in the next three months. Through the grapevine she'd heard that he'd found a new girlfriend; even though she wanted him gone, it was still a hard truth to swallow. "Good riddance," she thought, and felt sorry for whoever he was making miserable now that she was out of the picture.

Her dreadful marriage was over.

After that, it was just her, Nick, George, and Martha. With their support and her job at the station, she felt grateful, and as satisfied as she thought she'd ever be.

CHAPTER 7

During his tour of station operations, George had told J.P. that he could take a break both in the morning and afternoon. J.P. was accustomed to having a bowl of M&M's around his shop at home, and carried a freezer bag of them in his truck as he worked around the farm. So it was a surprise to George and Leah when their newest employee brought out his bowl of M&M's in the small room they used for breaks and lunch.

It varied from every kind of M&M: plain, peanut, almond, and — Leah's favorite — peanut butter. She remarked that first morning after taking a few, "These aren't healthy enough to have just laying around the break room all the time!"

J.P. allowed himself a small smile, and responded by asking Leah, "Haven't you heard that M&Ms can actually be a perfectly acceptable form of diet?" She gave him a puzzled look and J.P. went on, "Sure, all you have to do is *imagine* the reds are apples, the yellows are bananas, the green is lettuce, and the orange is, well, oranges." George shook his head and gave a chuckle while Leah *almost* smiled. It was more of a smirk, but she thought pleasantly to herself, "A country bumpkin who's also a wise ass, huh?"

The atmosphere around the station was usually quiet, the only noise being George and his regular buddies giving each other a hard time. This morning the only talking was George and J.P., getting acquainted with each other about the repair and service jobs at hand.

It was the *silence* that was different this morning around the

CHAPTER 7

station. George was comfortable with J.P., and had to admit he liked almost everything about him. Leah tried to concentrate on her work, but she found she had a hard time focusing with this new guy around. In fact, she was upset with herself because of the distraction. What was causing her to react like this?

J.P. himself was working at a steady pace, trying hard not to think about the farm, and trying to forget that he was living in the hubbub of the city.

When the noon hour came, J.P. excused himself to go to his pickup, and came back with his lunch box in one hand and a vase holding a red rose in the other. Much to George and Leah's surprise, J.P. set the rose on the break room table.

Leah scoffed, "What is that?"

J.P. smiled and simply responded, "For its beauty." Taken aback, they weren't sure how to respond, but it was clear the M&Ms and flowers were something of a ritual for J.P.

The break room was pretty quiet as they ate their lunches. J.P. and George were discussing a brake job that J.P. was doing on a Ford Explorer. The smell of the rose seemed to penetrate even through the smells of oil and gas that permeated everything in the service station. As Leah was finishing her lunch she couldn't help but comment on the rose.

"You know that flower will just die and you'll have to throw it away. You'll be lucky if it lasts a week."

J.P. studied her for a moment, and in a slow and deliberate voice replied, "We can't really compare the length of a flower's life to that of a human's. The way I see it, the job of the flower is to bring joy. I believe that if a flower brings any comfort or smile to anyone it has had a successful life."

Leah stood for a moment in silence, clutching the empty sack from her lunch. How could she respond to the philosophical ramblings of this stranger who'd come into their lives? After only knowing this stranger for a few hours, she had to admit her curiosity was piqued. What was it that created a man like this? A man who shares his ideas in the same way he held his physical presence — a picture of strength, full of consideration and deep conviction.

Realizing how long she'd been standing there, her cheeks flamed red with embarrassment. Thankfully, J.P. went on, for Leah's benefit, to say that, "On the farm, I see thousands of wildflowers. Some summers the pastures and road ditches are full of them. Sometimes I would think, 'What a waste,' when no one gets to see them. Now I realize that they are creations of God's and *He* sees them, so none of them are a waste." Leah raised an eyebrow at that, and J.P. continued, "But, I still think a flower that makes its way into a vase is the fortunate one."

She couldn't put her finger on it, but this explanation gave Leah a sense of ease, rather than furthering her embarrassment. She was trying to think of a label for this new guy. Was he good, bad, or just different? She hadn't decided yet. She also realized that she needed to think a little harder about the comments and questions she threw out at this new, surprising man.

Monday after work, Leah called her lifelong friend Julie. "Can we go for a walk? I have to tell you about my day." Best friends since Junior High School, Leah and Julie have walked every other day for years.

From the very beginning of their walk Julie could tell something was different, by the way Leah was rambling.

Finally, she took a pause long enough to mention, "We have a new guy at work."

"Oh, yeah?" Julie smiled, secretly. "What is he like?"

Leah had been *dying* to give Julie the details, and they all came spilling out. As she enthusiastically described J.P., her unusual excitement was easy to pick up. She told her about the M&Ms and the rose, how he always had a philosophy for something. The sudden, surprising reaction to a man was not lost on Julie, and by the time Leah was done talking, it was clear she was flustered. Julie could only grin; she'd been waiting a long time for this.

Leah caught the grin. "Hey! What's so funny?"

CHAPTER 7

"You!" She gave her a playful punch on the shoulder. "I've never heard you so excited about a man!" Leah got Julie back with a little nudge from her elbow. "Stop it!"

"Hey, I didn't do anything! You were the one rambling."

They kept walking and left the topic alone, but Leah couldn't deny it: she *was* excited.

CHAPTER 8

Tuesday morning at the station before they started work — and before Leah was at the office — George pulled J.P. aside. "Listen, J.P, I'd like to apologize for Leah's rude behavior when I introduced you yesterday."

"Ah, well, George, thanks for that, but it's not necessary."

"Well, I think it is. She went through a rough divorce about five years ago, and it's pretty common for her to feel cynical and bitter."

"That does explain the chilly introduction, but that's alright." He paused and looked his new boss in the eye. "We've all got a story we carry within ourselves."

George stopped still in his step, just as he had so many times in the jungles of Vietnam.

J.P.'s words sounded as sharp and clear as the rifle fire in the closeness of battle, and George fought the urge to drop to the floor. The safety of the ground still had a pull, even after all these years. Instead of giving in to the urge to take cover, George slowly raised his left hand and rubbed his cheeks; the left side with his thumb and the right with his forefinger. This was a ritual he had relied on thousands of times over the years, when the war entered his mind. He could still feel the physical scars that had *almost* disappeared with nearly forty years of healing. Most people didn't notice them unless they were very near, or were looking for them.

Each time he touched the scars, he felt the proof of his healing. Physically, George's wounds had been repaired, but his mind and

CHAPTER 8

emotions still needed more time.

George knew he had been watched over by heaven that soggy September afternoon. With the pouring rain and their movement at a snail's pace, the Marines and the Vietcong did not hear or see each other until only a hundred feet separated them. Their fight lasted two long minutes. After a hand grenade killed three 'Congs and wounded three more, they surrendered... but George had been hit. The bullet went through his cheeks; miraculously it didn't break his jaw bone. He would wear partial dentures the rest of his life, and suffered headaches and sinus problems for years.

George shook himself and came back to the present, rubbing his cheeks. He nodded at J.P. and thought to himself, "How did he know?"

When Leah awoke on Tuesday morning, still on her mind was the new guy. She was frustrated with herself, with her mind and body being affected by a man. She hadn't felt this way since her teenage years, overcome by a crush on some boy.

In her lighthearted mood, Leah chose a floral blouse filled with vibrant yellows and deep blues to wear to work. As she started the work day behind her desk, it was clear to everyone, most importantly herself, that her attitude was much different than the day before.

Yesterday she was suspicious, and today she was anxious — eager, even. Overnight, the rose had scented the office with a beautiful fragrance, adding to her optimism. The initial cool approach she had taken toward J.P. simply wasn't going to work.

At the morning break, Leah gave a cheerful "Hello!" to George and J.P. "That rose did a wonderful job of freshening up the office."

J.P. smiled in surprise, but warmly added, "And that colorful blouse adds a picture that matches!"

The compliment was all Leah needed to send her from "feeling positive" to "over the moon." She blinked and stared for a few moments at J.P., and there it was: a smile on her lips. The next second there was some blush upon her cheeks, followed by a gleam in her eyes. There was no denying it: this country bumpkin had livened things up in what had become her monotonous life.

Her response caught J.P. off guard. "Quite the change from yesterday," he thought to himself.

To J.P., there was not a better human gift than the sweetness of a smile. He realized then that she was truly enchanting, and found himself very pleased with this encounter. It looked like the ice might be thawing.

Leah had come to realize that the abbreviation of his name didn't quite fit his charming nature.

"May I call you Joseph?"

Flattered, he replied, "Of course. My mom has always called me Joseph."

Something about the moment snapped her back to her senses. She had said too much, too quickly. "Look at me, wasting your time!" She laughed nervously as she made her way back to her desk, "Back to work!"

As she sat down, she shook her head in disbelief. She felt foolish, wearing that flowered blouse to work, and blushing at Joseph's compliment. The longer she thought about it, she turned mad. After only knowing this man for a day, even after working hard over the years to protect her feelings, she had let her curiosity turn to excitement.

As George returned to work, he could barely keep his mind on the tasks at hand. He was so pleased to see Leah smile and have a conversation with J.P.

He couldn't wait to tell Martha tonight about all the hubbub.

As the week went on, Leah was very careful to not be vulnerable with words or actions. She was able to keep it up until Thursday afternoon, during break. She simply couldn't let a certain question go unasked or unanswered. Earlier in the week, she had mentioned that Nick had baseball games on the Saturday and Sunday of the

CHAPTER 8

upcoming weekend. The weather Saturday was supposed to be nice, but Sunday it was to turn cloudy and cool. As of last night's forecast, there was no mention of rain.

J.P. had interjected. "It might not be forecast, but I believe there'll be some rain on Sunday."

She had raised her eyebrow a mile high. "And why do you think that?"

"Because of the way the ants are acting."

Against her better judgement, she asked, "What ants?"

J.P. beckoned her to follow him. He let her out the side door of the station and walked twenty feet down the sidewalk. He stopped and slowly leaned over, pointing at the small mound of soil and a furious army of ants that were moving in very orderly lines going to and from the mound. There were thousands of ants working in an orderly fashion. As J.P. pointed at what he considered a marvel of nature, Leah's only response was, "Yes. They're ants. So what?"

"Well, you see, the bigger the mounds, the more the rain."

Incredulous, she scoffed, "You have got to be kidding!"

He looked up and could see the sudden anger in her eyes. There was a look upon her lips like someone was trying to force feed her something she hated.

At the same moment, Leah could see the hurt on J.P.'s face, but she simply couldn't believe what she was hearing.

"I'm not kidding. I'm dead serious. The large mounds are a sign of lots of rain." He added, as if to be more convincing, "They make the mounds so that the water doesn't flow into their holes. This usually means rain within 24 to 72 hours."

With her temper controlling her, she couldn't help herself. She angrily spat out, "Where did you hear such a thing?"

With the shock of Leah's fury, J.P. surprised himself by standing up slowly with a cynical smile. "Now, didn't your fifth grade science book have that fact in it?"

Her face turned red with fiery anger as she glared at the smile on this country boy's lips. Before she could think of something to say, she spun on her heel and headed for the side door of the station. As she stomped away, he could her muttering words of "ants," "rain," and "crazy."

Unbeknownst to them, George had followed the two and stayed hidden inside the side door. To his delight, he'd heard the whole conversation. He hustled out of sight so Leah didn't see him when she returned to the office. As J.P. returned to work, trying to clear his mind of what had just happened, George walked by J.P. with a chuckle. "Fifth grade science!"
  J.P. was embarrassed, but he kept working with a small grin.
  George was *thrilled* to have another story to tell Martha tonight.

Leah returned to her office and sat down hard in her chair. She had many thoughts and emotions running through her mind. She was angry, that was for sure, but at whom and for what? Was she mad at Joseph? Again, for what?
  She was mad at herself, for acting the way she did about the damned ants. She was *embarrassed* for herself. What had she become? She barely knew this guy, and she was unloading her stored-up bitterness on him. She knew some of this attitude came from feeling jealous of Joseph — it was clear George thought very highly of him, and had mentioned numerous times how good his work was, how well he liked him. Adding to the problem was that *she* liked him. He had brought a rose to the office, he was soft-spoken, and he was quiet until you asked him a question.
  Deep down, Leah knew she harbored anger toward *all men*; she had decided to hold them all responsible for her bad marriage.
  This Joseph, however, was somehow compromising her promise to herself. And, how? By his manner, words, actions, and his physique? She didn't feel confident about any of this, but she knew for sure that after what she had just put herself through, she was exhausted. Her head was spinning as if she had just stepped off of a twirling carnival ride. Leah wanted to be alone, so she quickly opened her office door and said loudly, "George, I am leaving early."

CHAPTER 8

She didn't wait for a response.

Leah's drive home was short, as there was very little traffic at mid-afternoon. She was anxious to get into her house; for some reason she wanted to be safe in her home. As soon as the door was closed the tears began to flow.

She was standing within the walls that her emotions had been hiding for years. It felt as if everything was crumbling around her. The years of her ignoring men were being washed away, and she had not seen it coming. She hadn't wanted it, but Joseph was unknowingly chipping away at her barriers.

She made her way to the couch, laid down and she cried like she never had before. It lasted only a few minutes, but felt like hours. As she wiped at her cheeks, she wondered, "Why?"

She didn't want to admit it, but Leah knew the truth. She was attracted to Joseph.

After finally coming to terms with this realization, she closed her eyes. With some final, flickering thoughts, she drifted off to sleep.

CHAPTER 9

One of Leah's jobs at the station was to clean the restrooms on Fridays.

It was a job that went all the way back to when she began working there as a teenager. This particular Friday, when she went into the men's room to clean it, she found herself, yet again, in shock. An unbelievable sight greeted her. The restroom was as clean, if not cleaner, than when she left it after cleaning the week before. Most of the male employees over the years had been slobs to say the least. The sinks were typically black from attempting to wash grease-soaked hands all week, and paper towels would be tossed everywhere. Today the men's restroom was in order and wiped down; nothing was out of place. The sight left Leah in amazement and disbelief. As she walked back to the office, she once again glanced at Joseph working.

Yesterday at this time, she had been upset. Today she was full of wonderment. After coming to terms with her feelings and releasing the tension that had built during Joseph's first week, she was now looking forward to the weekend. Watching Nick's baseball games and working toward sorting out her feelings sounded almost pleasant.

Saturday afternoon as Leah sat at the baseball game, the weather was perfect. The temperature was 75 degrees and sunny with an eastern breeze. The sunshine seemed to be warming her soul. As she sat in the stands, she had a difficult time concentrating on the game, even though she typically watched Nick's every move.

CHAPTER 9

Her mind kept wandering back to the last week at work and what had triggered everything that she had felt during the week. To her surprise, the word "felt" came to her mind. Other than when she was with Nick, she hadn't felt anything but sad and bored for a long time.

Sunday morning, lightning and thunder interrupted Leah's sleep. She could hear the rain hitting her bedroom window as she lay there listening to the storm. Of course, her thoughts wandered to Joseph, who had predicted for her that it would rain sometime this weekend.

A smile crossed her face as she drifted back to sleep to the cadence of the rain.

As for J.P., after work on Friday he immediately headed back to the farm. His first week of work off the farm behind him, and his assessment was that it went better than he had expected. George was easy to get along with, and there were some regular customers who seemed to stop by every day, which created a friendly atmosphere. When the older regulars found out he was just off the farm, that really got the conversation going. The daily group had opinions on every aspect of life; it seemed that their expertise extended far and wide. Any given day, the conversation could include the weather, politics, and sports. If they had a connection to a farm they gave J.P. many detailed accounts.

Many first-hand stories came from Fred, who still owned his family's farm and rented it out. Pete had a nephew who was a farmer, and it was nice for J.P. to see that there were connections between rural life and the city.

J.P. stopped at Daniel's shop first. As he got out of the Dodge, Daniel's blue heeler Sadie bounded out and greeted him. Sadie was an offspring of J.P.'s dog, Tellie, who had died three years earlier at the age of twelve.

He found Daniel in the shop. His son had taken the planter off that day and was putting the small pieces in boxes, storing them under the back stairs of the shop. J.P.'s first reaction was to give him a hug, and tell him how proud he was. This affection surprised Daniel somewhat. He had no idea that this week had been an adventure in emotion for his dad.

If he was honest, the week had been much of the same feelings for Daniel. With his dad gone, he was changing from the boy who dreamt about nothing but being a farmer someday, into a mature young man who was *actually operating the farm*. J.P. had always known that Daniel's future would take him here, as the boy was a natural when it came to the farm. Daniel had been interested in the farm since he could walk. With continuous questions of "What's that?," "What are you doing?" and, "What are we going to do next?" J.P. always said Daniel displayed symptoms of "dirt in his blood."

More excited than he realized, J.P. then went to the water hydrant in the corner of the shop and filled a tin cup of fresh country water, drinking it in one steady movement upward. He filled it again and called back to Daniel, "They don't have water like this in the city!"

After a few more swallows of crystal, pure water, he took a moment to appreciate the quiet of the farm. On the county road their farms were on, the average traffic count per day were two dozen vehicles — including tractors. You could double that amount during planting and harvest seasons. In the city, it seemed a continuous scurry of people either walking, riding bicycles, or driving cars.

For the next fifteen minutes, they both talked about their past week. Thankfully, the conversation flowed easily between them. The two of them had always been able to talk, with their similar personalities and love for the farm.

As J.P. drove slowly out of Daniel's driveway, he stopped and looked at the long rows of this year's corn crop that was three leaf tall. Twenty thousand plants per acre, single file, and thirty inches between the rows.

To him it was beauty — not only the plants, but the art of the whole field. He looked beyond the field of near-black soil full of

CHAPTER 9

young corn plants, to the pasture which was a much darker green than the corn. In time, the corn plants would darken when their roots reached the fertilizer. Finally, he glanced at the blue sky to the west, starting to paint waves of orange as the sun was going out of sight.

At that moment J.P. sighed a breath of relief, and said *"I'm home."*

CHAPTER 10

For years, work provided nothing different or exciting for Leah.

This Monday morning, however, as she prepared to go to work, Leah was anxious about the approaching week. With Joseph at the garage, she knew there was going to be a difference. He had proven that in his first week at the garage.

The first exciting details she encountered upon entering the office were a fresh rose in a bud vase and the fact that the bowl of M&Ms had been refilled. Two fresh reminders that things were different at the station, and that just about anything could happen when it came to Joseph.

At morning break, J.P. asked George how much rain his rain gauge collected this weekend. "Two inches, actually! It started early Sunday morning and didn't stop until that evening."

"Good to hear. We got an inch and a half on the farm. Beautiful rain." He threw in a wink and a smile for Leah's sake, but she could only blush and smile back, her mind full of ants and rain and cancelled baseball games.

There it was, a smile. It caught J.P. off guard again. From no eye contact at all to that small, enchanting curve of her lips.

Leah blinked and stared for a few moments at Joseph. She suddenly felt embarrassed of her smile, and blushed even more. She had never had a private or social relationship with any of the other repairmen, and here she was flashing smiles at this one with a gleam in her eye.

CHAPTER 10

Tuesday morning J.P. was mowing the golf course at 5:30, just when there was a hint of the dawning of a new day. Slowly, the dark of night yielded to gray, and eventually the morning fog cleared off. He was enjoying the light show combined with the sweet smell of fresh-cut grass. The smell of this early morning reminded him of the alfalfa hay of the farm, and he was glad to have found a place in the city that brought back feelings of his home.

The atmosphere around the garage during his second week was far more comfortable than the first. Everyone was civil to each other, and at the breaks you could even call their conversations pleasant.

J.P. decided he was not going to the farm over the coming weekend, and when Saturday morning rolled around, he found himself finishing a brake job in the shop of the station. Leah also was at work that morning. During a short break, she mentioned that Nick had a baseball game at one o'clock that afternoon.

"I'll be happy to go watch, since I missed watching him play last Sunday," she added with a small, inside joke of a smile.

"You know, I happen to enjoy baseball myself. Would you mind terribly if I joined you?"

To his quiet delight, she blushed and said, "I — well, I — well, sure!"

To her own surprise, Leah had said yes because she had her own reasons for having him at the game. She was hoping to get to know him better.

They had just finished their second week of working together, and this would be a good chance to get to know Joseph away from the station. She was hoping that a social event out in the open, like a baseball game, would help them both relax a little, and that the conversation would flow more naturally.

Leah's son Nick had stopped by the service station during the noon hour on Tuesday to check in on his mother and to ask George if he could come in to change the oil in his pickup.

George started an introduction, "J.P., this is — " but Leah proudly took over and continued. "...this is my son Nick. Nick, this is Joseph, the new service man." J.P. stood while Nick immediately extended his hand for a strong, solid greeting.

"It's nice to meet you, young man."

Nick grinned, "Good to meet you, too! I had heard there was a new guy here."

J.P. was impressed with Nick's gentle voice and politeness. The boy was a couple inches shorter than him and had a stout, even husky frame. He did not have his mother's blue eyes or light hair; his eyes and hair were brown.

He glanced back at Leah after he sat down. She was beaming with pride as she and Nick chatted about their days. As he watched them, he noticed Nick grab a handful of M&Ms. When Nick had finished the conversation with his mother, he turned to George and asked, "Is there room for me to service my pickup this afternoon?"

George answered, "I will be done with my job by four o'clock, so any time after that you may have a stall."

Nick patted George on the shoulder. "Thanks, see you at four!"

J.P. watched Nick leave, and couldn't help but wonder what kind of pickup the boy drove.

At four o'clock, Nick stopped by the garage and sought out George.

"Any space for my pickup, George?"

"Yep," George answered. "In bay two."

To J.P.'s surprise and delight, Nick rolled in with a 1967 Chevy pickup. It was candy apple red with chrome wheels. He couldn't help himself, and walked over to Nick's pickup.

"Now, that is a nice pickup!"

"Thank you! My grandpa gave it to me." He patted the hood. "It had been sitting in his garage for the last ten years. When I told him that I signed up for a shop class for mechanics and body repair for my junior year of high school, Grandpa said, 'Could you use that old pickup in the garage?'" Nick added, "I finished the pickup two months ago after working for a year and a half on it."

With self satisfaction, he continued his restoration story of the

CHAPTER 10

Chevy pickup. "The original color was a copper tan. Its motor was a six-cylinder, now it has a 350 V eight." J.P. could tell that Nick's confidence was growing as he continued explaining his process of refinishing the pickup.

After Nick had completed his story, J.P. told him that in 1967 his dad bought a new Chevy pickup, just like this one. "It had a six cylinder engine and manual transmission, but its color was a sky blue with a white roof on the cab. It cost my dad two thousand dollars. It was a good pickup, and we used it daily for years on the farm."

Nick's eyes widened, "For real?"

"That's the truth. Needless to say, it was a good year for Chevy pickups!"

The two didn't see it at the time, but their 1967 pickups marked the start of a new bond.

Leah had heard most of Nick and Joseph's conversation about pickups as she stood by the office door. She had an almost delirious smile on her face, and was more than pleased by what she heard between the guys.

As they worked, Nick and J.P. continued to visit over questions about the vehicles, trucks, and tractors that were used on the farm.

As they closed the station Saturday noon for the weekend, J.P. asked Leah for the ball field location and then both of them headed for their homes. Skipping the housework she had planned, she applied a little makeup — something she had never done before a ball game — and put her hair in a ponytail, topping it off with a team baseball cap.

Arriving at the game early, Leah intentionally avoided sitting near anyone else. As J.P. looked into the stands for her, he hardly recognized her as she waved at him. He wondered if it was being outside or maybe the atmosphere of the ballpark, because Leah was smiling and waving like a happy little girl at a parade. He didn't quite know what to think. They both seemed excited to see each other, but it was a rather awkward moment. They both felt like Junior High kids, too nervous to start the conversation.

After their hellos and a comment on how beautiful the weather was, J.P. started scanning the players during their brief warmups prior to the game.

Joseph's intense interest in the game was apparent to Leah right away. "You know, I've never known anyone on the bleachers to pay so much attention to the players as they warmed up for the game. I really only care about the actual gameplay. "

Joseph grinned at her. "It's America's game! I like to pay attention to the way a player presents himself, how he wears his uniform, his concentration level, his focus on the ball — it's an important aspect of the game both defensively and offensively, in my opinion. Then you've got the player's effort. All the players out there have different abilities, and those are God-given. But effort? Now that's something produced by the player himself."

"You seem to know an awful lot about this," Leah commented, adjusting her baseball cap. "Did you ever play?"

"Yes! I've been around a lot of baseball and softball. I actually coached my son, Daniel's teams for six years."

"Really?"

"Yes ma'am. It's my one true love in the way of sports."

J.P. sat still for a few moments as a flashback of his childhood playing ball came to mind. "You know, as early as the age of eight I discovered that a barn was a great asset for a boy to have when he was a team of one."

Leah, tore her eyes away from the field in order to focus on J.P. "A barn. For baseball?"

He laughed. "Yep! That huge barn had a tall, long roof that seemed about as big as a baseball diamond to a young player like me." He rubbed his hands together, as though they were itching for a ball. "My dreams were filled with fantasy games that I'd play in. I'd throw that ball as far up the roof as I could, and I'd wait for it to roll back down." His face warmed at the memory. "Once it'd hit the edge, it'd shoot off and I'd catch it mid-flight."

"Well," Leah marveled, "You think you've heard everything!"

CHAPTER 10

"I actually had a perfectly-formed glove, just for those barn games. Many a night I'd put a ball in the web of the glove, right here." He stretched out his hand to demonstrate. "Then I'd wrap it tightly and stick it between the refrigerator and the wall until it was just the right shape."

"So you're a pitcher, then?"

"Not really. I loved to toss the ball up high, then swing my wooden Louisville slugger. If the ball landed at the predetermined spot, it was a home run." Leah tried to stifle a good-natured laugh, but it slipped out anyway. He smirked, but continued. "A hit off the side of the roof was a foul ball. Over time, my coordination and strength improved and, let me tell you, my first hit over the roof was as exciting as a World Series grand slam!"

J.P. was looking out at the ball field, but differently than just two minutes before. He wasn't watching anything in particular, simply recapturing his youth by dreaming of baseball. At that moment the umpire shouted "Batter up!", bringing him back to the reality of Nick's game.

As the game started, he watched intently. Trying to keep up the conversation, Leah asked him questions here and there about the game, which ended up turning into play-by-play commentary from J.P.

Between the second and third innings Leah mentioned, "This is the high school I attended."

J.P. looked cross the street at the school and asked, "How many kids in your grade?"

"312. I only knew about half of my classmates' names, and I only considered three or four of them friends." Leah shrugged, "I hung out with a small crowd."

J.P. gave a slight laugh and said, "There were thirty-nine in my graduating class."

In the fourth inning, Nick hit a pitch down the first base line, but the first baseman grabbed it and got it to the base before Nick could reach it safely.

The longer the game went on and the more they talked, the more comfortable they became. Leah basked in the fact that there was a warmth about Joseph. She could sense a strength about him that even made her feel safe.

In the fifth innings a sharp-hit ball flew toward Nick as he played second base. The ball took an odd bounce and zinged past him.

Next on the conversation roster were their hobbies. Leah sheepishly divulged that playing piano was her favorite hobby. She couldn't bring herself to say it to Joseph, but music was probably her fondest love besides Nick. How fortunate she had been at times to leave the reality of life and get lost in the music of her piano. "I actually took piano lessons for eight years, starting at an early age. I — I took a break for a while, though."

What she left out was that most of her love for the piano came from her mother. Her mother had been a fine piano player, and they had played for each other and together almost daily. But, suddenly, her mother died when Leah was thirteen. For months after her death Leah didn't play the piano; the pain was too unbearable.

Finally, after two years of missing what brought her joy, she resumed lessons despite having to play the piano through her tears.

At times the tears were because of sadness, and other times the tears came from breaking through the barrier that kept her from being happy.

"I play now, though, when I need it most." And she left it at that. The thought of the past pain crept from her subconscious and resulted in silence.

He glanced over at her, wondering why she had stopped talking. She quietly gazed at something past the outfield with an innocent, broken gaze. Almost childlike. He couldn't have known that in those few seconds of silence, some of the most vivid memories of pain in her life flashed through her mind: being teased by other children in grade school because she carried a little extra weight, the death of her mother, her marriage to a controlling husband and then the divorce — and struggling with her newfound feelings for this stranger.

CHAPTER 10

After Leah finally blinked her eyes, J.P. tried to lighten the mood. "I wish I could play a musical instrument. I like music, actually. Dancing, too."

She shook herself back to the present. "I played a little flute, too, during my school years. I'll admit, though, when it comes to dancing I've definitely got two left feet."

As the game was nearing its end, she was surprised at how fast the last two hours had gone by. She also realized that this was one of the most complete conversations she had with anyone in a long time, besides Julie. She marveled at how easy it had been to talk with Joseph. Two weeks ago, she didn't know who Joseph was and now she had come this close to revealing some of her most private thoughts.

The final score of the game was 4 to 2; Nick's team lost.

The pair remained seated in the stands as the other spectators filed out. Neither one of them suspected that a baseball game could have been so enchanting. As they stepped down the bleachers, Nick came moving sullenly toward them. He had seen J.P. sitting next to his mother during the game, to his surprise, as he didn't know he was coming.

Nick shook his hand, but not enthusiastically. "Thanks for coming to my game, J.P., but we lost and I had an error."

"It was my pleasure. I haven't been to a game for a few years... I miss it."

The boy perked up a bit. "Did you play baseball?"

"I played, yes, and coached some also."

Nick sighed. "That pitcher out there today was good."

Leah stood back and listened to the two guys talk ball, pleased to just observe. "Yes, he was a good pitcher, that's a fact. But that error wasn't really yours." Nick's confused expression prompted J.P. to elaborate. "I saw the wild hop the ball took on its second bounce when it was coming toward you."

As the last of the fans, players, and coaches dispersed in the parking lot, J.P. dusted off his jeans and said, "I'd be happy to show you what happened to the ball that caused the wild hop." he added, "If you want, of course. It's up to you."

Nick glanced at his mother and finally gave J.P. a nod.

Leah sat down again, this time on the first row of bleachers behind home base. She let his words sink in. Always a calm voice, always gentle. "I will show you what happened if you want."

She chuckled a bit and thought, "I sure hope this doesn't have anything to do with ants."

As Joseph and Nick took the second baseman position, Leah could see her new friend pointing a finger, then moving a foot back and forth like he was smoothing the infield.

"Now, before a game, the infield has been drug and it's nice and smooth. As the game goes on, though, there are holes or divots made by players either running the bases or making defensive plays. Right?"

"Yeah, J.P. That makes sense."

"Well, that's what happened on your error; the ball hit a hole and took an unexpected bounce." J.P. patted the ground next to the base. "My players and I would do our field repair before an inning started. You can look for the uneven spots and discreetly smooth them with a shoe."

Nick was watching and listening to J.P. with his full attention. "Now, it may sound crazy, but it happens. It did to you today."

"It sure did."

"The game is about small things, so to prevent a hob or an error here or there can make a big difference."

Nick was just absorbing, not saying a word.

"You know, as long as we're out here, I have another thought about infielders: most play too deep." J.P. pointed out to the grass. "It seems to me if you play too deep, you wait for the ball and the ball plays *you* instead of you playing *the ball*. I always liked to play shorter and charge the ball, or attack it."

J.P. and Nick walked slowly toward home plate. When they reached it, J.P. said, "The pitcher *was* good today. Baseball is about rhythm and at times he was humming. Your first at-bat was like zoom, zoom,

CHAPTER 10

and zoom; three pitches and it was over."

Nick nodded his head, "Exactly!"

"After every pitch, step out of the batter's box, break his rhythm, and you take control." J.P. continued, "In all levels of baseball a high percentage of missed pitches are because of late swings. Most players believe you need a big bat for a big hit, but you don't. Usually the lighter the bat, the better... or at least choke up on the bat." He gave the boy a warm smile. "You see, Nick, baseball is about you and the ball. The simpler you make it, the better!"

Nick's head was spinning from the three minute crash course on J.P.'s baseball philosophy.

As J.P. and Nick were out on the ballfield, Leah stared in quiet awe. She didn't know quite what she was feeling, or how to process the sight of Joseph and Nick together.

Nick had been taught how to fish by her brother, Chuck. The two had been on many fishing excursions, from as short as an afternoon to as long as a week's trip. Nick and his uncle Chuck were real pals... but this was different. Joseph was virtually a stranger to Nick. She couldn't hear every word, but she could see both of the guys were concentrating on every detail. In even those short minutes, Leah could feel emotions swelling in her eyes, and was happy to be wearing sunglasses.

Nick was receiving a caring lesson like he had never received from a male figure, and that included his father.

"Sorry about leaving you all by yourself," J.P. drawled as they returned to the stands. To keep from crying, Leah waved off the apology. "That's okay!"

"I'm sorry that I was so forward, Nick. I know I'm not your coach, but those are some things that seemed to help me playing ball."

"No need to apologize! Thank you. It really was interesting; I can't wait to try it all out!"

It was one of those moments: they all stood there a bit too long, each knowing they should move, wanting to acknowledge that something special had happened this afternoon. They all had made an unexpected connection — a bonding, a start of friendships.

J.P. made the first step toward the parking lot. They all wanted to say something, but couldn't quite find the words, so he broke the silence with, "Good luck with the rest of the season, Nick. I'm sure you'll do just fine."

"Thanks for coming... maybe you can make it to another game?"

"I hope so, I enjoyed it." He turned to Leah, "And thank *you* for your company. It was a nice visit."

Leah, who was still managing to keep her emotions in check blurted out, "Thank you! It— it seemed as if time went by quickly!" As J.P. walked off he called out over his shoulder, "See you at work on Monday!"

She closed the door of her Blazer and smacked her forehead with her palm. "Is that all you could say? Time went by quickly?" She leaned back in her seat and stared for a moment at the roof above her head. Could this guy really be this nice? The flowers, the clean restroom, and the fact that he was so good to Nick. She felt like she should pinch herself to bring her back to reality.

Why was she tearing up in the baseball stands? What was happening to her? No guy had ever done that to her before. Until today, she had truly believed that she was immune to such a thing. Her head was spinning and her heart was racing, and she felt silly, like she'd transformed into a giddy teenage girl, falling for the prom king.

Her instinct was to think, "Not me, no, I don't have those types of feelings," But she couldn't deny it. She did. They had simply been misplaced, buried somewhere in her mind and hidden from her heart.

Joseph, by the simple act of being himself — so caring and kind — was chipping away at the wall that she had put up around herself, and in turn, the coolness of control she valued so much.

Today, however, watching Joseph extend that warmth to Nick was too much. It made her feel vulnerable, and there didn't seem to be a way to stop it.

Leah went home to finish her housework. Before the game, she had been wondering about Joseph and how the game would go, and

CHAPTER 10

now she found herself distracted by the memories of the good times she had with him.

The following week at work everything seemed different. Leah and J.P. were no longer strangers. In fact, they were quickly becoming friends. And when a person is working with a friend, the whole atmosphere around them changes. There was more chatting during break times, and smiles whenever the two came in contact.

George was happy to have J.P. as an employee; he was quite positive that J.P. had to be the best repairman he'd ever had. The conversations at work seemed to be an extension of the one that Leah and J.P. had shared at the ball games. Banter flowed easily and allowed them to learn even more about each other. It all seemed very natural.

George was also happy to see Leah smiling a little more. She was regaining a sparkle in her eyes that he hadn't seen since her divorce. She had always been polite to the customers, but never appeared to enjoy the contact the way she had in the past. To a bystander, she might not have looked *angry*, but she sure didn't look happy either. That was beginning to change.

Leah's personal and social lives were restricted to her siblings and Julie. And while she cherished raising Nick, there was soon to be a hole in her life when he went off to college. Nick starting a new chapter in his life would certainly change Leah's. If she were to be completely honest, she was not looking forward to Nick's moving on and away from home.

J.P. was planning to return to the farm during the upcoming weekend, leaving directly after work. On Friday, Leah happened to mention to him that there wouldn't be any baseball game that coming weekend, and that she wasn't sure of her plans.

He wasn't usually the compulsive type, but in this case he spoke up right away and suggested that they go to the golf course after work, hit some balls on the driving range.

"I can use the range anytime I want," he told her. "It's one of the perks of my cutting grass there." He was looking forward to being in the outdoors for a while, getting some exercise, and having some fun.

"Oh, gosh, I can't remember the last time I hit a golf ball! When I was a teenager I joined a golf league for several summers, but I'm pretty sure my last time on a course would be considered ancient history."

Leah was only stalling; she really wanted to go. "Why don't you leave your truck here? We'll go pick up your clubs."

That evening, on the driving range, they each hit a few short shots to loosen up. Then J.P. let loose with several big swings. When he connected, the balls would travel three hundred yards.

Leah watched in amazement. "Where did you learn to swing like that?"

He shrugged his shoulders. "Well, I'm not sure, but I've been swinging to hit things for a long time." He laughed, a quiet, amused rumble. "It's been mostly baseballs getting the pounding, though." He left out the fact that he'd only been golfing about a dozen times in his life.

She found herself wanting to lean back and watch Joseph swing away at the balls. The way he swung the club moved his body into a smooth, muscled line, powerful and attractive. In times past, Leah would have felt self-conscious being in public, feeling carefree and having a good time. This evening she was oblivious to anyone besides Joseph.

She hadn't had this much fun in a long time. They would take turns picking out yardage signs and seeing who could get the ball the closest. Sometimes, one of them would hit the ball and challenge the other person to get close to it.

Time seemed to simply swing away, and it had soon been an hour since they had reached the range. They had been enjoying themselves and each other, their time together filled with laughter and smiles. Neither of them wanted to leave, but they knew their out-of-practice bodies were going to feel that hour of drives in the morning.

CHAPTER 10

As they drove away from the driving range, they decided upon a pizza for supper. They had been having so much fun they had forgotten that they were hungry.

They were able to take the enjoyment along with them to the pizza parlor, where there was a long meal of more laughter. Unlike their previous conversations, nothing serious entered their minds that evening, and they both felt lighter for it.

As Leah pulled up in front of the garage, they were temporarily silenced by the joy of having such a great, carefree time with each other.

Neither of them had experienced this kind of abandonment of worldly cares in a long time.

The conversation between them still flowed easily, allowing them to get a little more acquainted, but it was clear the outing was nearing its end. Quickly, J.P. considered a kiss, but decided it was too soon; at this point yet, he thought, a kiss was out of line.

On Leah's side of things, she frantically considered a handshake — immediately knowing it was far too formal for the situation. "Damnit," she thought as she awkwardly shoved her hands in her pockets, "nothing was awkward at all until this moment." With a small smile, J.P. reached for the door latch and quickly got his golf clubs from the back seat. Both of them had looked forward to the fun, but neither had thought about how the day would end. Finally, he took a deep breath and added, "I hope the rest of your weekend treats you well," and, after a slight pause, "Thank you."

"No, thank you!" Leah quickly answered, pulling her hands back out from the denim pockets of her jeans. "It was fun. Really." J.P. nodded thoughtfully, and turned for his pickup. She watched him carry the golf clubs with ease, and let her thoughts wander back to his display of power on the driving range. As she recalled his athletic finesse and the broad lines of his shoulders, she couldn't help but feel a twinge of disappointment as she drove away slowly.

J.P. drove back to the farm that night, and didn't make it home until after midnight. The next morning in the light of day, he noticed that the crops were off to a good start. The farm had received another inch and a half of rain that past week. As usual, he happily checked the cattle and the fences, but his mind was 130 miles away, thinking of his new city life, and a certain brilliant smile. As he filled Daniel in on the details of how things were progressing in the city, he stuck to the facts: It was a good job, a fine house… but he kept Leah to himself.

CHAPTER 11

When Leah got out of bed on Saturday morning, she could feel every swing of the golf club from the night before. After a slow, exhausted walk down the hall, she took a long, hot shower to soothe her aching muscles.

Throughout the day, Leah's thoughts kept circling back to watching Joseph swing that golf club. "My God," she thought, "Now that's something I could watch all day." As she nursed her sore body while completing work around the house, she decided every powerful swing she watched made the soreness worth it.

On Sunday, Leah met Julie for lunch. Her friend could tell something was *up*. With easy smiles and tinkling giggles, Leah seemed like a different gal — or rather, she seemed like a gal Julie hadn't seen in a long time.

"Alright, Leah, what's with all the talking?"

Leah, coughed, surprised. "What?"

"Lots of talking, lots of smiling. Something is going on!"

"Oh stop it. I smile! I talk! You act like I'm Eeyore or something."

"Not like this! I'm looking at a sudden, overnight change." Julie dramatically stabbed a cherry tomato with her fork and popped it in her mouth, giving Leah her best stare-down.

"It's nothing! Work's just going... really well right now."

"Uh-huh."

Leah began to squirm under the practiced stare of her best friend. She knew Julie was like an old film noir detective — she'd get her to crack eventually — so she finally gave in. "Okay, fine! I just can't get my mind off that new guy."

With a whoop and a slap on the table, Julie laughed. "I *knew* something was up! Have you been holding out on me?"

With blushes and embarrassed laughter, Leah filled her in on the past week. Baseball, golf, and all... and Julie hung on to every word, over the moon for her friend whose life had known mostly gloom for the past ten years. With a twinkle in her eye, Julie pointed her fork at Leah. "I'll tell you one thing; I'm gonna need regular updates on this guy."

Leah matched the twinkle with her own. "I'll do my best!"

As she got ready for bed that evening, Leah felt like she was 100 pounds lighter. She was actually thrilled to be able to share her excitement with someone, and who could be a better confidant than Julie? She'd been bursting at the seams, and getting to live it all over again made the whole situation feel more real.

His philosophy on wildflowers, the ants and the rain — all the things she had written off as hoaky — were quickly becoming some of his most endearing traits.

She was nervous to admit it, but there might just be something there, after all.

Leah's muscles had mostly recovered by Monday morning. She didn't say anything to Joseph about the soreness she felt from their Friday night adventures, however.

The jovial atmosphere of the break room from the week before had spread into the service areas of the garage this week, and it showed in everyone's moods. At break on Thursday, J.P. was thumbing through the newspaper looking at the entertainment section.

Speaking to himself out loud, he said, "There's a movie out on DVD, of a book I read last winter."

Excited to learn more about J.P.'s interests, Leah sat down across from him with her glass of iced tea and asked, "What's the movie about?"

CHAPTER 11

"It's a WWII film. About the end of the war, the struggles of the people of Europe and their recovery."

Interested, Leah leaned into J.P.'s arm to get a better look at the newspaper. "I wouldn't mind seeing that! My father enlisted when he was 17. October of 1945, near the end of the war."

Fully aware of how close Leah was to him, J.P. shifted a bit in his seat. "You don't say?"

"He actually spent three months in Italy helping maintain order. Assist in cleanup, helping people recover from all the destruction, you know?"

"Well, I'd invite you over to watch it, but I didn't bring my DVD player to town when I packed up."

With what felt like 400 butterflies in her stomach, Leah tried to nonchalantly stir her coffee and suggested, "Want to pick it up after work tonight and watch it at my place?"

Realizing how personal the conversation had become, George gathered up his things and quietly excused himself from the break room.

J.P. smiled. "I'd grill burgers for supper before we watch the movie, if you've got a grill."

She nodded quickly. "Yes, I've got a grill! And I'll make a salad, too."

"I should probably be honest with you; burgers are about the only meal I can prepare."

With the remaining butterflies and talk of supper making her stomach growl, she added, "I think I'll chance it."

They both smiled to seal the deal.

J.P. rushed to his house after work. He grabbed a packet of ground beef that he'd brought from the farm from the freezer. He also took the time to shower, shave, and put on some clean clothes. After looking through the few clothing options he had in his closet, he wished that he'd brought more things from the farm. Even with all the decisions and excitement racing through his head, he managed to arrive at Leah's home on time. She greeted him warmly and let him in, and J.P. couldn't help but smile at how much things had changed since that first day at the station.

Leah watched with approval as J.P. grilled the burgers to perfection on the back deck, and she made a tossed salad in the kitchen. With the smell of the finished burgers on the kitchen counter and the scent of sliced onions, cucumbers, and tomatoes for the salad, both J.P. and Leah were pleased with each of their contributions to the evening's meal. The anticipation of this evening was growing into excitement for both J.P. and Leah.

After Leah's first bite of burger, she exclaimed, "Oh my gosh, this is delicious! What kind of burger is this?"

J.P. gave a little smirk, proud of his finished effort. "This is my famous potato burger. They've got potato hash browns added in with a little onion and garlic seasoning."

While they enjoyed their supper, they talked about everything from favorite movies to stubborn customers. It was a wonderful meal — the perfect excuse for them to be together outside of work.

After dinner, they settled in on the couch for the movie. Careful not to sit too close, while only leaving a small amount of space between them, they enjoyed the historical film, even through the giddy nervousness of their intimate evening.

After the movie, J.P. filled Leah in on the differences between the book and the film while she listened intently. She scooted just a little bit closer on the cushion, telling him stories her father had shared over the years from his time in Italy.

Showing genuine interest in the real-life experiences of her father, he asked question after question — if he was honest, it was probably just to keep her talking as long as possible. It had always been a hobby of his to research the happenings of WWI and WWII, but it was starting to look like his hobbies were taking a turn in a personal direction.

J.P. got off the couch to stretch his legs. He slowly walked around the room, looking at pictures both on the wall and displayed on the piano. There were many of Nick, including his senior pictures, some after successful days of fishing, proudly showing off a catch. There

CHAPTER 11

were a couple of him in varying baseball uniforms.

He believed one group photo was Leah's family picture. He pointed and said, "Tell me about your family."

Leah smiled wistfully. "In that picture I was twelve years old. That's my sister Sally, she's divorced, has two grown daughters, and lives across the city. My brother Chuck is married, no children. He's a deputy sheriff." She swallowed. "Those are my parents. My mother passed away when I was thirteen, and my dad is retired." She touched the frame briefly. "He actually lives only six blocks away."

J.P. turned to Leah and said, "I'm sorry about your mother."

Leah, who was seated on the couch, answered, "Thank you. To be honest, I don't know if I ever got over that loss."

She was surprised that she'd revealed that, something she'd been holding back all those years. There was something about Joseph that was allowing her to open up to him.

After her mother's death, Leah had a difficult time comprehending love. Losing her mother and the love she felt from her had left her emotionally hungry, longing for love and attention. Her emotional growth felt stunted. Leah did not know God, in fact, she wasn't even aware that there *was* a God. If there was, he didn't seem to be present in her life. Her days seemed to be always gray and overcast. Only the playing of the piano helped to clear the gloominess from her days. It was with the birth of Nick that she began to process growing emotionally again. With his arrival, she suddenly had someone to whom she could give her love, and to receive love from in return. As he grew older, the love they shared as mother and son became even stronger. For Leah, this was as close to a spiritual experience as she understood.

Leah had been baptized, but couldn't remember ever going to church. Not even her marriage had taken place in one.

As J.P. continued looking at the pictures, he said with the same certainty in his voice, "When I was eighteen, I lost a sixteen year old brother in a traffic accident."

J.P. still remembered the pain of his brother's death, but no longer felt the immense anguish of it. The wound of this loss had healed, but he was still aware of the scar. He never blamed God, as some people wanted to, for the accident. He had made peace with himself, and Him. He opened his heart to God and became more aware of His love, and everything He had created. J.P. had always been comfortable with his God. It didn't matter if he was in church, or out in the openness of the farm; he was reminded of the beauty in everything.

Leah rose from the couch and walked over to the piano bench, sitting down on the familiar surface. J.P. had his back turned to her as he browsed photos, so as she hit the first note, he jumped in surprise.

Leah was feeling lighthearted. She began playing "Linus and Lucy," the Charlie Brown theme song. Suddenly, J.P.'s heart was leaping to the music. For some reason, though, his feet were dragging as he stepped toward the piano until he was standing directly next to it. His heart may have been telling him to go for it, but his mind wanted to be cautious. As Leah continued her melody, his pulse was racing and his mind was spinning in delight. No one had ever serenaded him before, and he was truly enjoying the performance. As he looked at her face, he saw there was more to her than the smile on her lips. There was a joy and pride radiating from her heart. He couldn't have known that the piano had been the only thing that made her feel good since age thirteen. J.P. was one of the few who were privileged to be a part of this portion of Leah's life.

Over the years, Leah had grown to be stoical and restrained in her life. When she was with the piano making music, however, she was warm and spontaneous. It was about the only thing in her life that she let flow naturally.

As Leah finished, J.P. clapped. No one had ever played music one-on-one for him.

When Leah looked into Joseph's eyes, she could see the welling of unshed tears. Since they'd met, this was the first time he'd seen her show such confidence.

"That was very nice. You are an excellent pianist!" With emotion still trying to surface, J.P. was struggling with keeping his voice from cracking. He continued, "I really do enjoy music, and that was

CHAPTER 11

one of the nicest things anyone has ever done for me."

J.P. meant every word. No woman had been so kind to him for a long, long time. This was different than his mother baking him cookies or a home-cooked meal. His relationship with his wife had turned from cool to frigid years ago. This act warmed him to his bones.

Leah had performed with such grace that she seemed to glow. A gentleness and eloquence had surfaced that he didn't know she possessed. As they glanced at each other's eyes, hers were filled with delight while his were sad with tears. He wasn't sad for what Leah had done. He was sad for his failed marriage and what he had lost in years past.

As quickly as Leah had made the split decision to play the piano, she asked Joseph without hesitation, "Is everything alright?"

J.P. was breathless, as if he had run a steady mile, and at the same time speechless from a guilt that he had never admitted to.

His heart had temporarily lost its joy, and a tear rolled down his cheek. He moved his heavy feet and sat next to her on the piano bench, facing away from her and the keys.

In a trembling voice, he said, "I'm married, Leah." He took a moment, and they both let it sink in. "But it's been over for a long time. Truly. We haven't seen each other in years."

They sat in silence, knowing that their trust in each other was growing, their bond becoming stronger. They could feel the unspoken gratitude they had for meeting, for becoming friends.

"I met her when I was 17, and, that's honestly the last time I remember loving her. Those first few weeks. Suddenly we were both in our 40s and couldn't stand to look at each other." He told her everything about his marriage, there on the piano bench. When he was finished, Leah took her turn, and told him about Heath.

At the end of the evening, they parted with an almost nervous energy — the butterflies were still there, "Thank you for the burgers." Leah said, as they moved toward the door.

As he stepped out onto the front porch, he turned to her, and met her gaze warmly. "Thank you for the music." A tiny smile crept to her lips.

They said good night, adding a habitual "See you at work tomorrow," and they separated with the memory of what they had learned from each other's eyes.

CHAPTER 12

J.P. and Leah had come to enjoy each other's company so much that the time they spent together passed like a flash of heat lightning, while their time apart felt like the second half of a Nebraska February — cold and grueling, and with no end in sight.

One sunny Tuesday afternoon, he poked his head into the station's office and briefly tipped his hat out of habit. "I'm in need of a quick break, Leah, and I hear it's beautiful out."

She smirked a bit, and leaned back in her chair. "You hear that, huh?"

"I do. I mean, I feel like I haven't seen the sun in ages. Want to come out and see if the rumors are true?"

Trying to play it cool, but secretly thrilling at the thought of spending some alone time with Joseph, she put the cap on her favorite pen and set it next to her computer keyboard. "You think there's even big, fluffy clouds out there?"

"Won't know unless we go investigate, will we?"

And with a small giggle of excitement, Leah popped up from her chair, grabbed a light jacket off the coat rack, and took her favorite station employee by the arm as he led her out into the sunshine.

"I love being out in the fresh air… if you can call city air 'fresh,' I suppose."

She gave him a playful punch in the arm. "Hey, now."

"I'm just calling it like I see it — or smell it, rather! Besides, I like being outside, and I like being with you, so I'm getting the best of both worlds, if you ask me."

Blushing at such an honest, open compliment, Leah steered their attention to a young woman and her two children, enjoying a picnic on a large blanket printed with cartoon characters. "That looks lovely. You know, I can't remember the last time I've been on a picnic!"

J.P. stopped walking and dramatically placed his hand on his heart. "What? Why that's terrible!" Seeing the small smile growing on her face, he continued with "Why, I tell you what, I think that might just be a sin!"

Another playful punch in the arm brought him down from his theatrics, and he chuckled. "Really, though, I don't think it gets much better than a picnic. I've eaten many a meal picnic style, because out on the farm... when you're working with planting or harvesting, you're usually miles away from home. You can't just drop what you're doing and drive home to eat when time is of the essence."

"Now, see, Joseph, I think you underestimate how strongly I feel about food."

"That's what snacks are for! I'd carry a whole day's worth of this or that. Nuts, apples, granola bars... sometimes a meatloaf sandwich from my mother. When I need a break or a stretch, I just hop out of the tractor, pick something that looks good, and picnic under the clouds."

She sighed wistfully, "You make that sound awfully nice."

"Well, I'm not lying. I've had picnics weekly — spring, summer, and fall for the past 30 years. One of those 'joys of life' you hear people talking about."

They walked quietly for a few minutes, simply enjoying one another's presence and listening to the breeze. Leah couldn't help but dwell on the silence — her past was full of long, quiet stretches of time... but they were always full of tension and the promise of an argument. This was a new experience for her, simply *being* around someone without feeling the need to fill the silence with small talk or nervous babbling.

"I don't much like the sound of regret in your voice," J.P. gently broke the silence, leaving Leah wondering if he could read her mind. "So I think you and I need to go on a picnic together."

Despite the blush forming at the top of her collar, she tried to sound nonchalant. "Oh yeah? When?" Hoping she wasn't grinning like the Cheshire Cat, she did her best to calm the butterflies in her stomach.

CHAPTER 12

She and Joseph had spent a lot of time together in the past month, the casual movie night and golf out included. But a picnic? This felt more official. An honest-to-goodness date. "When?" She repeated.

J.P. paused to think for a moment, then, "This Saturday evening."

She gulped quietly. "Evening?"

"Sure. There's no limit to when you can picnic. To be honest, I've put some thought into this already." He smiled devilishly. "I've got some plans up my sleeve."

"And where would we be having this picnic?"

"Now, that'll just have to be a surprise."

The butterflies in her stomach had turned into a full-on bee swarm. "What do people bring on a picnic? Drinks? Potato salad? What should I bring?"

He came to a full stop and turned to meet her eyes. "Just your pretty smile."

She blushed, smiled, and nervously tucked her hair behind her ear. She couldn't help doing any of those things, and he felt just fine about that.

"Seven o'clock sound alright?"

"Sev— seven o'clock. Saturday?"

"Saturday it is."

J.P. had noticed a beautiful area fifteen miles northwest of the city, and decided to investigate it a bit further. He had even turned off the highway onto the gravel road, driving a couple of miles into what felt like the middle of nowhere — just the way he liked it. Out here, there probably weren't many other people who knew about the abundance of picturesque scenery. Every vehicle on the highway sped past the turn, in too much of a hurry to notice the local beauty of the countryside.

When he felt homesick during the week, J.P. would head out north of the city to clear his head. Driving the highways, taking note of the cattle and crops, he was able to breathe in the clean country air and get in touch with his roots. It was on one of these drives a few weeks past that he discovered where the scenery changed from flat farmland to rolling hills of corn. As J.P. was maneuvering a turnabout in a field drive, a rusty-but-cared-for pickup pulled to a stop on the side of the dirt road. J.P. figured it was the farmer who owned the land, and decided to take the opportunity to introduce himself. After a quick greeting and a handshake, J.P. gestured out at the fields surrounding them.

"That's a beautiful field you've got here, sir."

The old farmer took off his cap and ran a hand through his sandy hair. "I appreciate you sayin' that. Not many people think of a field of corn that way."

"Well, I'm a farmer, but the drought's pushed me to the city for the time being. I can't tell you how nice it is to watch the crops wave in the breeze."

"I might not have experience living in the city, but I know what you mean."

"Would you mind if I came back here, next time I need a break from all the hustle and bustle?"

With a friendly smile, the farmer assured him, "Sure. You're welcome anytime."

As he drove away, J.P. started to truly get excited. On an instinct, he reached for the roll of Rolaids he kept in his glove box, but stopped. "Come on, J.P. This isn't stress — this is the good stuff." Pulling his hand back to the wheel he began making a plan in his head. Picnic location? Check. Beautiful picnic companion? Check and check. Next on the list was food and transportation.

After stocking up at the grocery store, he took the time to wash and wax his red Dodge pickup. Not only did it give him a sense of pride to see it sparkle in the sunlight, but it was a comforting ritual that helped calm his nerves, just a little bit. After it was shined up to his liking, he finally began to load it up with items for the picnic: two lawn chairs, charcoal grill, card table, and utensils. For the menu, J.P. started a beef roast in the crock pot, later adding fresh potatoes and carrots. His plan was to warm them on the grill, and top it all off with some fresh, grilled sweet corn — it doesn't get much better than that. "Well," he thought as he smiled to himself,

CHAPTER 12

"it *can* get better if you make a few s'mores on the hot grill."

J.P. was equal parts nervous and excited. He hadn't felt this way in a long time. Long enough he could barely remember what to be nervous about. To be honest, he couldn't remember the last time he'd had to impress a lady on a date. Had he and Claire ever even gone on a date together? He shook that thought from his head and continued hustling to get everything in order. He wanted the evening to be perfect, and was genuinely looking forward to some time outside the city in the country air. He was used to being out in the open this time of year, and longed to take in the beauty of nature — especially with someone special by his side.

Leah was nervous and tense as soon as her eyes opened on Saturday morning.

The minute hand on the clock seemed to be in slow motion as she fiddled around the house in an attempt to do her weekend chores. As she was washing dishes, her favorite coffee mug slipped out of her hands and, as it headed for certain doom on her kitchen floor, was miraculously intercepted by Nick, who had just walked into the kitchen for a Pop-Tart.

"Morning mom. Want to talk to me about why you're so fidgety?" He handed her the coffee mug covered in music notes, with a small smirk on his face.

"I'm not... *fidgety*. You're fidgety!"

"Ha, okay mom. Keep telling yourself that. I'm off to practice." He kissed her quickly on the cheek and added on his way out the door, "Say 'hi' to J.P. for me!"

"Very funny!"

After an empty sink, two loads of laundry, and a squeaky-clean toilet, Leah finally plopped down on her couch. "I give up!" She breathed out, exasperated, and dialed Julie's phone number. After not even one full ring, Julie picked up singing the theme song from *Dirty Dancing*.

She let her friend finish out her silliness, and blurted, "Julie, do you know what time it is?"

"Um, no? Lunchtime?"

"Yes. It's only noon. I've got all my work done and Nick says I'm antsy. What am I supposed to do until 7:00?"

Sensing the rising tension in her friend's voice, Julie knew just what to do. "Tell you what. I'll swing by your place in 20 minutes and we'll go to the mall, just like a couple of teenagers."

Leah sighed loudly with relief. "That sounds incredibly silly, and I think it's just exactly what I need right now."

"Good! I'll be by in two shakes. Nothing like window shopping with your best friend to get your mind off what's making you nervous. Five bucks says you'll even have a good time."

As they walked around the local mall, lunching on soft pretzels and admiring clothing in the display windows, Leah finally filled Julie in on *all* of the details. Up until today, she'd stuck close to the surface; what they'd been up to, how handsome he was. Today, though, she just had to tell *someone* about the feelings he was stirring in her. The ones she didn't know how to handle.

"At first, I thought he was so strange. Going on and on about ants and flowers, and 'country air.' I thought he was a regular— well a regular country bumpkin. Like an extra on *Andy Griffith* or something." She brushed some excess salt off her pretzel absentmindedly. "But, I realize now that he's just... unique, you know? He's different from all the other men I've spent time with."

Julie nodded quietly, knowing not to interrupt.

"I had him stereotyped — and the image of him I had built in my head made me feel, I don't know, defensive. I'm not sure why." She smiled, wistfully. Now, having him in the station every day is — and don't make fun of me — it's calming. It feels comfortable."

"Well, good. I can't remember the last time you felt that way about someone."

"I can't either! I mean, I said it feels comfortable but sometimes it's the opposite! I'm excited, I'm nervous, my heart's pounding... I feel so mixed up right now."

Julie knew her cue. "You remember when Stetson Schutz asked me

CHAPTER 12

to prom senior year?"

Leah laughed, "How could I forget? We talked on the phone about it all week long. I swear my phone felt permanently glued to my ear."

"Well, now, this isn't much different. I was so nervous all week long. I was worried I'd say something stupid, or *he'd* say something stupid, and it'd all be a disaster. But you know what? We had a great night."

"I know. I'm just... I don't know. I don't have a great track record."

"Honey, you don't really have *any* track record. You're practically just getting started. J.P. seems wonderful, and kind, and it sounds like he really likes you. Don't let your past muddle up the present. Good things can happen to good people." She stealthily ripped off a piece of Leah's pretzel and popped it in her mouth. "And you're my favorite kind of people." She chewed thoughtfully for a moment, then added, "I want a full report on that picnic."

As they made their way around the mall, Leah's feelings transformed from nervousness to excitement, and she found herself feeling grateful for her friendship with Julie. It may as well have been 1974, because she was starting to feel like a kid again.

CHAPTER 13

At seven o'clock sharp, there was a knock on Leah's door.

After a few frantic, deep breaths, she opened it, and found herself caught breathless by the sight of Joseph.

She was used to seeing him in a cap and a buttoned-up, loose-fitting shirt supplied by George at the station. This evening, there was no cap — simply a recently-groomed, flat-top haircut. He wore a pullover shirt, tucked neatly into his Wrangler jeans. Trying not to focus too hard on the Wranglers, she noted that the shirt fit him very nicely — putting emphasis on what she had come to think of as his "near perfect" build. She wouldn't have guessed that this was hidden under the clothes he wore at work — although she certainly had wondered. In truth, she thought Joseph looked the image of a career army officer in top condition.

Leah had pulled her hair up into a ponytail, leaving some longer bangs on the side to frame her face. Putting makeup on earlier, she had asked herself in the mirror, "Since when do I get all dolled up for a picnic or a baseball game?" After putting on the finishing touches, she smiled at herself and said, "Since a man named Joseph came into my life, that's when."

After what felt like hours digging through her closet, she finally came to a decision. She chose a red-and-white-checkered blouse with the bottom tied casually in a knot at her midsection. She added her favorite pair of jeans (so as not to look *too* formal) and a comfortable pair of white canvas shoes, since she wasn't entirely

CHAPTER 13

sure of what he had planned.

Joseph's first thought when he laid eyes on Leah was "Well, looks like I've got a date with Daisy Mae."

Leah had never paid much attention to the truck that Joseph drove, but now she noticed that it was a well-kept Dodge — and tonight it looked almost new. Little did she know, he had cleaned and worked on it tirelessly to make it look presentable for the night.

After a few moments of nervous small talk, Leah grabbed her purse and locked her front door. As they made their way to the pickup, Leah noticed that the truck's box-end was nearly full of equipment and supplies for the picnic.

"Two coolers? A grill? Lawn chairs?"

He gave her a half-grin. "Well now, this isn't exactly your ordinary picnic."

She smiled back. "I'm not surprised at that. I'm starting to think that you're no ordinary man."

A little surprised by her forwardness, she felt a blush creeping up from the collar of her shirt. Thankfully, Joseph simply chuckled and walked Leah around to the passenger side of the truck, opening the door for her and offering her a hand. He walked back around, turned the key, and they were soon on their way to a picnic in the country — J.P. style.

After a while, it was clear their journey was taking them outside of the city limits. Leah decided she had no choice but to sit back and enjoy the ride. She was so excited, she felt like a young girl going to the circus for the first time — although she was looking forward to having more than stale popcorn and cotton candy to eat. With the windows rolled down just enough to let in fresh air without ruining the time she'd spent on her hair, she did her best to listen to the breeze and relax.

When Joseph turned the pickup off the highway and onto a gravel road, she found herself pleasantly surprised by the change in scenery. "Oh, wow," She breathed, "I had no idea all of this was out here!" As she looked around, she delighted in the rolling hills of fields, the canyons of grazing cattle, and the patches of cottonwood trees huddled together at various points of the rural countryside. J.P. pulled off the already out-of-the-way gravel road onto an even less-maintained dirt trail. They drove past a tangled row of trees, and Leah laughed.

"I'm so used to the trees in town, I always forget there are so many different kinds."

"Yep, looks like that's quite the mix there. Oak, cedar, pine. Probably some ash trees, too."

After about a quarter of a mile, the pickup rolled quietly to a stop at a lush, green patch of grass next to a thriving cornfield. He turned to her and grinned. "We've arrived."

The two got out of the pickup, shut the doors, and stood still for a moment, taking in the breathtaking beauty around them. Joseph took a deep breath and sighed quietly. He was clearly savoring the fresh, rural air he loved so much. Leah slowly began to realize that she was looking at a near-replica of where Joseph had lived most of his life, and it gave her a new understanding of this man she was getting to know. She hadn't ever put any real value in the areas outside the city, and she certainly hadn't thought twice about the smell of the countryside.

And it wasn't just the scenery — she had always thought of rural people and the areas they came from as boring and lacking in personality. But it was hard to keep thinking that way after spending time with Joseph. He had a mysterious, almost magical kind of personality that came to life as he took in the beautiful landscape around them. After a few more seconds, J.P. pulled his hands out of his pockets and clapped them together. "'Bout time for a picnic, don't you think?"

"You read my mind, Joseph," she lied, good-naturedly.

J.P. got busy unloading the supplies, first getting a chair for Leah and offering her something from one of the coolers. "You like cream soda?"

She let out a surprised laugh. "Cream soda? I haven't had one of those in an awfully long time. I'd love one, thanks." He handed

CHAPTER 13

her an old-fashioned looking glass bottle of caramel-colored liquid, and she sat back luxuriously into the canvas chair he'd provided. "Cicadas buzzing, tree branches swaying... this feels like a TV show."

As she relaxed, J.P. got the charcoals going in the grill. They talked casually about his days on the farm; what time he woke up, what he thought about during long hours on the tractor. When the charcoals were nice and hot, the thick cuts of roast beef and potatoes were put on the grill to warm up. "I started them at home with the notion of finishing them up once we got to the picnic site. Just need to get it all up to heat and ready for eating." He put the lid on the pot-bellied Weber grill and wiped his hands on the towel he had brought with him. "Looks like everything's on schedule, Leah. How do you feel about going for a walk?"

Leah was quick to jump up out of her chair — the fact was that she was willing to go anywhere J.P. wanted to take her. She wasn't sure when it had happened, but she had come to trust him completely, and wanted to be with him as much as possible.

They walked slowly in a westerly direction down a long, sloping hill. The tree shelter they had driven by on the way to their picnic was on their right, and an alfalfa field spread out to their left. A sweet, grassy smell floated on the gentle breeze as they ambled to a small creek with even more trees, a quarter of a mile ahead of them. Leah felt the familiar urge to fill their silence with rambling words. From her experience, a long lull in conversation usually preceded a knock-down, drag-out argument or a week of even more tense, silence. She knew that wasn't the case here, with Joseph, but a habit is hard to break.

"It's such a nice evening... I was a little worried it might —" Before she could finish her aimless comment about the weather, it was replaced with a startled shriek. A sleek doe and her spotted fawn had jumped out of the trees about fifty feet in front of them and abruptly stopped to gaze at the human invaders in their wooded home. Her heart pounding, Leah had been quick to seek shelter close to Joseph; even through her surprise she felt herself blush knowing their shoulders were touching. The incident seemed to stretch for at least five minutes, when in all actuality it was probably only about five *seconds*. The deer and the humans stood motionless, staring at each other. Finally, the mother deer deciding J.P. and Leah were unwelcome intruders, she snorted at them in what seemed like annoyance. This changed Leah's initial startled awe into actual fright, and she grabbed one of Joseph's hands. The deer, choosing to spend their time elsewhere, bounded away with high leaps and white tails flashing in the air.

Leah could hear her heart slamming in her ears, but she wasn't sure if it was from the deer or realizing she was holding Joseph's hand. This was the first time they had really and truly physically connected. She had ignored J.P.'s offer of a handshake the first day they met... she again found herself wishing that she had not been so cool toward him. Not that an initial handshake would have felt or meant as much as this did right now. She could feel his strength through his calloused hand, felt his confidence in his stance. She tried to catch her breath, swallowing discreetly because it felt as if her heart was in her throat.

J.P. put his arm around her shoulders to try and calm her, and left it there as they watched the deer bound out of sight.

Finally, Leah couldn't hold it in anymore. "Wow! I mean... wow!"

"You alright, there?"

"Joseph, I have never been near something so... so wild!"

He smiled and simply murmured, "Beautiful weren't they?"

"Yes, yes, they really were," was all she could force from her lips. She was suddenly more focused on the fact that she still held Joseph's hand... and did not want to let go.

They continued walking toward the creek. Once they reached the rippling water, they could see the many wild flowers lining both sides of the creek. Leah was amazed by the flowers — it looked like a painting you saw in a museum. Bright splashes of color, rich textures of green and brown. This was the type of scene J.P. had described to Leah on his first day at the station. He picked a handful

CHAPTER 13

of wild roses, blue phlox, and white asters and offered them to Leah. She accepted them with her free hand, bringing their sweet scent up to her nose for a quick inhale. Slowly, they headed back to the picnic site. Leah's head was spinning with excitement of the beautiful country setting and the joy of the gift of fresh flowers. J.P. found himself almost giddy that the evening was off to an excellent start.

When they reached the picnic site, J.P. rinsed out the cream soda bottle and filled it with water from a jug sitting in the back of the pickup. Leah handed him her new bouquet and he placed it in the makeshift vase before put the finishing touches on supper. He added more charcoal to the grill and then laid sweet corn, still in the husks, onto it.

As she watched him from her canvas perch, J.P. went about setting up the card table and dinnerware. In a matter of minutes, dinner was served. It worked out just as J.P. had planned it: sliced roast beef, flavored by the grilling to finish it, new baby potatoes, and sweet corn cooked right on the grill.

"Well, I feel downright spoiled," Leah remarked as she reached for another ear of corn. "Everything tastes just right... but I had no idea you could just toss ears of corn on the grill and have it turn out like this."

"You're happy with it, then?"

"Color me impressed, Joseph. With everything." Feeling like a completely different person, she reached over and placed her hand on his. "The setting, the nature walk, this incredible meal. The whole evening."

The sun had advanced to its lowest point in the western sky as they finished what was left on their plates. The sunset was filled with colors of blue, orange, and brilliant pink. "This evening is one of Mother Nature's works of grandeur," J.P. announced as he collected the plates from the table. Leah couldn't help but smile at his dramatic declaration, mostly because she couldn't agree more. To her delight, she noticed that a full moon was rising into the eastern sky as the sun disappeared in the west. It was a twilight

Leah had never known existed. Out in the country, away from the light pollution of the city, it was sure to be a gorgeous night.

J.P. set about preparing dessert. After digging around in the pickup, he brought out the marshmallows, Hershey's bars, and graham crackers.

"S'mores? On a grill?"

"Yep! I can't imagine ending a picnic with anything else."

Giddy again, Leah thought back to the beginning of the night — feeling like a kid headed to the circus. "I'd take s'mores over cotton candy any day," she thought to herself.

After dessert, J.P. moved the lawn chairs up and on to the back of the Dodge where they could relax and let their meal settle while they enjoyed the rest of the night. Offering her his hand, he helped Leah up to her chair before easing into his own. As darkness took over and the moon became their only source of light, they melted into the sounds of nature at night. Insects buzzed and chirped, wind rustled the surrounding crops and, Leah swore, if you concentrated, you could hear the creek, babbling away in the distance. The darkness brought the daily cycle of dawn, light, dusk, and darkness to completion. Leah thought about the fact that, in the previous two hours, she'd experienced all of those phases with Joseph, except dawn, of course. The thought of seeing the sunrise with him brought a shiver she tried to hide. She could feel the darkness heightening her other senses — the decadent taste of their meal lingering on her tongue, the haunting calls of owls in the distance, and the smoky crackle of the burning fire in front of them all seemed richer, more intense than they should be.

As they sat in the back of the Dodge, neither one of them could think of something to say. She felt the old fear of a tense, volatile silence creeping quietly up her spine, making the hair on the back of her neck prickle. With some deep breaths, she tried to remind herself that this silence was safe, and that there was so much around her to savor. Their eyes were gazing upward to see a blanket of stars in the night sky, so many more than the night sky in the city. Focusing on her senses instead of her memories, she closed her eyes. Smelling the scent given off by the burning logs and the sweet aroma of the alfalfa and wild flowers, it wasn't difficult to understand that nature had a firm influence in the events of the evening — just like it had shaped Joseph and the beliefs she had come to admire.

The air had become cooler, which was in sharp contrast with the warmth generated by J.P. and Leah's proximity to each other, in the folding chairs in the back of the Dodge. With a private quirk of her lips, she marveled at the fact that J.P. had even thought to bring a jacket for each of them, if the evening air became uncomfortably cool.

They stretched backward in their chairs, relaxing, taking in the mesmerizing kaleidoscope of nature as it danced around them in the calm and quiet of the night. Silently, but together, they paid homage to Mother Nature and the gifts she had bestowed upon their evening.

Leah had always been cautious about being vulnerable. With the comfort and security she was feeling with Joseph's jacket around her, she was finding it hard to keep up the walls she was so used to maintaining. In the moonlight, she reached hesitantly for Joseph's hand. The hand she would not shake at their first meeting, the kind hand that carried a rose each Monday into the garage. Leah was ready to accept the warmth from Joseph's hand and ready to let it melt away the coolness that had gradually grown in her over the years. Leah glanced at Joseph, but his eyes were gazing into the night sky.

J.P.'s thoughts were about Leah, not the past, but the future. He was listening for a message in the whisper of the breeze.

Neither of them spoke, for fear of breaking the intoxicating spell that held both of them, bound to each other in that twinkling moment. They were so content that time seemed of no consequence — they felt motionless, as if they were free from gravity's restraints.

Later they'd swear that neither one of them had dozed off, but by the time J.P. looked at his watch, it was nearly midnight. Gingerly, J.P. began cleaning and repacking their makeshift picnic area. When Leah realized what Joseph was up to, she stood up and let him help her down from the box of the Dodge. All of this happened in silence, almost out of respect for what they had experienced together. Neither one of them had the words, so they let the sounds of night capture their feelings.

As they started back to the city, Leah did her best to catalog the details out the window. The dimmed crop rows fanning out endlessly, the breeze turning cooler by the speed of the pickup. As they turned onto the highway and approached the city, the glow of the lights dominated over the stars, and Leah was surprised at her disappointment. They were quiet all the way to Leah's house, where J.P. walked Leah to her door holding the wildflowers in one hand and Leah's hand in the other.

As they stood under the porch light, gazing into each other's eyes, neither of them could find the right words to end the evening. When J.P. finally handed Leah the cream soda bottle of flowers, he realized it was the perfect moment.

The kiss.

It wasn't crazy with passion — nothing sloppy. Not the frantic smack of wild teenagers, but the timid, hopeful first kiss of two people who wanted nothing more than to feel young and free again.

Though it was late, Leah's senses were on fire. As she watched Joseph walk toward the Dodge, her heart flooded at each of his steps. The only sounds she remembered were the closing of the pickup door, the starting of the engine, and then the crackle of the tires as they rolled across the pavement.

Once she was inside her home, Leah practically stumbled into the first available chair. Her legs felt weak, but her mind and heart were emboldened — fortified with a surprising strength. She briefly wondered if the last six hours had all been a dream. Exhausted, yet coursing with energy, she could barely admit to herself that she was hoping for something more than a kiss.

J.P. drove slowly to his little house. He didn't want the evening to end. He felt like he'd been planning the evening for years, never once expecting the reward of a memorable, perfect first kiss. As he parked the Dodge, turned the key in the lock, and got himself ready for bed, he replayed the perfect twilight picnic in his mind, analyzing each comment and movement for hints of meaning. Finally, with a smile on his face, he drifted off into a much-needed slumber.

CHAPTER 14

After a short but satisfying sleep, J.P. headed for his hometown.

Being a practicing Catholic, J.P. wanted to reach Frankton in time for Sunday morning Mass. He had attended Sunday Mass his whole life, only missing church because of illness or, occasionally, a blizzard. He wasn't about to allow the move to the city to interfere with the practice of his faith.

Being back home for Mass gave J.P. the opportunity to see and visit with a lot of people from his church community. He knew everyone and their families, all two hundred of them. After the service, there were many hellos and handshakes for J.P. at the front of the entrance of Saint Peters. Still beaming from the previous evening, he couldn't remember the last time he had felt so content.

He then headed for his parents' farm, where there would be a massive Sunday meal prepared for any family members who happened to stop by. With gratitude in his heart for being home, and last night's dinner on his mind, J.P. couldn't put a damper on the smile that had settled in on his tanned face.

As he watched his mother dig through kitchen drawers for a serving spoon, he realized that she and Leah had something in common. As the only two people on Earth who insisted on calling him "Joseph," they shared a bond they weren't even aware of. Considering both women were the main reasons for his joy that day, it seemed entirely appropriate. Kate's home-cooked meal was satisfying his *actual* hunger, and Leah's company had control of his emotions — he simply couldn't ask for more.

Being back on the farm didn't give J.P. any respite from his thoughts about the night before — or that he really wanted any, but they were affecting his mood as he interacted with his family. They commented on the fact that he was smiling more, that he was laughing in a way they hadn't heard in years. Different members of his family quizzed him about his change in mood, but he just shrugged them off with another laugh. *He* knew what had changed, but he wasn't yet ready to share this new development with his family. He had a feeling, though, that they'd be finding out eventually.

J.P. spent part of the afternoon checking things out around the farm. The cattle and the crops looked like they were happy and thriving, and there was plenty of grass in the pastures to keep the cattle satisfied. The farm had received more moisture in the first six months than it had in any of the last six total years, and everyone was in a much happier mood, thankful for the precious gift of rain. People who make their living off the land understand — it's water that makes everything grow.

With an unpredictable partner like Mother Nature in the struggle to make a living off the land, it looked like she had chosen this year to be gracious. J.P. knew enough to be grateful.

That evening, before heading back to the city, J.P. stopped to visit with Daniel. It was nice to sit on the front porch with his son, cans of Coke in hand, talking about the ins-and-outs on the farm these past few weeks.

"You know, son, I'm real proud of you. While I know all the rain is helping, I also know things wouldn't be running so smoothly if you didn't have such a good head on your shoulders."

Daniel smiled at that. "Thanks, Dad. I appreciate it. The rain does

CHAPTER 14

help." He took a slow, thoughtful sip of soda, "What about you? How's the country mouse liking the city?"

"Ha, I guess I *am* a bit like the country mouse, huh? You know, it's not as bad as I thought it'd be. I've got a good job that pays me well, a boss I can trust, and — and I've even been to a few baseball games."

Daniel leaned forward in his chair, a suspicious glint in his eye. "Baseball games? Like, at the college?"

"Ah, well, no. Just — just some legion games at a field near my place."

The younger Dreuel simply raised an eyebrow at the elder. "Interesting. You haven't been to a game in... a while."

J.P. hadn't missed the look in his son's eye — he couldn't fool the boy. "Well, Daniel. I— I've, well —"

"You've found yourself a city mouse?"

He laughed, "Actually, yes. I think. Maybe."

"Yes, you think, maybe?"

"Yeah, that about sums it up."

Daniel thought for a moment and stared out at the fields that filled his vision, then turned and stuck out his hand. J.P. looked down at it in surprise, then took it for a firm shake. Daniel grinned. "I'd say it's about time, Dad."

Back in the city, Leah had gotten together with Julie on Sunday afternoon for a walk, and Julie was desperate for details.

"You *know* why we're here." Julie distractedly tried to push her too-short bangs behind her ears, and her 4 foot, 11 inch body struggled to keep up with Leah's fast steps. "*Spill it.* Spare no detail. Leave no stone unturned, and let no heavy petting go without detailed description."

With a squeal, Leah playfully punched Julie in the arm. "There was *no* heavy petting!" The two friends started off on their usual route as Leah described the picnic as best she could. She recalled everything from Joseph's appearance, to the scenery and the surprise deer, to meal in the twilight, and — finally — the kiss and silent departure from the front door. As Leah recounted the story and her heart rate began to climb, her walking speed increased quickly and surely, until Julie finally nudged her with her elbow.

"Alright, Speed Queen, I need a break. I can focus on your sweeping fairy tale romance a little better if I'm sitting!" She dramatically flopped down onto the park bench a few steps away and patted the spot next to her.

Leah, giggled. "I'm sorry — I must have gotten excited!"

"I'll say!" After a few deep breaths, Julie gave her friend a sly smile. "You know, after hearing about this guy's first week of work, I thought he sounded like quite the odd duck."

"You and me, both."

"But, I've got to say, after hearing about this dinner-cooking, heart-fluttering, country bumpkin, I can't wait to meet him."

CHAPTER 15

A person would have to be living under a rock to not realize that there was a romance going on in George's Service Station. J.P. and Leah were like two birds in a National Geographic special, strutting around each other to show off their feathers and follow the mating rituals of their species.

George and two of the other good ole boys who hung around the station were getting a kick out of the show that the two lovebirds were putting on. Besides George, there were Pete and Fred, and they all felt quite fatherly toward Leah, and since her divorce, they had taken it upon themselves to stand forth as her protectors. Fortunately for J.P., all three of these gentlemen liked him. In fact, they were delighted to see Leah experience so much happiness.

"Why, that's the happiest I've seen her since before her marriage to that bum," Fred declared as he took a sip of old afternoon coffee.

Pete agreed with a nod of his head and a drink of his own. "We've all seen it, that's for sure. And I reckon I'm just fine with that."

Another nod, another sip, this time from George. "And it doesn't hurt that he takes the time to talk to you two geezers." The geezers in question chuckled. "He even takes what you tell him seriously. Shows respect."

"Way I see it, George, the fact that he can get through your stories without keelin' over is damn near a miracle. He's got a friendly disposition, too."

"You're not kidding there, Pete. I swear I don't think I've seen him get frustrated even once. If something's not going right on a repair, worst I've heard is 'Oh, heck!'"

Fred smiled and held out his favorite coffee mug, old and faded, with a picture of Herbie Husker winking out at whoever took the time to look closely enough. "Here's to the young lovebirds!" And with a couple of jolly clinks, J.P. was given the official seal of approval.

Meanwhile, J.P. was enjoying his relationship with Leah so much, he felt like his heart was going to burst out of his chest. The way he cared for her was filling the void that had opened up sometime during his marriage to Claire. Having someone who *wanted* attention and kindness from him wasn't a feeling he was used to. That being said, J.P. was struggling with that side of his blossoming romance. How could he have these feelings for Leah when the fact remained that he had a wife?

This thing with Leah had caught him off guard, that's for sure. Had he run away, hoping he could leave that messy part of his life on the farm? Or had he simply left the farm to experience the parts of life he'd never had the chance to? Experiences that had eluded him by being faithful to the farm and his family? He wasn't sure. It was probably a big, messy mixture of all of it, and he wasn't quite sure how to clean it up.

On Wednesday, Leah invited J.P to another of Nick's baseball games. As was his way, J.P. was paying attention to even the tiniest details of the game.

"So, slugger, I see you giving Nick tips, but that's about all I know of your baseball career. Tell me about *your* playing days." She smiled behind her sunglasses and snacked on her popcorn, waiting patiently for him to peel his eyes away from the game.

"I always made time for it, no matter how busy I was on the farm. I started playing organized baseball when I was about thirteen,

CHAPTER 15

which was a relatively late start compared to kids nowadays."

"You're not kidding, there! I feel like I've been buying Nick uniforms since the dawn of time."

"Yep, uniforms aren't cheap, that's for sure." He sneaked a kernel of popcorn from the small brown bag she had in her hands, popped it into the air, and caught it deftly in his mouth. "I played until I was eighteen — that's as old as they'll let you play legion baseball."

Distracted by the crack of the bat, J.P. turned his attention temporarily back to the game, allowing Leah to admire the strong curve of his jawline while she waited for him to rejoin the conversation.

He turned back to her and grinned, "Sorry about that. Once I hit the age limit, I took up fast and slow-pitch softball. You know, there were some summers where I played in a hundred games between three different teams. The year I quit is when I started coaching my son, Daniel's, team. Coached them for six years and made it to the state tournament my final season."

"Sounds like the perfect way to end your career."

"It sure was."

Leah thrilled at these tidbits of Joseph's history. No wonder he paid such close attention to Nick's games. She thought of the powerful way he hit the golf balls at the driving range and added, "I bet you were pretty good!"

Joseph merely shrugged his shoulders, smiled a mischievous smile, and said, "I played a lot."

In the second inning, while Nick was playing second base, there was a hard-hit grounder toward Nick's right. He charged the ball, fielded it, and tagged the runner going to second base, then threw the ball to first for the out to end the inning. Nick's teammates and the team's fans cheered loudly, and Leah and J.P. joined from the stands.

As the game continued, J.P. turned to Leah, "Now that I've told you about my favorite hobby, I'd love to hear more about yours."

Not prepared to talk about herself, she blushed. "Well, you already know about my piano playing, which I like to do as much as

I can. It calms me, helps me... process things. To be honest, I don't have many more hobbies than that. Being a single mom took up most of my time and energy the past five years, and before that... well, my ex never really allowed me to have any time of my own."

J.P. didn't like the sound of that, and felt himself bristling at the mention of Leah's mysterious ex-husband.

"Don't get me wrong, though. Nick's my pride and joy. I'm thankful I had those five years to raise him the way I thought best. Away from the... negative influences of his dad." She focused on the field for a bit before continuing. "Nick was always an 'A' student and, besides the normal growing pains of a teenage boy, he had never been a problem."

"That's good to hear... but I don't think your son counts as a hobby."

Leah held out her hands, "Alright! Yes, you're right. Definitely not a *hobby*. I guess you could say my best friend is my other hobby. Julie. We've been joined at the hip since junior high."

"Junior high, huh? That's quite the friend to have around."

"Yep, we still talk at least twice a week. You know, I don't think we've ever gone more than two weeks in all those years without at least spending *some* time together... which is something of a miracle considering what things were like with Heath."

Heath. Joseph was startled by the mention of his name, and the hatred that seemed to drip from the way she said it. Realizing that the conversation had turned darker than she wanted, Leah perked herself up. "She wants to meet you, you know. In fact, you might say she's *dying* to meet you."

"Who, Julie?"

"Yes, Julie!"

"Well, I can't say I'm not a little nervous about it, but I think that sounds like a fine idea."

In the third inning, Nick had struck out. In the fifth inning, he was up to bat again and there were two runners on base. J.P., ever-vigilant, noticed that Nick's hands were choked up on the bat. On the second pitch, he lined a hit over the third baseman's glove and

CHAPTER 15

the ball rolled to the corner of left field. The two runners scored and, to his team's delight, Nick managed a triple.

When Nick took the field the next inning, J.P. noticed Nick smoothing the infield with his shoe.

Leah glanced at Joseph and saw him intently watching Nick, and remembered the game two weeks earlier, when Joseph had talked to Nick after the game. "What's Nick doing, moving the dirt with his shoe?"

"He's smoothing the field, so hopefully he doesn't get a bad hop." Leah nodded seriously, pretending to understand his baseball jargon.

J.P. smiled, and glanced sidelong at her. "A bad hop is when the ball hits uneven ground — it shoots off in a direction you can't anticipate."

Grateful for the explanation, she smiled right back.

After the game ended with a win for Nick's team, he bounded across the field and over to his mother and J.P. His team had won three-to-one, with a few of Nick's plays being important factors in the game. Nick gave his mother a happy hug and then turned toward J.P.

"Good game, Nick!" This new man in his mom's life flashed him a proud grin, and Nick produced his hand for a shake. J.P. took it and shook heartily.

"Thanks, J.P.! And thanks for coming!"

Leah and J.P. exchanged amused glances. Nick was practically beaming with excitement and pride. It was clear that J.P. had taught him some important lessons in those few short minutes, two weeks ago. But Leah could see that what he'd *really* gained from the conversation was confidence.

Nick clapped his hands together. "I'm hungry! Let's go for pizza! What do you say? J.P. you want to come?"

The two looked at each other and smiled again. The evening couldn't have worked out any better. With Nick doing all the planning, neither of them had to make an awkward decision, or come up with an excuse to spend the rest of the day together. Still chattering excitedly, Nick and Leah piled into her car, and J.P.

hopped into his truck to follow them to the best pizza in town.

"I'm telling you, J.P., this is the best pizza you'll ever have," Nick chimed in after their server walked away with the menus.

"I believe you!" J.P. took a sip of his water and relaxed into the booth. As they were waiting for their pizza, he could see that Nick was full of questions.

"So, how did you know all those things about baseball? Like the stuff you showed me a couple weeks ago?"

"Baseball is a game, you know? So try to keep it simple. The game is you and the ball. It seems most guys want to complicate it."

Nick thought for a few moments and looked thoughtfully at him. "No coach has told me anything like that before."

J.P. nodded and shot a meaningful look at Leah. "Most things are simple if we let them be."

Leah heard that, loud and clear. She hadn't realized their picnic had been so "simple" at the time, but of course it was. They had watched the sun go down, the moon come up, and the stars twinkle as they came out in the darkness. They had simply let everything *be*, and enjoyed it. There was no attempt to control — from the encounter with the deer, to the scents and sights of nature, to their extended-but-comfortable silence... and, of course, the ending. That delightful kiss.

Leah sat next to Joseph in the booth waiting for pizza and realized, to her astonishment, a fact about Joseph that had been hidden in plain sight. From the very first time she decided to pay attention to him, it was clear that he was different. She had been leery of it at first, when she thought of him as a hick, some podunk farmer from the sticks. Now, in this booth with her son, she knew that Joseph was *simple*, in the purest sense of the word. Not simple-minded, but brimming over with simple and honest thoughts — the complete opposite of what she had become used to from men. What had kept her away from him that first week was now what was drawing her in. At that moment, Leah found she couldn't help

CHAPTER 15

herself, and reached for Joseph's hand under the table. When she found it, she gave it a squeeze.

J.P. looked at her with surprise. Leah, though, gave him a sweet smile, and chuckled quietly at his jolt.

Even in his anticipation of pizza and residual excitement from the baseball game, Nick noticed that little moment between the two people sitting across from him in the booth. This added even more fun to Nick's already excellent evening.

As a seemingly-starved Nick devoured slice after slice of pizza, he asked J.P. questions about his son Daniel, and the farm. The conversation went into the evening, comfortably and without hurry. As they said their reluctant goodbyes in the parking lot afterward, Leah winked at Joseph — a bold move for her — and chimed, "See you tomorrow morning at work!" Her face warm with nervousness, she ducked quickly into her Blazer and shut the door. What she *really* wanted to say was "I can't wait," but she kept that to herself.

She and Nick pulled out of the parking lot and headed home, silent for the first mile as an 80s rock ballad crackled out of her car's aging speakers. Nick leaned over and nudged her with his elbow. "That was pretty cool of J.P. to come to my game again."

"Hmm. Yeah, it was." Leah felt her embarrassment creep up again, as she kept her eyes on the road, tapping her fingers to the music on the steering wheel.

"I really like him, Mom."

Knowing it was one of those quiet moments, the kind where honesty is always the best choice, she replied, "You know, I think I do, too."

When Leah arrived at work the next morning, she found an envelope bearing her name waiting on her desk. Apprehensively, but with growing excitement, she opened it and read quietly to herself:

I cannot wait!
Could we go on a date?
I would like to take you Saturday night
To the dance hall, Starbrite.
I am as excited to dance
As a horse trained to prance.
I will not press,
But I hope you do not make me wait and guess...
And that your answer is a quick, YES!
J.P.

Stunned, Leah gasped and dropped into her office chair, reading the simple poem over and over again. Without really knowing why, she looked around to make sure that no one was watching her. In fact, she felt like she had done something silly or wrong, just by reading it. Stifling a giggle, she remembered what it felt like to be caught passing a note to someone, and being forced to read it in front of the whole class.

Luckily, George was the only one on guard, and he didn't suspect a mission of this sort to be carried out on this hot, summer morning. After Leah had gotten beyond the blushing, she smiled at the honesty of the poem and decided to take decisive action. She straightened her blouse, ran a hand through her hair, and practically marched out of her office and into the shop. She made a direct line for Joseph, who was under the carriage of a car doing some kind of repair.

The sight of his strong legs sticking out from under the car was enough to *almost* break her determination with a laugh, but she muscled through the giggles and tapped him on his knee. He noticed her at the last moment, and rolled out to see what she was up to. He grinned up at her with a smudge of oil on his forehead and opened his mouth to greet her. Before he could say anything she got straight to the point. "So you want to go dancing?"

He swallowed. "Yes ma'am."

"Good. So do I, but I need you to understand something." Her

CHAPTER 15

heart pounded as she put on her toughest face. Of all the things she was confident in, her own dancing ability was *not* one of them. She wasn't going to let that stop her, though. The truth was, she was willing to give just about anything a try when it came to Joseph.

"The last time I went dancing was New Year's Eve, and it was awful."

"Well, I would like to think that this time would be different."

"I would like to think that, too."

"What happened? Can you tell me?"

Joseph's gentle voice and concerned gaze managed to calm her down enough to sit on the floor next to him. "I went out with a group of friends. Honestly, they're not even really friends. Acquaintances." She picked up a wrench and absentmindedly scraped some grime off of it with her fingernail. "One of the men with us drank too much, grabbed me by the arms, and tried to dance with me. I told him to back off, he called me a 'Debbie Downer,' and I ended up getting a cab home so I could avoid having to be around him anymore."

He didn't make a big deal of it, but J.P. instinctively reached for the roll of Rolaids in his pocket. Instead of expressing the anger he was feeling, he popped one in his mouth, and let Leah continue her story.

"Now, I'm sure a night of dancing... with you... will wash that bad taste right out of my mouth. I'll bet you're a much better dancer, for one, and I know you'd never try to force me into something I'm not comfortable with."

"You're absolutely right."

"The thing is, though, dancing is *not* my strong suit. I feel like you should know that ahead of time."

He blinked at her for a moment, and then let out a laugh he couldn't stop. "After what you just told me, you think your *dancing* is the problem?"

"It's... not good, Joseph." She cracked a tiny smile. "I'm concerned for your toes."

He laughed again — a hearty belly laugh that made butterflies dance in her stomach — and took her hands in his. "We haven't talked much about drinking, but I never have more than one drink."

"That's good to know. You just don't like it, or what?"

"I'm not a fan of the taste of alcohol, honestly, and I usually get a headache... even after one drink."

"I appreciate you telling me that."

"And besides, if your dancing is as bad as you're making it out to be, one of us is definitely going to need to be sober."

She gave him a light punch to the shoulder, and he thrilled at the contact. "You know, New Year's Eve was the last time I went dancing, too. By my way of thinking, that's too long ago."

"Oh really?"

"Sure is. Fact is, I love to dance. If I had the opportunity, I'd go out once a week."

She pulled herself up off the ground and dusted off her jeans. "How about let's take it one dance at a time, huh?"

He grinned. "Deal."

She turned on her heel and headed back into her office, trying hard not to frolic the whole way to her desk. She was feeling sneaky and feisty — she had completed her mission. She found the note, read it, and made contact with the sender before anyone was the wiser.

The idea of dancing, being that close to each other made Leah's heart rate speed up. Once she was sitting down, she realized she had many unfamiliar feelings running through her body. It had been years since Leah had felt even a semblance of desire for a man. There was an appetite — one she had completely forgotten about — from deep within trying to make its way to the surface. Was it her body telling her mind, or her mind telling her body?

Leah didn't care what it was; she was feeling *something*. If she was going brutally honest with herself, she couldn't even remember the last time she had felt *anything* remotely physical for someone. She liked this change, and was hoping for more.

CHAPTER 16

Saturday afternoon, the clouds thickened and it rained steadily. Leah thought to herself with a quirk of her lips, "Not picnic weather," and she wondered playfully, "Think the ants had forecast this rain?" She poured a steaming mug of tea and allowed herself to daydream as she stared out the window. Last Saturday had been picture-perfect weather for a picnic, and she couldn't wait to go on another. Overcome with a giddy feeling, and empowered by the fact that Nick was still in bed, sawing logs, she called out through the window screen, "Let it rain!"

Nothing short of a natural disaster was going to dampen her spirits about the coming evening. A week ago, Leah had been anxious and nervous about the whole ordeal. Today, her feelings were bouncing from wall to wall with excitement and a growing confidence in herself and her relationship with J.P.

To help get her mind off the time, she sat at the piano and played some of her favorite pieces. She closed her eyes while tapping the keys, enjoying the transformation from notes to music, so sweet to her ears. Lost in the swells of her favorite tunes, she let herself escape from reality for what seemed like half an hour. When she opened her eyes, she was startled to see Nick leaning against the wall, smiling at her.

"So why the good mood?" he asked, with a smirk on his face.

"Oh, nothing, big. Just enjoying the morning."

"Enjoying the morning, huh? What's there to be happy about on a rainy Saturday?" He crossed his arms. "Our baseball game has been canceled, and we can't even practice." Huffing like a twelve year old, he muttered. "What am I going to do all day?"

Leah was glad he had gotten distracted by his own plight, and had forgotten to pursue his previous line of questioning. "Why don't you call Becka for lunch and take in a movie? Seems like the kind of day for that." She began to absentmindedly play a few notes, bringing his attention back to her.

"So why *are* you so happy today? Bet it has something to do with J.P."

She turned to him dramatically with a roll of her eyes. "I don't know what you're talking about," she joked.

Leah wasn't prepared for his honest response. "Good for you mom, I mean it. I really like J.P., and you deserve something nice to happen in your life."

Caught off guard by both his emotions and hers, she felt tears begin to sting her eyes. That stinging evolved into rolling tears, and she struggled to keep from audibly sobbing. She covered her face in her hands. With his face changing from soft happiness to a sort of terror, Nick backpedaled. "Gosh mom! Oh jeeze, I didn't mean to make you cry!" Nick slid onto the piano bench next to her while she continued to cry quietly and put his arm around his mother's shoulder. He nudged her gently. "Play me that song. You know, the one you used to play to cheer us up on rainy days?" He clumsily plunked a few notes of the song out with his right hand. Her crying began to mix with laughter, and Leah began to pound out *You Are My Sunshine* on the piano. She felt a sense of freedom and contentment as she and Nick sang together, as loudly as they could. Had there been dogs in hearing range, they would have set up a howling. As the song finished, Nick gave his mom a long hug.

"Thanks, Mom. I think I'll take your advice and call Becka."

As Nick left the room to find his phone, Leah got up from the piano and moved into the sun porch. She watched the rain come down while she daydreamed about the coming evening with Joseph. In her mind, beautiful music was floating around the room, and the

CHAPTER 16

two of them were seemingly lost out on the dance floor, unaware of anything but the music and each other. It was only a daydream, but it sent a warmth and desire coursing all the way to her toes. .

For the second Saturday in a row, J.P. washed and cleaned his Dodge pickup. He didn't care that it was raining; there would be no cutting corners. His plan was laid out, and he was going to follow it through. After the pickup, he polished his favorite cowboy boots — the ones that had been a gift from his maternal grandfather over twenty years ago. They were his good boots; their only job was attending church and enjoying the dance floor. J.P.'s cowboy genes came from this grandfather, who had taught him that when a man pulls on his boots and puts on that wide brimmed hat, he is elevated to a higher standard. "You are to be a gentleman, J.P.," his grandpa had told him, "and let your words and actions show 'em all that you're a cowboy." He allowed himself a moment to reminisce for a bit, and then set back to the tasks at hand.

When Leah answered the front door to greet J.P. that evening, she was once again surprised.

There stood a cowboy with a bouquet of brightly-colored flowers in his hand for her. Suddenly, her dream from that awful day so long ago surged back from the depths of her memory. With his boots and cowboy hat on, Joseph looked a full six inches taller. Here he was again, stunning, strong, and impossible to resist. She didn't ask questions, but figured that this was Joseph's favorite dancing attire. As she fumbled for her purse, she could once again feel the red glow on her face that had become a common occurrence as of late.

J.P. noticed the blush, and thought maybe it was because of the flowers. He knew it was the first time Leah had received flowers on a date, other than the wildflowers the week before.

"I hope you're not embarrassed by the hat, although I've got to admit I probably wouldn't take it off if you were."

"No! No, of course not, it looks nice!"

"Well, good. I can't help but feel the most comfortable when I'm wearing my hat, boots, and wrangling jeans." He beamed at her. "Simply put, this is who I am."

Leah pushed a wisp of hair behind her ear, and drummed up the courage to say, "I wouldn't want it any other way."

J.P. wouldn't say anything to her, but he was also surprised by Leah's appearance — not to mention his own reaction to it. She was showing more than a glimpse of her ample cleavage, and her hair was pulled back loosely, allowing pieces of her bangs to frame her face. The scent of her perfume had him thinking thoughts he hadn't entertained for years. Pulling his mind back to the moment at hand, he held out the bouquet. "These are for you, Leah."

Leah gratefully took them and put the flowers in a jar. Embarrassed, she laughed. "If you never get flowers you don't exactly have much reason for a vase!" She was dressed casually. In fact, she was wearing her most comfortable shoes, hoping they might bring her luck on the dance floor.

She couldn't believe it, but luck was on her mind, and it wasn't just limited to their time on the dance floor. She tried to shake the thought out of her head — it would be a *long* night if she was worried about *that* the whole time!

The rain had slackened to a drizzle, and J.P. commented that it was cool for this time of year. When J.P. opened the door on the passenger side for Leah, her attention was immediately drawn to the rose hanging from her sun visor. She also noticed the dream catcher hanging from the rear view mirror. Seeing this small glimpse into his life made goosebumps spring up on her arms. Was it the cool air? The rose? Or was it the cowboy walking in front of this immaculate pickup?

In a split second Leah made a decision. It was *definitely* the cowboy, and there was no doubt in her mind: she was going to make Joseph *her* cowboy that night. She grew ever more anxious to be in his arms on the dance floor... and otherwise.

Walking into the Starbrite Dance Hall is a thrilling experience. It's

CHAPTER 16

a step into the past, with all of its original beauty still intact. The Starbrite is a large, barn-style dance hall built at the end of World War II. After half a century, this historic venue has accumulated a rich ballroom history that includes the Lawrence Welk Orchestra and the Allen Miller Band. Even with the years of dancing, the oak floor was kept in prime shape through regular, expert maintenance. J.P. took in a deep breath of the dance hall air as they walked through the doors. Rich wood mixed with that little bit of cigarette smoke that refused to fully leave the premises (no matter what the law said) filled his head, and he felt almost drunk on the atmosphere. The Starbrite's history had to be read like a book, with dozens of pictures decorating the walls. The photos — mostly black and white — provided a marquee of the sounds and styles of dancing that patrons had enjoyed under this roof for nearly sixty years.

In recent years, most of the music is provided by DJs, this evening included, but occasionally a genuine band will take the stage.

It was already buzzing with dancers by the time they arrived. J.P. estimated the crowd at nearly one hundred and fifty.

She hadn't ever had a reason to give it much thought before tonight, but Leah was pretty sure that — before Joseph — she would have been embarrassed to show up with someone wearing a cowboy hat. The truth was that Leah liked to go unnoticed, and a cowboy hat tends to have the opposite effect.

But tonight? Tonight she was proud to strut into this dance hall with her cowboy. They managed to find a place to sit, sharing a table with two other couples they didn't know. Even the idea of sitting with strangers felt exotic to Leah — the whole experience felt like a trip to a faraway land.

As they waited for the music to start, J.P. leaned into her ear. "Do you see anyone here that you know?"

"Actually, I did recognize one couple when we walked in, but I don't know their names. Possibly from the station, or one of Nick's baseball games." She turned toward him. "Why do you ask?" "No reason, just curious."

The two had decided their first dance should be a slow one, in order to get acquainted with each other's body rhythm. Just hearing J.P. talk about *body rhythm* made her cheeks turn red. As the music slowed and Vince Gill's classic voice filled the room, he took her by the hand and led her to the dance floor. He smiled at her. "Typical Western theme, huh? Love and heartache."

She smiled back. "I don't know why, Joseph, but it feels perfect." As they swayed to the sad ballad, it felt like they were melting into each other — becoming one and the same. The song's subject matter didn't match their current circumstances, but it spoke to their pasts, and it felt therapeutic to give those feelings a new meaning — their previous lives had brought them to this moment, this music, this night.

The fact that they moved so well together wasn't lost on either of them. With their bodies close and swaying, their hearts pressed together gently, it became increasingly clear that this was going to be a night they would not soon forget.

J.P. couldn't believe it, but he realized the night was going to work out just the way he had planned and hoped it would. He could tell by the way Leah moved that she enjoyed being in his arms and following his lead on the floor. He felt his cheeks flush, and quickly pulled his thoughts back to the music.

After the first two songs, they made their way back to the table. They had barely gotten seated when the music changed and J.P. grabbed Leah's hand, excitedly pulling her back onto the dance floor. The song had a faster tempo than the one before, and as Joseph started two-stepping, Leah immediately got nervous. Her head shot downward in order to look at her feet and make it easier, but Joseph gently took her chin and brought her face back up to his.

"Don't worry. Just look into my eyes." He dipped his mouth next to her ear and began whispering, "Two, two and two, two." Mesmerized by his voice and the feeling of his breath on her ear, Leah instinctively fell into step with him. She couldn't believe how much she was enjoying the evening. The dancing, the music, the feeling of Joseph's body against hers — it felt like magic. She didn't

CHAPTER 16

have to pretend that she liked it, just to impress Joseph.

"You make this seem so easy. It's… fun." she murmured, breathlessly.

"Things tend to be easy, when you let them be simple." And they danced. It didn't matter which song or what kind of tempo, Joseph's timing adjusted to the beat automatically and she with his.

It *was* simple — it was simple and perfect.

A thought that occurred to Leah during one of their momentary breaks from the dance floor was that her choice of shoes had nothing to do with her ability to dance. In fact, if you had asked her then, she wouldn't have even remembered what shoes she was wearing. The truth was that Joseph had reached inside her soul and brought to life a latent desire to bring flesh to all those songs she had heard and loved on the radio. Suddenly, she realized that all those songs were written for *dancing*, not mere *listening*.

The feelings and desires expressed in the music mirrored what she felt toward Joseph, and adding the element of *dance* made all the old songs feel new. Moving together, breathing together, hearts beating together — it was like he'd given her the key to unlock a door she didn't realize existed. The music had given her a particular language through which she could express her love for Joseph, and allowed her to feel that love in return.

At the stroke of midnight, after hours that felt like only a few minutes, they decided to call it quits. It was difficult for Leah to let go of the dance — the movement, the connection, the new language she had learned — and she wistfully looked back at the other dancers, settling in for another hour. Joseph's hand on hers, however, snapped her back to reality as he gently led her out the front door. The quiet outside was startling, and as they left the dance hall she began to notice the tiredness creeping into her legs. There was still a cool drizzle in the night air as they walked back to the Dodge. As always, Joseph accompanied Leah to her side of the truck and opened the door for her. As he rounded the pickup and climbed into the driver's seat, he was surprised to see that

Leah had scooted all the way over to sit close to him. The air was practically crackling with electricity as he caught her eyes with an unquestionable desire. He didn't ask it out loud, but Leah heard his question, clear as a bell. She answered it with a long, passionate kiss, pulling reluctantly away after a few moments to catch his eyes right back. He cupped the back of her neck with his left hand, ran his right hand through her hair, and definitively answered her kiss with one of his own.

These were not like their first kiss, one week ago. These kisses were rough and primal; surprising passion and forgotten desire collided as they fumbled with buttons, hungering for more. Shaking hands feverishly explored trembling bodies, and ragged breaths began to bring a teenage fog to the edges of the windows.

Neither of them knew how long this went on, but eventually they needed a moment to come up for air.

Leah nervously raked her hair with her fingers. They both took a deep breath.

With a breathy chuckle and a pounding heart, J.P. turned on the pickup, then the heater to clear a spot in the foggy windshield on this cool night.

Leah continued to sit next to J.P. on the way home, keeping her left arm flush with his right. The cool, damp night air had been quickly replaced by their hot breath, and J.P. had to turn up the blower to finally clear the windshield fully. The drive home didn't cool them down; it, in fact, had the opposite effect. As he focused intently on the road, Leah placed her hand on his thigh… dangerously close to his favorite belt buckle. He inhaled sharply. The passion continued to build as they drove along the highway, letting their hands continue to roam over unexplored territory.

The ten minute drive was like a double-edged sword — a blissful, new adventure laced with the torture of restraint.

As they pulled up in front of Leah's home, and before the Dodge

CHAPTER 16

came to a complete stop, Leah blurted, "Do you want to come in for a drink?"

J.P. didn't answer. With that smile, he didn't need to. Giggling, they scrambled out of the pickup and into the house. It was well after midnight and Leah hadn't seen Nick's pickup in the drive. Her son had mentioned something about spending the night at a friend's house, and she couldn't have been more pleased.

The "drinks" amounted to a hurried glass of water.

J.P. smiled mischievously at her from behind his water glass. "Full night of dancing will knock you flat if you're not careful." Leah's eyes grew wide at that comment, and she abruptly set her glass down. She took J.P.'s glass right from his lips and crushed her mouth against his.

Everything seemed to happen in a flurry: their minds, lips, and hands were frantically busy. Leah was quite sure that if they kept this up much longer she was going to explode, so she broke away, took Joseph by the hand, and led him into her bedroom.

Neither of them had to say a word.

In the midst of her racing thoughts, Leah was able to pause for a moment and think, "There's that silence again," before her momentary clear-headedness drowned in the rush of heat and disorienting desire. They were caught up in the urgency of it all.

And, yet, despite the blood pounding in their veins and the knowledge of what was to come, J.P. was still J.P. He hung his hat on the doorknob and lined his boots up by the wall. Leah found this to be endearing and reassuring, and surprisingly attractive.

She let out a throaty laugh that she hadn't heard from herself in a long time, and gave her dancing shoes a kick toward the closet. Finally, they simply stood there, face to face. Leah reached up and began slowly popping open J.P.'s pearl snaps. His spry, calloused fingers had no problem with the tiny, delicate buttons on her blouse. As she dragged the fabric off of him, she noticed that J.P.

had his cattle brand tattooed high on his left shoulder. A 'D' lying on its back with a bar above it. She cocked an eyebrow at him as she traced her finger over the small, perfect-for-him tattoo. As he carefully removed the silk of her blouse, he, too, cocked an eyebrow at the small rose nestled just below her collarbone. In a quick, silent decision, they both decided not to begin a discussion about tattoos.

With his hand resting solidly on her lower back, J.P. laid Leah gently on the bed. While she desperately wanted to move things forward, she knew that Joseph was rarely in a hurry; he was sure, direct, and caring in everything he did.

Leah was certain that Joseph would not be any different in making love.

Everything that had led up to this moment — her initial stubbornness, his disarming honesty, their aching needs for a sense of safe belonging — brought an almost monumental fulfillment to the moment. The months of dancing around one another's desire to love and be loved brought a satisfaction to this night that neither could ignore. This moment was worth the wait.

The feelings they couldn't keep at bay were a little confusing, but in a pleasant way. In one sense, they felt like a couple of hormonal teenagers, and *really* wanted to act like them.

They *weren't* teenagers, though, and they knew it.

J.P. stopped for a moment and murmured into her ear: "We don't have to do this."

Leah's dreamy-eyed gaze was replaced with a playful panic and she responded in an almost desperate plea, "*Yes*, we do!" Relieved, he smiled, and she settled back into her languid anticipation. "Let's not stop now."

Emboldened by this, he brought his face close to hers and kissed her deeply. Just like on the dance floor, they felt they were getting a glimpse into each other's souls. With nervous hearts and almost ceremonial agreement, they came together in the ultimate pleasure of one another's body.

As they moved in tandem, practically dancing to the matching beat of their hearts, Leah felt as if she was melting. Her senses reeled at the forgotten feelings, the building tension. As she reached the point she thought she might simply float away, an earth-shattering shudder overcame her, and she found herself letting out a triumphant cry.

Surprised, satisfied, and utterly exhausted, Joseph dropped onto his elbows next to her and let out a long exhale. Pulses slowed, beads of sweat began to turn chilly, and the roaring momentum of desire began to fade in the quiet bedroom. As they lay facing each other side-by-side on the bed, small smiles of affection and shyness began to punctuate the silence, and was soon replaced with lazy giggles of contentment.

Leah was the first to say anything. "So you're branded, huh?"

"Yup. Looks like I'm not the only one." J.P. smiled and traced a line up from her elbow to her shoulder with his index finger, then let his hand rest there. It felt as if they were sharing a secret. "Oh, that." She blushed, even though she didn't think she could possibly blush anymore than she was already. "Only two other people know about that silly rose; my friend Julie and the tattoo artist."

He raised his eyebrow. "So it sounds like I'm part of a very exclusive club."

She scoffed. "You're right about that. I'm not sure what I was more drunk on — tequila or the fact that I didn't have to answer to anyone but myself that night."

"That sounds like quite the story!"

She chuckled lazily. "I don't think right now is quite the time for it."

"Probably not." He laid down on the pillow below him and put one hand behind his head. "Way I figure it, there's probably 10 or 12 folks who know about mine."

It was her turn to raise an eyebrow.

"What? It gets hot outside! It's common practice to take off your shirt when the heat's too much."

She laughed, "For you, maybe!"

J.P. smiled, and slowly moved his finger away from the rose, letting it find its way down to her nipple. To his delighted surprise, she breathed out a sigh of arousal. Leah reached for Joseph teasingly and whispered, "If you want to... play some more, I'm up for it."

It only took a few minutes of slow, lazy fondling before it was clear that J.P. was also ready for more. Their meandering hands found their way over all of the exciting, new territories of each other's bodies until, eventually, their lips met again in reignited hunger. With less urgency this time, J.P. pulled Leah close and entered her again. The two moved together in a fog of contentment, oblivious to the world around them.

This was something totally new for J.P.

Even in the early days of his now loveless marriage, his wife never initiated any kind of intimacy. It was always the same. An obligation on her part, complete with J.P. providing the only sense of excitement.

Nervous to break the silence with anything other than satisfied sighs, he brushed some strands of hair out of her face. "After tonight, I've got half an inkling that you're a wildcat in disguise."

She stretched languidly and smirked at him. "Meow."

They fell asleep shortly after the second round. It was nearly three o'clock.

J.P. only dozed for a short time. The sun's rising set off his inner alarm, and he was out of bed and buttoning up his jeans by the time Leah opened her eyes. Exhausted from the night before, her eyelids only partially opened as she rolled over to get a better look at him.

"Looks like the sky cleared up overnight. It's going to be a sunny day."

Leah grinned. "In more ways than one."

He blushed as he snapped up his shirt. "I'll hopefully see you at Nick's game. Two o'clock?"

"Mmhmm." She murmured and rolled back over onto her

CHAPTER 16

stomach, her foot poking out from the bottom of the blanket. Joseph put on his hat, pulled the comforter over her exposed toes, and gave her a kiss on the forehead before he quietly walked out the door.

As he turned to close the front door of the house, he caught motion out of the corner of his eye. Thinking it was Leah, he re-opened the door... and found himself face-to-face with Nick.

The teen's eyes widened. "Oh, I thought you were Mom going somewhere! It's so early in the morning, I wondered what was up."

For the first time in a long time, J.P. found himself feeling embarrassed and a little tongue tied. After a few awkward moments, Nick cleared his throat and made steady eye contact with his mom's new boyfriend. "You'd better be good to her."

Before J.P. could reply, Nick grabbed a box of cereal off the kitchen counter and headed back to his bedroom.

Joseph gently closed the door and stood on the porch, feeling a little sheepish.

He had never even given a thought to Nick being home. He shook his head and muttered, "Need to be more careful in the future." He started his Dodge and headed back to his little house. He couldn't chastise himself for long, however, as he found himself overcome with happiness from the night before. With the sun shining and the windows down a crack, he realized then that he was in love with Leah. Nick didn't need to worry; he intended to be good for her. He knew he would never have taken such a huge step if he didn't intend to follow up on it.

J.P. hadn't heard Leah's mumbled farewell as he left the bedroom. "Goodbye, my country pumpkin," had been barely audible from beneath her tangled hair. As she drifted back to sleep, she found herself hoping she didn't dream, as what she had experienced in the past twelve hours would have fulfilled any woman's imagination.

She didn't open her eyes again until noon, she couldn't recall ever sleeping that late into the day.

It took her a few minutes as she lay there to realize that she was naked. The sudden flood of memories sent goosebumps all over her body, nowhere near as powerful as the feelings that Joseph had triggered the night before, but it was enough to wake her up.

So much had happened during the night, and the fantasy played on a loop in her head as she remembered each moment.

She knew it was natural, the things that happen between men and women. But Leah had *not* been living the life of the women she saw on TV. Flowers, dancing, and sex were not part of her routine... but she was starting to think they *could be*, with Joseph.

Leah clumsily felt around on her bedside table for her phone and put it up to her ear, moving a swath of mussed up hair out of the way.

"Julie, you are not going to believe this."

J.P. headed back to his house, showered, and then went to church.

As the 7:00 am Mass progressed, J.P. found himself struggling with what had happened the night before. This was the first time he had been unfaithful in his marriage, and no matter how he justified his circumstances, he couldn't shake the feeling of guilt.

He stayed after Mass to have some private prayer time, and a long-overdue talk with his God. J.P. believed that his God was a God of unconditional love, and ultimately didn't think God would condemn him for one incident like last night.

How could this be a sin when a true love was growing from his friendship with Leah? He didn't know the answer, but he knew in his gut that his feelings were genuine. As people started coming in for the 8:30 Mass, he figured God had probably had enough of his reasoning and negotiating for the time being. He believed God had aligned everything that had happened over the past two months. He reminded himself firmly: nothing was by chance, but by God's will.

Leah and Joseph met at Nick's ball game.

They touched hands discreetly — nothing too outwardly obvious, but with great meaning for both of them. It meant they mutually felt good about last night. It meant that last night was the beginning

CHAPTER 16

and not the end. This baseball game wasn't peppered with constant talk like the others had been, and they were both content in that. They had learned much about each other last night, and needed some silence in order to process it.

As the game continued, Leah couldn't help but glance at Joseph. She wondered how a fellow who looked so rugged and tough could be so considerate and gentle. She had never met a man like Joseph, and was beginning to recognize a feeling she had written off as a fairy tale. *Love*, she thought in amazement. *I'm in love with this man.*

J.P. turned and met her gaze, flashing her a comforting smile. From the first time J.P. had met Leah, he had noticed her pretty eyes. Now that happiness had replaced that cold stare, he couldn't help but think that she was even more beautiful than the day they first met.

Leah and Julie grew up in the same neighborhood, and had even gone to the same elementary school. In Junior High, many of their classes overlapped, allowing for plenty of time to chat between and during classes.

It was in the seventh grade when Leah's mother died.

Though they had known each other most of their lives, they weren't exactly close. When Julie heard of Leah's loss, however, she knew how important it was to seek out Leah's home and offer whatever comfort she could. From that day on, they were the best of friends.

Julie had been Leah's sounding board about J.P. for weeks now. She knew the details of every conversation, every encounter — anything that happened between the two lovebirds the previous week.

She had mentioned many times how much she wanted to meet J.P. But while Leah was willing to divulge information about Joseph, she couldn't help but feel protective of him, and was nervous about sharing him with the world outside of George's Garage.

Now, of course, Julie understood that, but she was extremely eager to meet J.P. This man was rapidly changing the life of her dearest friend, and she'd eat her purse if she was going to have to wait much longer to meet him.

The Friday after the couple's magical night of dancing, Julie presented herself at George's Garage over the noon break.

As she strolled in the break room, Leah stood up and gave Julie a warm hug. Though she was surprised by her visit, Leah found that she was actually relieved at Julie's walking in unannounced; there was no anticipation of a formal introduction. She didn't ask her for an explanation, either. It was clear what was happening: Julie had the afternoon off and she had decided to take the initiative and finally introduce herself to J.P.

The two women turned toward the man in question, who stood quickly from his chair.

Leah blushed slightly, and said, "Joseph, this is my friend Julie. Julie, this is Joseph."

Because he was blocked by the table, Julie crossed the room and came to him instead of waiting for him to come out from behind it. As J.P. extended his hand, Julie gave his hand a small grip, then surprised J.P. by throwing her arms around him in a long, happy hug.

Leah and George watched on in awe — Julie's forwardness never ceased to amaze them. The sight of 4'11" Julie giving the six-foot-tall-J.P. a full-on, arms-all-the-way-around hug was amusing, to say the least. The significance of their embrace warmed Leah's heart in a way she didn't realize was missing. Two of the most important people in her life were coming together, and she realized there had been no reason at all to feel nervous.

J.P. had been caught off-guard by the hug, but he didn't feel any instinct to pull away. He had a huge smile on his lips, but his eyes were fixed on Leah.

Leah was smiling, too.

CHAPTER 17

Leah invited Joseph to her extended family's picnic on the 4th of July. It was an annual family event. Besides being the 4th, it had also been their mother's birthday, and they always made a point to get together and remember her.

This year, the picnic was being held at Leah's brother Chuck's home. J.P. had briefly met Leah's father Charles at the station already, and he obviously knew Nick. The other half of the party was made up of Leah's divorced sister, Sally, and her two daughters, Heather and April. Leah had given Joseph the address to Chuck's house and J.P. drove himself to the cookout. When he arrived at the house around five o'clock, he met Chuck, Sally, Heather, and April for the first time. It was overwhelming, to say the least.

It was immediately evident to J.P. that the family had been doing some considerable drinking before he got there. He learned that the three women, Sally, Heather, and April had started with mimosas a bit earlier that afternoon, and were showing the effects of it. During the introductions, J.P. could feel their eyes blatantly peering at him with curiosity, and possibly something more. He'd always heard people talk about being "undressed with their eyes," but had never experienced it firsthand until now. He was getting especially uncomfortable feelings from Heather, whose flirting was far from discreet.

After ushering him away from the other women, Leah filled him in a bit on her niece. "Heather's twenty five years old, and still lives with her mom. She's not making any moves to further her education, and she can't seem to keep a job to save her life." She sighed. "I don't know. I love the kid, but she's got problems."

To J.P.'s relief, the men retreated to the back patio while the women stayed inside the house.

He was thrilled to discover that the conversation was centered around baseball. The Yankees had drafted a pitcher from the University of Nebraska, and he had just been called up to the majors. "He's a local kid from Lincoln. He pitched for the University." Chuck said in between bites of popcorn. "I've been paying attention to his move up in the Yankee Organization."

With the Yanks being Nick's favorite team, he filled in all the details about this new guy. J.P. enjoyed getting to know Leah's family, and he found himself feeling a sense of pride as he listened to Nick share his baseball knowledge. After the baseball talk was spent, J.P. couldn't quite help his curiosity.

"Charles, do you mind telling me a bit about your time in the army?"

Leah's father leaned back and smiled. "Got an interest in it, have you?"

"I do, sir. Very much."

Charles was more than willing to share his stories. While serving a ninety day duty in Italy after WWII, he had seen the effects and destruction of the War firsthand.

"Our most immediate task was the care of the wounded and sick. Getting food to the citizens became the next order of priority." He recalled that all the people were thin and sickly, with a haunted look in his eyes. He recounted that so many of the people they came upon, especially in the countryside, seemed lost, starving, and shell-shocked.

As Charles got warmed up to the storytelling, he shook his head. "Even the earth seemed wounded. The landscape was spotted with the wreckage of war. Reminded me of a direct hit from a tornado." Shaken by the tale but excited for more information, J.P. took a sip of his iced tea as Charles took a moment to remember. "I was horrified to see the craters in the ground from the artillery shelling. The most eerie thing was the total silence. There were no animals; no pigs, cows, goats, chickens, dogs. Not even wildlife, like rabbits or squirrels." He

CHAPTER 17

looked down at his hands. "Everything was dead or gone. It felt as if we had gone to another planet, not just foreign soil."

The four guys on the back patio had grown quiet, but they could still hear the voices of the women in the house and the traffic on the street out front. J.P. found himself looking up into the tree for a bird or a squirrel. The picture of destruction that had been painted by Charles' stories seemed to come to life right there. He noticed that Chuck didn't seem phased — he had heard his dad tell this story many times before. But for Nick and J.P., it was a harrowing story that was fresh and raw, heard for the first time.

"Thank you, Charles. I've read many accounts of war stories, but there's something different about hearing from someone who's been there. It's a fitting story for July 4th."

J.P. stood up and excused himself to the restroom in the house. Riding the adrenaline of Charle's story and feeling a sense of warmth and belonging, he winked at Leah as he passed through the kitchen. She winked back with a playful smirk.

The hall to the restroom was lined with old high school photos of Sally, Chuck, and Leah, and he couldn't help but chuckle at a picture of Leah in bright orange bell bottoms. After a few minutes in the restroom he washed his hands whistling a chipper tune, and opened the door to a surprise he didn't see coming. Leah's niece, Heather, was propped up against the door frame, her hip cocked to the side. She was close enough to him that the strong smell of beer filled his nostrils.

"Heather, I—"

Before J.P. could say anything more, Heather slapped her hand clumsily on his chest and slurred, "Do you like doing my aunt?"

With warning signals flaring in his head, J.P. tried to step around her, but Heather stepped forward, blocking his escape route. He was perplexed, despite the way she acted when they were introduced. He had figured the flirting had all been in his head, but now he was truly uncomfortable.

"Heather, if you need to use the facilities, all you need to do is let me through."

She laughed and scrunched up her nose "Use the facilities? Who talks like that? No wonder Leah likes taking you to bed." She stumbled a bit, but righted herself up against the door frame again. "You're a regular old-fashioned country boy."

Though he was worried about the immediate situation, J.P. couldn't help wonder about the 'doing her aunt' comment. *What had Leah told her family?*

"Heather, I'm just trying to be polite. If you'll just move aside so I can get back to the party…"

She did not budge. Instead, she leaned into him, exhaled loudly with her rancid beer breath, and whispered into his ear, "If you liked her you should try some of this." To his horror, she squeezed him close, angling her body so her breast rubbed against him. Finally to his breaking point, he got ahold of her arms and broke her grip on him. As gently as he could, he moved her away from him and stepped into the hallway.

At that moment, Heather's face turned white as a sheet as she realized that her plan was not going the way she wanted. She had been positive that J.P. would have wanted to return her advances, but it was clear that she was sorely mistaken.

So she turned to plan "B."

Catching J.P. off-guard again, she wound up and slapped him point blank across the face. As his hand flew up to his cheek in shock, she took a deep breath and let out a horror movie-style scream. Tears sprung to her eyes, and she threw herself to the floor, her body wracked with hysterical sobs.

No matter how hard he tried, J.P. couldn't bring himself to move. He was paralyzed and stunned.

Sally and Leah were the first to investigate Heather's scream and sobs, followed by the guys who could hear all the commotion, even outside.

After half a minute of stunned silence, Leah was the first to speak. "What happened?"

CHAPTER 17

While Heather continued to rant and rave incoherently, everyone turned to J.P. "She— she slapped me," he sputtered.

With a guttural, rage-filled sob, Heather shouted, "He felt me up, and— and groped me!"

Shocked eyes turned on J.P. as she went on. "I was going into the bathroom and we met in the doorway and, and his hands were all over me!"

Deep down, Leah knew that Heather had a history of being a drama queen. It had become evident to everyone in the family — except Sally — that she may have a drinking problem. Leah's sister had spoiled her and it showed. Heather was lazy and self-centered. Leah did her best to push back the searing anger she had for her sister and niece as everyone moved into the living room.

The situation became all the more heated with Sally jumping to her daughter's defense. "So when do I get my chance to add a slap to his face, huh? That's the only way to deal with a brute!"

Finally, Chuck stepped in. As a deputy sheriff with the education and experience to handle a situation such as this, he could make a pretty accurate guess as to what happened. He knew that J.P. hadn't had any alcohol that day. He'd chosen iced tea, and had even made a comment about not liking beer at all.

Heather, on the other hand, had been on his radar for a long time now. With each family gathering getting more and more out of hand, her drinking was no longer something he could ignore. He loved his niece, but this wasn't the first time she'd made inappropriate advances on a houseguest, and it was time to do something about it.

Leah, on the other hand, wasn't feeling quite so compassionate. She could see the reddening handprint on the side of his face, and that was awful enough on its own. What made it worse was that she could see and feel the sadness in J.P.'s eyes, and it was killing her to know that someone in her family had caused it.

J.P. said nothing, as he figured there was enough shouting and talking going on.

Sally was shouting for Chuck to take J.P. to jail, and Chuck's attempts to settle the two women down were turning the whole situation into a dysfunctional circus. Finally, Chuck had had enough.

"Alright then, Sally. How about we take Heather down to the Sheriff's office to give a statement? She might need to take a breathalyzer test first, of course, make sure she's on the up-and-up."

Sally balked. "I'm not letting Heather go anywhere, and certainly not to the sheriff's office!"

"Then *settle down*, Sally." Chuck handed both her and Heather cups of coffee and stalked back to the kitchen.

As things quieted, Leah took the opportunity to say her piece. "Joseph would *never* do what Heather is accusing him of. Heather, on the other hand, hasn't been the picture of stability lately, has she?" Sally shot Leah a death glare and, for a moment, Leah felt truly scared. Sally was like a mother bear whose cub had just let out a cry for help.

Sally slammed the coffee mug on the end table, splashing dark liquid onto the carpet. She screamed "You don't know this guy! We're family. I see where your loyalty lies!"

This last accusation filled Leah with both anger and sadness. She *did* know Joseph. At this point, she felt like she knew him better than she knew many of her family members. He was the most caring person that she had ever known, and she hated that she had gotten him involved in this screwed up mess. She wanted to stand up to Sally and tell her so, but with Sally so out of control, she knew it would just make things worse.

Leah and Sally had always gotten along — except when Heather was involved. Her sister had tunnel vision when it came to Heather. Leah knew that Sally harbored a lot of guilt for Heather's youth, but she was tired of this tired old song and dance. Today was the perfect example of Heather as the poor angel who just happened to always be the victim of someone else's actions.

J.P. was feeling sick, and regretting the fact that he'd left his trusty roll of Rolaids at home. He hated conflict, and would do just about anything to keep himself out of situations that were uncomfortable.

CHAPTER 17

He couldn't imagine being accused of something like this, and yet here he was.

Fortunately, it was clear to him that the rest of the family was beginning to see his side of the situation. Feeling desperate, J.P. quietly asked Chuck and Leah if he could leave. Both simply nodded, Leah with tears in her eyes. She wanted to give Joseph a hug, but knew it would make matters worse. Giving her hand a meaningful squeeze, J.P. turned to let himself out the door. As he made his way back to the Dodge, he could hear Sally shouting after him through the open window.

"Where is he going? Oh, I see! That's how we treat criminals, is it? Just let 'em walk!"

J.P. quickened his pace, and once he was finally inside the pickup, he could still hear Sally shouting, even over the engine. He laid his head on the steering wheel for a moment and sighed, "Something is loose in that woman's head,"

When J.P. got to his little house, he went directly to the sink, ran cold water on his hands, and splashed his face time and time again. With every splash, he tried to wipe his mind clean of what he had been through in the last hour. Unfortunately, he knew he'd be playing all of the events on repeat for the rest of the night, and probably longer. He dropped onto the small sofa in his living room and stared up at the ceiling.

The evening had started out so nicely. He hated to think what this had done to Leah's family's image of him. He knew it wasn't his fault, but he was kicking himself for how he handled Heather in the hallway. He should have done something other than grabbing ahold of Heather to get her off of him.

He sighed. No matter how many times he ran it through his head, he couldn't see a different outcome, and that was hard for him to grapple with. He was a man who was in control so much of the time, that it was difficult for his brain to accept any other way.

The sun had started to set, and was casting long shadows in his living room. He thought about heating up a frozen casserole his mom had sent with him last time he visited, but he just couldn't bring himself to turn on the oven. J.P. had been alone many times in his little house, but at this moment, he felt lonely. Between being slapped across the face, enduring chaos and verbal abuse, and finally being by himself, he was overcome with a need for someplace familiar. It was cooling off outside, and there were firecrackers and fireworks being lit up and down his street. Normally, he was energized by all of that abounding neighborhood activity, but not tonight. Loneliness was the theme of the evening, and it didn't look like that was going to change.

After only a few minutes at the little house, he decided to go home. Back to the farm.

As J.P. climbed into the Dodge to leave, he stopped to watch families on the lawns and sidewalks, enjoying their Fourth of July celebration. The kids were laughing, the adults were smiling and having a good time — not a single family drama as far as he could tell. Seeing the families lightened J.P.'s heartache, but it only made him more determined to go to the farm. He put the pickup in gear, pulled out of his driveway, and turned toward home. The darker the sky became, the more fireworks he could see in his rear view mirror. While it hadn't been a banner Independence Day, he was grateful for all of the colors in the sky, providing a comforting distraction for his burdened mind.

After an hour and a half of driving, when he was nearly back to the farm, J.P.'s phone rang. When he saw the phone number on the caller I.D., his heart lurched a bit. As much as he wanted to hear Leah's voice, he wasn't sure he was ready to talk about what had happened. He answered the phone, regardless.

"Where are you? I am sitting in front of your house. It doesn't look like you're home."

J.P. sighed, "Yeah, I know. I'm actually almost back to the farm." There were several seconds of silence, then with a crack in her voice,

CHAPTER 17

Leah rushed on. "Joseph, I'm so sorry for what happened today. Everyone knows that none of it was your fault. I know you, and I know you're worried about what my family thinks of you and —"

"Leah, Leah, slow down. It's alright."

"No, it's not alright! Heather finally told the truth. I need you to know that she admitted it, and no one thinks any less of you." She took a deep breath, and let it out slowly. "I wanted to tell you all of this face to face... but I understand you wanting to head back home."

J.P. was exhausted and confused. He had been desperate to leave the conflict and chaos at Chuck's house, but he hadn't thought about what it would be like to leave, either. Being excluded from the outcome, being by himself, and not knowing what was happening felt almost as draining as being right in the middle of it. He had so many thoughts, but very few words.

Scared of his response, Leah quietly added, "I would really like to see you Sunday sometime so we can talk."

J.P. said. "Sure. I'll call you on my way back Sunday, and we can set something up."

Leah had left Chuck's completely exhausted. Even though she didn't play an active role in their lives, she loved her sister Sally and Heather, too. It was painful to see them put through such an awful night. *"Tough love,"* she thought. *"That's what people call it."* Her shoulders sagged as she drove. Leah felt tough, alright. Tough and beaten up. All she needed was to be around someone gentle for a while. She felt so bad for Joseph — he had basically been the sacrificial lamb, given up by the whole family for the betterment of themselves.

She was scared of how the night would affect her and Joseph's relationship. She was in love with Joseph — that much she knew — and she hoped he still felt the same way about her. She was afraid he would judge her, based on the rest of her family, and she didn't want him ending his day with this impression of her. She *had* to stop to see Joseph that night, or she wouldn't sleep a wink.

Her disappointment at seeing his little house dark and empty was overwhelming. Talking to him on the phone hadn't been ideal, but it had been nice to hear his voice. She would hold onto that until she talked to him again.

After the events and turmoil of the day, Leah found herself crying as she crawled into bed. Once calm, she slept so soundly that it felt like her eyes fluttered closed, only to immediately open again in the dim morning sunlight. The sound of Nick fumbling around in the kitchen had her curious. She got herself out of bed, still feeling dead tired. She climbed into the shower, dressed, and finally made her way out to the kitchen.

As her slippers padded onto the tile kitchen floor, Nick emptied his version of scrambled eggs onto a plate, complete with breakfast sausage and toast. "'Morning!" He greeted her cheerfully, but with a nervous air of anticipation. "I was just about to knock on your door." he pulled a dining chair out, waiting for her to sit. "I thought that, after last night's mess, you might need a good breakfast to get a new start on the day."

Leah took a sip of surprisingly good coffee and thought back, realizing that yesterday's lunch was the last time she had eaten. She finally broke out into a big, grateful grin."That's an awfully wise philosophy. Wherever did you learn something like that?"

Nick dropped a spatula into the sink and turned to her. "'Dunno. I seem to remember one of my friends quoting his mother whenever he needed a little help in his life."

"Hmm…" Leah murmured as she stirred some cream into the black liquid in her mug, "Sounds like a very smart lady."

"Smart enough," he smirked, "to eat this food before it gets cold!" Leah graciously accepted the plate, buttered her toast, and waited for Nick to fill his own plate.

After a few minutes of general small talk, the two finally decided to talk about the awful 4th of July party. Nick had left Chuck's house when the trouble started, after Leah quietly told him to head home.

"You know, I've got a lot of questions, but I mostly want to know if everything turned out okay last night."

CHAPTER 17

"I appreciate that. I promise I'll fill you in on the details later. I'm just so tired." Leah gave Nick an abbreviated version of the events, leaving out a lot of heated words. She added, "Joseph left soon after you did." She morosely pushed some eggs around her plate, trying to decide how much more she should say. "Afterwards... Afterwards, I called him, but he was already on his way back to the farm."

Leah didn't look up from her plate, and Nick could tell she was still pretty upset. He pushed his plate aside, reached across the table, and took his mom's hand in his. "I knew last night J.P. didn't start that trouble. He's a good guy." Leah continued staring at the eggs on her plate. "Is everything going to be alright with you and J.P.?"

Finally, she looked up. "We're going to talk when he gets back tomorrow."

Nick patted her hand. "Good. He's a good guy, and you're a good gal, too, mom. Try not to feel guilty, okay? None of that was your fault, either."

As Leah watched Nick take his plate to the sink, she felt her heart repairing, just a little bit. A heartfelt talk with a teenager is rare, and she was grateful for this opportunity to visit with Nick. "Enough about all that nasty business. What do you have planned today?"

"Not much. Video games, maybe? A nap?" He took her plate from her hands before she could reach the sink.

Before he could say more, she blurted out, "How would you like to go over to the country club and hit the driving range with your old mom?"

"The driving range? Like golf?"

"Yeah! I could try using Joseph's name... that might get us a bucket of balls."

Nick smiled and studied his mom for a moment. It was clear that she didn't want to spend the day moping around alone. "Sure, Mom. Sounds like fun!"

"Really? Great! I'll call the range!" As she shuffled away in her slippers to find her phone, he briefly thought about asking if he could invite his girlfriend, but thought better of it. His mom needed some time alone with him, and he couldn't bring himself to say no.

By nine o'clock, they had their bucket of balls and were swinging away.

Since neither of them had golfed much as of late, it ended up being a hilarious experience. With a lot of missed golf balls and even a club that went flying out of Leah's hands, the two of them laughed harder than they had in a long time.

After leaving the driving range, they ended up at the mall. Shopping for items and supplies that Nick would need for school, they leisurely walked from store to store, simply enjoying the outing. They then stopped for Chinese food at Nick's favorite restaurant, right in the mall. After a contented silence, bellies and hearts full, they both decided it was probably time to call it a day.

"You know, Nick, I believe I could go for a nap." Leah smiled at him as he drove back to their house.

"Too much strenuous activity, Master Golfer?"

"Yeah, that must be it! You're free to go do whatever it is you do with your friends. Thanks for humoring me and hanging out all afternoon."

Nick pulled into the driveway and he leaned over to give her a kiss on the cheek and said, "I had a great time, Mom. For real." She hopped out of the pickup and shut the door, giving it a solid pat before Nick pulled away. As Leah turned for the house, she wondered *"What is it about my guys and their pickups?"* Her amused smile froze as she suddenly became worried all over again. *"Is Joseph even 'my guy' anymore?"*

Now, Leah wanted to do more than take a nap. She wanted to check in on Joseph to see how he was feeling today, about everything. She still felt skittish about the day before, and knew from experience that feelings can come with a delayed fuse. She couldn't wait another day to talk to Joseph — not being able to see him after yesterday's happenings felt like cruel and unusual punishment. After closing the front door and kicking off her shoes, she decided to call Joseph on his cell phone.

CHAPTER 17

J.P.'s nerves felt frayed all day. He had tried to keep himself busy so his mind would stay away from the previous day's fiasco, but his heart was hurting and it showed. Daniel and Kate could tell something was wrong, but J.P. didn't feel up to confiding in them.

When his phone rang, it nearly startled him out of his skin. J.P. was overjoyed to see that it was Leah calling him, and glad that she took the initiative to call him.

"Leah." It was the only greeting he could think of.

"Joseph, I — I'm so sorry about what happened yesterday."

In that moment, J.P. didn't care about yesterday's fiasco. He leaned against the side of his pickup, focusing on the conversation. "How are you doing?"

On the other end of the line, the physical and emotional exhaustion finally broke with that small, caring question, and Leah started to cry.

"Leah, Leah, please — it wasn't your fault. You've got to believe that." For a few seconds, though, he let her cry, knowing she needed it. After some final sniffles and a very distinct, deep breath from her, he asked, "You up to filling me in on what happened?"

"Yeah, I think so." And, after another deep breath, she launched into the details of the night before.

"Apparently, Chuck's had enough of Sally and Heather for a while now. Thank goodness for that; I was so happy when I realized he believed you! I guess he already had a plan in place with another detective from work — Dallas — and had given him a call right after you left. Dallas is trained in facilitating interventions where alcohol and drugs were an issue. So, once he showed up, we all moved to the living room and did our best to get to the root of the problems. It was exhausting — time and time again, Heather just denied and lied. Eventually, though, pieces of the truth would start to surface."

J.P. moved his phone to his left ear and reached into his pocket for a Rolaid. It'd been a while since he'd kept them there, but the past 24 hours had been something else. "That sounds like quite the ordeal."

"Hmm, yeah. It was. Neither of them wanted to hear what we

had to say, at first, and threatened to leave multiple times. Chuck and Dallas had taken the lead, though, and wouldn't let anything or anyone go. Finally, Heather broke. I know it was good for her in the long run, but it was really hard to watch. She wasn't ranting or raving or wallowing in self-pity — just quiet and sad... talking about her deep feelings of inadequacy and insecurity."

"Well, it sounds like some good might come of it, at least. I'm grateful for that."

"Me, too, I suppose. I'm not grateful that you bore the brunt of the drama, though."

Still feeling raw from the incident, but wanting to move past it, J.P. decided it was time to shift topics. "I hope you didn't spend the day moping around in your slippers." She could hear the smile creep into his voice through the phone. "You do anything fun?"

"You know, I actually did a bit of both. Moping in slippers and a little fun. A lot of fun, really."

Leah then shared with him her morning and afternoon spent with Nick. J.P. found himself laughing when she told him about going up to the country club and using his name as their pass into the place.

"I can't tell you how happy it makes me to hear that," he said. "You deserve some fun, especially with your son." He shared his day with her up to this point, even though to him it was all routine. Leah expressed surprising interest and asked detailed questions.

"Well," he answered, "So far today I've checked and counted cattle, checked water supplies in tanks and ponds, and looked the crops over. All pretty normal stuff."

"That all sounds *completely* foreign to me. I can't believe that's just another day for you!"

"Well, that's just part of it! As much as I hate to cut this short, I've got a lot more of that to do before the sun goes down."

"Oh, of course! I don't want to take too much more of your daylight." She quietly smiled at how silly that sounded, and found herself awash with relief at the pleasant turn of conversation.

CHAPTER 17

"I'll see you tomorrow, Leah. You can count on it."

And they both hung up smiling, nervous dread having been replaced by genuine excitement.

Sunday evening, when J.P. got back to the city, he went directly to Leah's house.

When she opened the door, they immediately pulled each other into their arms, embracing as if they hadn't seen each other in months. Feeling the comfort in each other's arms was something neither of them had experienced in a long time.

"Come in, please!" Reluctantly, she pulled away and moved out of the doorframe. "I'd like to talk a bit more, if that's alright."

They sat on the couch next to each other, Leah fidgeting with nervousness. She started by blurting, "You'll never know how sorry I am about what happened at Chuck's."

Out of instinct, J.P. started to say something kind to her, but she put her finger up to his lips. "Please, just let me get all of this off my chest." She took a moment to gather her thoughts, and continued. "Chuck has ordered my sister and Heather to get family counseling. Sally usually does whatever Chuck tells her to do. The power of an older brother, I guess. What ended up coming to light was that... well, one of Sally's live-in boyfriends molested Heather when she was eleven. Sally had known what was going on and had done nothing to stop it. It only ended when Heather told a friend at school about what was going on, and Sally lost custody of Heather for almost a full year."

Not wanting to interrupt, J.P. simply put his hand on hers. "So now she's overprotective and Heather's been taking full advantage. And you just happened to be there for the big blow-up." Leah, in turn, put her other hand on his, and looked him fully in the eyes. "But there's something I learned going through all of that craziness on the 4th of July. So much of life is about control. Heather and Sally, with all their dysfunction, have controlled my family. My ex-husband was someone who was different from one minute to the next... and that controlled how I lived my life. The last five years, I thought I could get back control of my life by isolating myself." Determined not to cry, Leah blinked a few times, and held his hand tighter. "I realize now that that's not control — that's just just letting life pass me by. And that realization? That's from meeting you. You're one of the most interesting, caring men I've ever met, and I'm so lucky to have you."

Joseph wasn't used to a lot of compliments, and could feel his cheeks reddening as Leah poured out her heart to him. Underneath this new, uncomfortable feeling, though, was joy. He'd given up on love like this a long time ago.

"The past few months have been full of the best surprises, and they've gotten my attention. You've won my heart. Most of the time I'm so excited about this, but Joseph, sometimes it scares me to death."

J.P. reached for Leah's hand and gave it a light squeeze. Leah continued, "I have fought hard the last five years, but after meeting you, I've started to ask myself, 'Who have I been fighting with?' And the only answer I can come up with is, *'My past and myself.'* The past and all of the bad decisions I made, and myself for not forgiving... myself for those decisions." She laughed a little, feeling embarrassed. "Does that even make sense?"

J.P. nodded, but let her continue. "I'm so happy that you're in my life, but that's a big change, and change is hard for me. I just want us both to be prepared for that, you know? With you being the main ingredient of my change in my life, we may have differences... but Joseph, I never want to resent you for what we have." After a few seconds, Leah decided she might as well continue being assertive. "Joseph, I love you."

Overcome with happiness at her honesty, and surprised by her forwardness, all J.P. could think to say was, "Thank you, Leah."

Rather than keep talking — as there wasn't much left to say — he cupped her face in his hands and kissed her, hoping to communicate what he was feeling without having to come up with the words. Among comforting embraces, honest words, and passionate kisses, the night was exactly what they needed to heal their hurts.

CHAPTER 17

J.P. didn't go back to the farm once in the coming two weeks. The crops were in, fertilized, and growing with timely rains.
So much had happened so quickly between him and Leah. It felt like they were cruising smoothly along quietly into the month of July. They went to Nick's baseball games and even visited the golf course for another round of fun.

He had been thoroughly enjoying himself, but something was missing. The truth was, he had been living in *Leah's* world for three months, and he felt it was high time to change things up a bit. He was going back to the farm the last weekend of July, and he had decided to ask Leah to go back with him... back home to *his world*. It was going to be a big weekend — it was the annual rodeo celebration in the neighboring town of Washburn. There would be a deep pit barbeque, a rodeo, and a street dance on Saturday.

Initially, Leah didn't show too much interest in Joseph's farm life. The closer they got to each other, however, she found herself wondering what kind of people and places had shaped Joseph.

So when Nick's baseball team lost their district game on the third Sunday of July, J.P. asked Leah if she was interested in going back to the farm the following weekend.

Surprised but pleased, Leah reasoned out loud, "Well, Nick's baseball season is over, so I can cross those commitments off the calendar..." She thought for a moment, knowing J.P. wouldn't mind the brief silence. Up until then, her relationship with Joseph had been mostly within her personal boundaries; in her home, at the garage, and sitting together at baseball games. It was a nice, comfortable safety zone, and leaving it was intimidating. It's easy to blend in and get lost in the city. With 200,000 people bustling about, you can virtually go unnoticed. If you don't get involved in neighborhood, school, community, or church groups, you just stay in the crowd, and she had to admit she felt much more comfortable that way.

Not long ago, Leah wouldn't have even had the will to think about accepting an invitation like this. She didn't know *when* she had become satisfied with such mundane life, but she'd been feeling that way for years.

Leah had taken risks with Joseph. She went on a picnic in the country, danced the night away at the Starbrite, and had two of the most memorable nights of her life in the process.

Her Joseph had lifted the window she had been looking out of, the one that she used to keep herself apart from the world. Lately, she'd grown tired of watching from afar. In fact, she felt like shouting out that open window at the top of her lungs. She was starting to love living in this new world of hers, and she knew it was all because of Joseph.

Suddenly, as if desperate to not miss her chance, Leah snapped up the opportunity. "I would *love* to go back to the farm with you. Besides, I've never actually been to a rodeo. It would be an... educational field trip!"

He grinned, and teased her dramatically. "You poor girl! You couldn't remember the last time you went on a picnic, and now you tell me you've never been to a rodeo! Once again, it's my job to rescue you from such a deprived existence!"

Relieved and nervous, Leah laughed and laughed.. but deep down she thought that was probably true. She had never felt or lived life as she was then with Joseph in her life.

CHAPTER 18

As soon as Leah agreed, Joseph was making plans for the upcoming weekend in his head. He was learning that he had a gift for planning everything with a touch of intimacy, and wanted to top their last two big outings. With a brief pang of sadness, he realized Claire never cared for elaborate surprises, so he hadn't ever really had the chance.

The week seemed to drag by as he thought of details, perfected his plans, and went over the schedule. He was excited and anxious — it had been three weeks since he had last been home. He was eager to see the development of the crops and the growth of the cattle, but if he was honest with himself, he knew it was more than that.

He was nervous for everyone to see Leah. When his thoughts were of only him and Leah, life seemed like paradise. But when J.P. considered the whole picture — the farm, family, community, his faith, *and* Leah, he got anxious. After all, he was still a married man according to the law of the land and the eyes of the church. But, as his mother would have said, that was a whole different can of worms. The way he felt toward Leah, and the pure joy he had experienced these last few months had created more than a few questions in him regarding both the law and the Vatican. He knew, though, that there wasn't anything he could do about that at the moment, and decided to choose a positive attitude.

The atmosphere at work more closely resembled a junior high dance than it did a garage. The two of them shared secret smiles and thrilled at innocent things like holding hands on their lunch breaks and exchanging notes disguised as work documents.

Despite feeling like a kid in puppy love, Leah couldn't help but also feel like a real 'grown up.' An adult with confidence, satisfying relationships, and an idea of what love is *supposed* to resemble. Respect, excitement, and tenderness — together they had grown emotionally into the adults they hadn't realized they could be.

George was also enjoying the changes happening at the garage. For so many years, he had wished for something better for Leah. He shook his head and laughed as he watched them pretend they weren't all starry-eyed for each other. He would have never dreamed that someone from *his* garage could present such a positive change in Leah's life.

Before Leah left work Friday afternoon, George couldn't help but tease her. "Five dollars says you come back to work on Monday wearing cowgirl boots."

She let out a throaty laugh, so happy-sounding that it caught him off-guard. "Oh, George, I don't think I'm *that* far gone!"

"Well, if you would have told me three months ago that you were going to a rodeo, I would have checked you into the hospital for observation! I don't think boots are that far-fetched!"

Expecting another snappy comeback, George found himself speechless when Leah threw her arms around him in a heartfelt hug. Delighted, he didn't really care what the hug was for, but he asked anyway. "Now what's that for?"

"For everything, George. Everything you've done for me." She gave him a quick kiss on the cheek and waved goodbye as she practically skipped out the door.

J.P. had planned for them to leave for the farm directly from work at the end of the day. He had packed what little he needed in the Dodge that Friday morning. After work, J.P. followed Leah to her home so she could drop off her Blazer and grab her bags.

"I've got two suitcases. Did I overpack?" She asked, as he carried

CHAPTER 18

her luggage out to the pickup.

"I've got to admit, I'm so excited I'd load your kitchen table in here if you asked me to."

As Joseph turned around from loading the suitcases, Leah reached for his hand. "Joseph, are *you* sure that I should go with you to the farm?"

The question took J.P. by surprise, but the answer came easy for him. "I'm more than sure, Leah. This is for you and me. There are people and challenges back home that I need to face in order to move forward. I've been avoiding a lot of uncomfortable conversations for a while now, and it's time to take you home."

Leah hadn't realized she'd been holding her breath until it whooshed out in relief. She put her arms up around his shoulders and leaned into him, resting her head on his chest. He leaned forward and whispered into her ear, "I'm sure."

She looked up to find comfort in his eyes, and let him wash away her nervousness with a deep, reassuring kiss.

J.P. was headed home, to the area he had lived in his whole life, until this last year. The place that had molded him into the man he had become.

From the moment Leah met Joseph, no matter what he was talking about, his words were always under control and direct. The two hour drive to Frankton, however, was a different story. J.P. talked and rambled as they traveled the highway, and Leah could tell he was excited, nervous, or both. She looked out her window to try to conceal her amused smile. She heard about everything from his cattle, to his machinery, to how much land they farmed... who his schoolmates were and which ones were still around... anything, really, to squash the nervous thoughts from his mind. The farm was ten miles west of Frankton, and they were coming into town from the south. This meant the farm was not going to be the only stop of the night. The town of Frankton would come first.

As they crossed the Loup River bridge a mile south of town, J.P.

officially began the tour of his hometown.

"This bridge was built the same year I was born," he mentioned, as he felt a part of himself relax, knowing he was finally home. "You know, Frankton's unique in that a mile north of town there's another river, the Cedar, and the two join up a few miles east of town. Some people in town can look and see both rivers from their front porch."

Leah beamed at him. Rivers and bridges weren't exactly at the top of her list of favorite conversation topics, but she could listen to Joseph's hometown pride all day long. As they passed the city limit sign, she read aloud: "Welcome to Frankton, population 1451." She whistled. "1451? That's barely a neighborhood in the city!"

They drove past the sign marking the road to the cemetery on the left, and then the high school football field. "That track's been resurfaced recently, and they got a donation for the new bleachers. A lot of the work was done by volunteers — myself included. It was hard work, but it was fun."

As scenes from J.P.'s past whizzed by, Leah realized she was going to have a lot of information thrown at her this weekend. He was home — really and truly home — and he was excited, proud, and eager to share his stories with her.

Originally, she thought she would be the nervous one, but she was finding that her nerves were fine. She felt calm and safe when she was with Joseph, no matter where she was. This was a very new feeling for her; feeling safe and happy in the presence of a man didn't come easily to her, and she was overcome with gratitude. Until now, her love for Nick and the sweet feeling of her fingers on the piano keys were about the only things that brought out any intense emotion in her. She decided she was quite happy with the change.

They drove through the town on the highway slowly to the north. J.P. pointed out some of the houses of importance, and Leah found herself in awe of the beauty of the structures. One of the homes belonged to later generations of the town's founders, who had built Frankton into an important community in the early settlement of

CHAPTER 18

the area. As they neared the northernmost edge of town, Leah could see how the landscape opened up into a wide river valley. With a quiet gasp, she turned to J.P. "This is just gorgeous. I've lived in Nebraska my whole life and never dreamed it could be this pretty."

"Yep, that's a nice view, there. Those hills in the distance turn that valley into an awfully pretty picture." He pointed to a specific area Leah couldn't quite focus on. "The Veterans' Memorial is to our right, about halfway down that sharp drop-off of the highway into the valley."

J.P. drove the one mile north of town and, as they crossed the river below, she could see the sign that read 'Cedar River.'

"Wow, the Cedar's a lot smaller than the Loup."

"Sure is. You know, there are actually three branches of the Loup - they all converge west of here."

Leah nodded, amused. It was fun to watch him, and she felt more relaxed than she had in a long while.

Turning back toward town, J.P. turned east at a blacktop road, so that Leah could see a grain elevator straight ahead of them. As they neared it, J.P. passed a divided street and pointed absentmindedly out his window. "That's Broadway Street - the main drag. Runs straight through the business district."

He drove right up to the cement tower of the elevator, and pulled up close enough for her to get a good view of the base. "These walls are 18 inches thick and the whole thing is 20 stories tall." He chuckled. "Farmers like to call 'em the 'towers of the plains.'"

"I can see where they get that!"

"I figure I've delivered hundreds of truckloads of grain to this elevator over the years," he added, as he put the pickup into reverse and headed back on Broadway to the business district.

She was a little lost in all the sights and sounds, but could tell that J.P.'s voice was growing excited as he continued to rattle off facts about the town. She turned her focus to the road ahead when she realized they were approaching a baseball diamond. No wonder she could practically hear the smile in his voice.

"Now, it's unusual for a small town like Frankton to have a covered grandstand like this. They built this one in 1940 during the depression as part of the W.P.A."

She scooted a little closer to him on the bench seat, eager to soak up some of the enthusiasm she had come to treasure. "W.P.A.?"

"Works Progress Administration. Part of the New Deal. Designed to create jobs and improve the country. It sure improved Frankton, that's for sure."

J.P. pulled the Dodge over to the side of the field and put it in park, taking a moment to give Leah's hand a squeeze before he hopped out of his side and around to hers.

"We're going in, huh?"

"Sure are! How else are you supposed to get acquainted with one of my favorite places in town?" Holding hands, the two headed down to get a better look at the field.

"The season's over, so it looks like we're meant to have a little alone time. You're going to get your very own personal tour!"

As she watched J.P. transform into an enthusiastic young boy right before her eyes as he chattered away, she had to stop herself from shaking her head in disbelief. She wasn't much of a baseball fan herself, she had to admit. She loved Nick, and she loved J.P., and she couldn't get enough of the pure joy the game brought to them, so here she was at home plate. It was clear the field was a significant landmark in Joseph's life, and she was grateful to be a part of it. He led her up into the grandstand to where a spectator had a clear view of every play from first base to third.

"This grandstand can seat 600 people."

"Six hundred, huh? Seems like a lot for such a small town."

"You'd be surprised what kinds of crowds we pull out here for a big game on a perfect summer night. Popcorn, a cold Coke, and maybe a styrofoam dish of homemade ice cream made by booster club moms."

She looked up at him. "Doesn't get much better than that, huh?"

"It really doesn't." He turned to her and grabbed her hand again.

CHAPTER 18

"Let's go check out the field." J.P. and Leah headed down the steps and out around the backstop fence, walking slowly from third base to home plate and then out to the pitcher's mound.

As they turned to face the grandstand, J.P. began to replay highlights of the many seasons he played and coached on the field. Leah had a hard time following all of the plays he described, but she could have watched and listened to him all night long. The memories alone were giving him a visible adrenaline rush — the color on his cheeks, the power in his body, and the brilliant smile across his face — and she let him play out his past in front of her. After a few minutes, she quietly reached for his hand, not wanting to take the moment away from him, but wanting to be a part of what he was feeling and reliving.

J.P.'s smile only got bigger as he looked down at her hand and then into her eyes. "Some of my best memories and some of the most fun I've ever had in my life have happened right here. I'll never forget the freezing shower of Gatorade I got from my little league baseball players after we won a league tournament," he pointed out toward first base, "Right over there in front of our home dugout." J.P. continued, "It doesn't get more satisfying than a double play from shortstop on my softball teams, or hitting a ball into right field and getting a stand up triple." Finally, he fell silent. Smiling, buzzing with life, and surveying the area as if his life was complete.

Leah leaned in toward him and whispered, "I can feel it, you know. All of the sudden, I can see the red, white, and blue of the grandstand." She leaned into his shoulder. "I can hear the roar of the fans echoing, probably even miles away."

"It sure is a beauty, isn't it?" He lifted an arm up around her shoulders and pulled her close to him, and they spent a few minutes enjoying the silence in this beautiful monument to America's favorite sport. The spirit of bygone games seemed to permeate the grounds, and it felt right to be quiet, just for a little while. Leah had known from watching Joseph at Nick's games that he loved this game. But being here — on his home field — allowed Leah to share in Joseph' love for it. They stood there on the pitcher's mound, holding each other, giving tribute to Joseph's experiences and the fact that they could share them here, together.

With a quick squeeze, Joseph indicated that he was ready to head back to the pickup, if she was. As they gradually made their way back to the Dodge, Leah soaked in the warmth of the experience. She had expected to learn quite a bit that weekend, but hadn't expected the tenderness and importance of their trip to the ballfield. Her nervous anticipation of the weekend was gone, and was replaced by a feeling of comfort and hope.

J.P., while overcome with happiness, was feeling a little less calm than his companion. Now that their romantic moment on the diamond was over, the possibilities of the evening were beginning to make him nervous.

He had, of course, considered the consequences of bringing Leah back to Frankton and to the farm when he first asked her. Caught up in the excitement of the new relationship, he figured those consequences were worth it, for he and Leah to be happy together.

Even though he knew, deep in his heart, that he was right, he couldn't stop the butterflies from having a hoe-down in his stomach. His past considerations flashed through his mind as they climbed into the pickup and headed toward their next, very public, destination.

J.P.'s feelings for his wife had started an irreversible slide even before Claire took the job that had her traveling weeks at a time. She had hated the farm and its lifestyle. When she found her off-the-farm job, it became her answer to happiness. When he realized that, for Claire, "happiness" meant being as far away from the farm for as long as she could be gone, he knew their marriage didn't have much of a future. Claire held her job and lifestyle as her priorities, while J.P. had to admit to himself that his love for the farm and its way of life ranked above his marriage.

For all the years of turmoil in their marriage, the strongest emotion J.P. felt over the whole thing was disappointment. Sure, he had bouts with fear, anger, and loneliness, but when J.P. realized

CHAPTER 18

his marriage was over, the loss of it had turned him numb. After a winter of blurred days he could barely remember, when tiny green buds finally started speckling the tree branches, he knew it was time to close that chapter in his life. Leaving the farm was about more than a simple change of scenery — he needed a stark change in perspective. And, boy, did he get one.

In a small, rural community, one of the hardest things to do is keep your personal life a secret. Family, friends, and most of the community knew something of his estranged marriage. When and if J.P. brought a gal into town, it wouldn't be a huge surprise to most of the people he knew. His friends and acquaintances had all suspected that J.P.'s move to the city was about more than the job.

These thoughts were flooding J.P.'s mind as he and Leah climbed into the Dodge to leave the ballfield.

They headed south on Broadway, past the swimming pool and the dairy freeze. As they drove by the pool J.P. lowered his drivers window, and the sound of dozens of young people having fun filled the cab. He turned to Leah. "These two blocks of town are the mainstay for the youth in the summer." He took a quick final glance at the pool, and tried to focus on the warm breeze and the happy yells of all the splashing kids.

The word "simple" floated again to the surface of Leah's mind, triggered by the wistful tone in his voice. After the first time he brought "simple" to her mind — back in the city — Leah looked the word up in the dictionary, out of sheer curiosity. The meaning for the word was, "Easy to know, unaffected, not complex, and honest." Leah smiled all the more, knowing that she had been right. Joseph was simple, and that wasn't a bad thing at all. He was straightforward, practical, and honest, like the hometown he was so proud of.

As they entered the business district they passed the blacksmith, mechanics shop, and feed store.

"Blacksmith? Is that even a thing anymore?"

J.P. shook out his nervous shoulders and turned his attention back to Leah; the whole reason he was giving a tour. "Well, it's not quite the career it used to be, but there are still a few around. That's the flower shop, liquor store, bar and grill."

He drove, and rattled off each store on the main three blocks of businesses. "Grocery store, pharmacy, lawyers office, cafe, hardware, beauty shop."

"You could probably recite all these with your eyes closed, couldn't you?"

"Sure could. Seeing as how I'm driving, though, I probably shouldn't." He winked at her, and continued. "Medical clinic, service station, post office, and two banks."

"Is that it?"

"That's it. Just about everything you could possibly need."

"That's pretty true! I noticed everybody waved at you, or stuck their finger up off of their steering wheels. Do you really know everyone in this town?"

He laughed, a genuinely happy sound, realizing how different their worlds really were. "Well, I *do* probably know most of these people, but they'd have waved at me even if I didn't."

"What? Why?"

"That's just what we do around here. Think of it as a friendly greeting. Besides, everyone knows everyone else — or they're at least acquainted — so people don't want to offend anyone."

"That blows my mind. Seriously, knowing everyone in your whole town? Or even most of the town? I can't wrap my brain around that."

"We're definitely different, you and I."

She smiled up at him. "I kind of like that."

"Me, too. I'll bet we can both wrap our stomachs around being hungry, though, don't you think?" He took a deep breath. "Want to stop by the Cage for a burger?"

"You read my mind."

Stepping into the Cage Bar & Grill was like walking through a time

CHAPTER 18

machine. The swinging old-style doors you had to pass through once you got through the outer door was only a hint of what was to come — a one-of-a-kind mix of baseball memorabilia and an ode to the Wild West.

It was a big building, and the owners had spent years adding decor to the walls that they'd found at various places. One of the first things to catch a person's eye was a balcony in the rear of the bar, reminiscent of the old movies where the show girls would hang out when they weren't onstage.

To the left was the frontier saloon, with a standup piano next to the wall and a jukebox next to that. There were round tables with a symbolic deck of cards at each table. The wall was lined with mirrors overlooking a small dance floor, and in the back stood the pool table.

And an oval-shaped bar sat right in the middle of it all.

Adding to the unique atmosphere of the place was a modern sports bar. In the front right corner, you could see a wire baseball backstop, The Cage.

There was a home plate painted on the floor in front of it, then an outline of first, second, and third base, and finally, a pitcher's mound. There was a table sitting at each of the bases and the mound, which made table service very simple. Three big screen TVs, video games, and sports memorabilia were mounted on the walls.

J.P. and Leah had barely gotten through the front door when people began enthusiastically greeting J.P. from the bar. After a flurry of introductions and slightly uncomfortable laughs, they finally sat down at one of the small round tables. Their waitress, Deedee, gave J.P. a hug and said, "Good to see you, J.P. I haven't seen you lately."

Avoiding an explanation, J.P. simply replied, "Good to see you, too, Deedee. How are the kids?"

Deedee hadn't been born yesterday, and she knew a man who didn't want to talk when she saw one, so she played along. "Kids are great, taller than me now. You guys here for the burger special?"

"We sure are. Thanks, Deedee."

"Sure thing, J.P."

He breathed a sigh of relief as she turned toward the kitchen. No one had seen J.P. and Claire together for at least two years, so seeing him here with a different woman didn't come as too much of a surprise to the other patrons. That didn't mean, of course, that they weren't curious.

Oblivious to J.P.'s nervousness, Leah was soaking in all the charm of the Cage. Not just the decor, but also the way J.P. interacted with everyone. It was clear that life was different here for Joseph — much different than in the city. In the last fifteen minutes they had visited the baseball field, been greeted by the driver of every vehicle coming down mainstreet, and said "Hello" to everyone in the Cage. J.P. had even gotten a hug from somebody. This was more of a connection with people and life in general than Leah had in a whole day in the city.

She found herself thinking back to the first week she had met Joseph. She had wondered, "Was this guy good, bad, or just different?" Turned out, he *was* different in a very good sort of way. And maybe this small town would turn out the same way.

The food was good and the atmosphere was friendly. Best of all, Leah could tell that Joseph was in his element; he was home. Two couples were out on the dance floor, so J.P. turned and held out his hand to her.

"You up for a dance?"

She nodded happily. "You bet. Hopefully I remember how to move my feet."

"Nah, it's just like riding a bike. You'll get it figured out."

"What if I told you I don't know how to ride a bike?"

If Joseph had been taking a drink of his coke at that moment, he may have spit it across the table. He looked at her first in shock, and then in pity. Leah threw her head back and let out a peal of laughter.

"Got ya. You should have seen the look on your face!" She took his hand and happily joined him on the dance floor. It was their first dance since their night at the Starbrite ballroom, and it felt just as heavenly to Leah as it had that night. They danced to four songs, finished their french fries, and finally decided to continue their journey out to the farm.

It had become Leah's custom when they were together in the Dodge to slide over next to J.P. on the bench seat. It had become a very natural position for the both of them, and J.P. especially liked how cozy and comfortable it felt. He and Claire had gone from dating to boredom in what felt like a flash, and feeling content next to a woman still felt fresh and exciting.

"It was already dark when they left the Cage. "It's a ten mile drive, eight miles west on blacktop, and two miles south on the dirt."

She snuggled up next to him, and leaned her head on his shoulder. "I'll take your word for it."

When they finally pulled into the driveway, Leah noticed the "Joseph P. Druel" on the mailbox as they slowed and turned left into the farmyard. Between the pickup headlights and the yard light, Leah could just barely make it out on the barn: the tattoo that Joseph had on his left shoulder, the lazy D with a bar above it.

"You know, in this dim light, that white brand on the red barn reminds me of a welcoming smile."

The corner of his mouth curved up, and he looked up at the barn, too. "A welcoming smile. I like that."

As they stopped alongside the house, Leah gave Joseph a kiss on the cheek.

He was taken by surprise, and asked, "Now, what was that for?"

"For trusting me enough to bring me home."

The impulsiveness of the kiss was as surprising to Leah as it was to J.P. In those few seconds, she marveled that she would ever act on her feelings so quickly. She even seemed to be developing something of an imagination, and it was growing just as quickly as her love for Joseph.

He stood just outside the cab of the Dodge, and as he opened Leah's door, he gave a deep, dramatic bow. "Welcome to my home, Leah. My real home."

Walking into the house, Leah was struck by how lovely it all was. It wasn't exactly how she imagined a man kept his home.

"This is... so much cleaner than I expected it to be! And it's really gorgeous! The curtains, the floors — it feels like a country cottage on a home and garden show." She continued to gush about it to Joseph who stood back and ate it all up.

This shouldn't have surprised Leah because, as she reflected, Joseph was not your ordinary guy.

"I'd like to say the house has been in my family since it was built, but that's not how it happened."

Leah did her best to listen intently as she wandered from room to room, immersing herself in this house that Joseph had turned into his territory. "Oh, yeah?"

"Yep, the family that built it back in 1926 lost it during the great depression in 1930, along with the farm."

"Oh, well that's sad."

He nodded. "The banks and insurance companies took over many of the farms in the area." The topic was heavy, but he was still enjoying the conversation. Seeing this spark of energy in Leah was a good reminder that there was plenty he didn't know about her, either. Who knew what kind of hobbies and interests she had before she let them slip away?

After a quick tour of the main floor, J.P. grabbed Leah's luggage and escorted her to the basement, which held two comfortably-sized bedrooms. One had been J.P.'s room for the past year, and the other a guest room. He put her suitcase on the bed in the guest room, as he planned to sleep in his own room during the stay. After getting ready for bed that evening, they met in the hallway between rooms.

Leah rested her arms on his shoulders as he clasped his hands behind her waist.

"Lights out time, huh?"

With a flutter in his chest, he leaned down and gave her a small, sweet kiss. "Yep. Early day tomorrow."

"Hmm. Does it have to be an early day for me, too?"

CHAPTER 18

A laugh rumbled in his chest as he drowsily nuzzled his face into her neck. "Nope. In fact, I insist that you sleep in as late as you possibly can."

"I can definitely agree to that. Good night, Joseph." She locked her lips onto his one last time, before trapping him in a bear hug. Once she finally released him, she turned into her bedroom, quietly shutting the door behind her.

CHAPTER 19

The next morning, J.P. was out of the house by 5:30 am.

He took a short drive around the farms, and confirmed that the crops were looking good. He was happy to see that they had received timely rains over the summer, and now that fall was approaching, the benefits of the moisture could be clearly seen. With full ears of corn hanging from the stalks and the plump-looking bean pods on soybean plants, he felt like he could breathe a sigh of relief.

When Leah awoke two hours after Joseph, she could smell the bacon frying.

The aroma filled the whole house, and she thought to herself, "What a wonderful invitation to get out of bed."

When Leah made her way up to the kitchen after doing her best to tame her hair and splash her face with water, she found that Joseph had a breakfast of bacon and hash browns waiting for her. Next to the deliciously-steaming plate was a fresh bouquet of wildflowers, and she leaned in to smell the beautiful purple and yellow blooms.

She could see that he had been out already that morning, judging by the dusty boots next to the front door. She sat down and took a little sip of piping hot coffee, then looked up at him washing dishes at the sink. "How does everything look around the farm?"

"Looking mighty good, as a matter of fact."

"So are you going to give me a tour?" She asked, excited.

"Yup," was all he said in reply, but as he turned to her she could

CHAPTER 19

see that there was a big grin on his face.

"I'm in for quite the whirlwind, aren't I?"

"Sure are. And maybe a few history lessons here or there. Better finish that breakfast if you're going to keep up your strength."

She smiled and dug into her breakfast, feeling like quite the lucky lady. She felt lucky for a lot of reasons: Joseph loved her enough to want to share his life with her, he felt comfortable enough to joke around, and he could cook a mean plate of bacon. It didn't get much better than that.

As she finished her coffee, she noticed that Joseph was dressed in a way she hadn't seen yet: old, unpolished boots, and faded jeans with pliers hanging from a holster on his right side.

She chuckled to herself, thinking about pliers replacing the six-shooter for the men on the plains in these modern times. A twenty-first century cowboy. Eventually, she was grinning from ear to ear.

He looked at her curiously. "What's so funny over there?"
She looked at him and raised an eyebrow. "If you're a good cowboy today I'll tell you about it tonight."

Caught off-guard by her surprising combination of secrecy and forwardness, but still up for some fun, he decided he'd play along.

"I'll be good today, I promise you that ma'am." They both laughed like they'd known each other for years. When J.P. put on his gray cowboy hat out of habit, the picture was made complete and Leah couldn't help but let out a girlish giggle.

"Come on now!" Joseph protested "What is going on? You think I look funny?"

She shook her head quickly, "No, no! I promise. You look the *opposite* of funny. I'm just so unfamiliar with all of this."

He gave her a sideways glance, not sure that she was being totally square with him and finally gave in. "Okay, I'll believe you." After a moment, he added, "You know, a person can't just buy them like this." He reached up and patted his hat. "It's taken me eight years to get it just right."

"Ha! I guess I was right in thinking it looked like it had been run over!"

"You sound like you're joking, but it has indeed been run over, a number of times! Four wheelers, cattle hooves, not to mention getting tossed around by the wind."

Leah felt a little overdressed, as she didn't have any clothes to match Joseph's farm-working attire. This was much different from the service station, where they both wore a basic uniform-style shirt. As they stood at the east window, Leah looked at the barn, and smiled when she saw the smile.

"So what's that mark on the barn all about?"

"That is my brand. It's called the 'Lazy D.'"

"The Lazy D?"

"Yep. See, it's laying down? It's lazy."

Leah laughed, temporarily satisfied with the explanation.

Upon stepping out of the house, the two were bombarded by two slobbery, excited, bounding canines. J.P. happily introduced her to the farm's dogs, who were very excited to have him home.

"Looks like you missed them, too!" She observed, as he scratched and pet them while she tried to protect her face from dog slobber.

He straightened up and smiled. "Sorry, guys, you don't get to ride along today. I've got company." To Leah's surprise, the dogs acted like they understood, and sat on their haunches, staring longingly toward the truck as she and J.P. walked toward it.

For that day's drive, they climbed into the twenty-year-old Chevy pickup with a flat bed box. Leah noticed the big white blocks and bags stacked neatly in the back of it. She looked around the farm site one more time, catching the brand on the barn in the corner of her vision, and thought, "Yup, it still looks like a big smile." Another grin rose on her face, and she wondered if this weekend was going to be full of smiles. So far, there hadn't been any disappointments — nothing to frown about.

As they left the farm site, they turned north, then right again into a cornfield where they followed the dirt road that cut through it.

"This is the best-looking corn we've had for maybe ten years," he

CHAPTER 19

mentioned, with a sound of relief in his voice. The corn stalks they were driving through were between eight and ten feet tall.

"This is something else that's totally new to me! I've never driven through a cornfield, and I've definitely never been this close to a corn stalk before!" She let out a loud, boisterous laugh. "I feel like a little girl on a field trip from school!"

They drove out of the walls of corn into what J.P. explained was an alfalfa field. Leah remembered what alfalfa was from their drive out into the country for the picnic, so she sat quietly and contentedly instead of asking questions. They continued to drive on the flat field for about a mile.

"It's beautiful." She sighed.

There were ravens flying along a grove of trees, and she could see some higher hills off in the distance. She looked over her right shoulder, back in the direction of the farm site. Although she could still see the roof of the house and barn, they were slowly fading into the distance. She had no concept of direction or distance out here, where there were few buildings or road signs to help her navigate her surroundings.

This really was the great outdoors.

J.P. brought the pickup to a stop, and he pointed off into the distance where there were some cattle feeding on a hillside.

"Are those your cows?"

"Oh, they're our cows alright, and we're headed out to move them."

Leah jerked her head to look at him with a surprised expression. "How?"

J.P. gave her a feisty wink, then honked the pickup's horn a few times. He got out, placed his hands together like a funnel, and yelled several times, "Come Bossy! Here Bossy!" And honked the horn a few more times. Leah noticed the cattle raising their heads as they began walking toward them. He reached into the pickup, repeated his ritual again, and then leaned against the pickup door with a smile on his face. She watched the movement on the hills in amazement, and after only a couple of minutes, the first of the cows came running as if out of nowhere.

J.P. lifted a sack out of the back of the pickup and crossed a fence, so that he was standing among the herd. She heard him, in a soft voice, saying "Good girls, good girls." After he was surrounded by the herd, he took a few steps, opened a gate, and opened a sack of what he called "cattle cubes." The giant animals stepped through the opening of the gate into the new grass, happy for the food. The cattle and J.P. seemed to stop, as if they were enjoying each other's company. He explained that he was counting the herd and looking for any health problems among them.

After a few moments, the slow pokes of the herd showed up, bringing up the rear. Leah's 21st century cowboy was still talking to them, "Good girls, nice girls."

She started to call out to him, "Maybe I'm not so special —," but stopped mid-sentence. She realized she had startled the cattle; their heads raised quickly, and they started moving away from the pickup. She decided to simply watch the scene, rather than adding her two cents.

She knew that Joseph believed all humans and animals had a purpose in life, and that — while we may not understand everything about life — there is a reason for all of it to exist.

It was a touching picture of total trust and satisfaction between J.P. and the herd, for a few moments at least. Soon, though, the cattle were paying no attention to J.P., as they became more interested in the new supply of green grass.

It was a surreal picture of man and beast sharing a common ground. The cattle knew they were safe; their leader was among them. As she watched quietly, Leah thought that the scenic view was beautiful, but that its beauty was no match for this astonishing moment unfolding in front of her. She realized that she had been holding her breath, trying desperately not to disturb this moment, and was surprised to feel the wetness of tears stream down her cheeks. She felt a growing hunger to share in Joseph's life, to know more about his way of living it.

CHAPTER 19

It was clear that he had been doing this his whole life — that he really knew no other way. She wondered if she could assimilate herself into his experience. It would probably take a lifetime, she knew that much, but she found that she didn't care. Her gratitude for the moment swelled as J.P. started moving slowly toward the pickup, still talking to the herd. Quickly wiping her cheeks dry, she flashed him a smile, and called out "I know people talk to their cats and dogs all the time, but I never considered that it was something a person could do with cattle!"

When J.P. got back to the pickup, he moved four salt blocks and four bags of mineral over the fence and put it all in open-top boxes for the cattle.

"What are those big blocks? And what do you keep in the sacks?"

"Well, cattle crave salt and minerals — they do the same for them as vitamins do for humans."

"Oh. Wow. There's so much to learn. You're going to have to put up with a lot of questions," she said as he hopped back into the pickup. Once he was seated, she scooted over to his side, as usual. "Maybe if I get closer to you, I'll learn more?"

His chest rumbled with a laugh. "Like osmosis?"

"Yeah, just like that." She sighed and laid her head on his shoulder as he started the pickup's engine.

"You remember what I said about the life of a flower? That God may be the only one who sees the hidden ones?"

"Of course I do." She answered, fondly thinking back on the first time Joseph had ever caught her unaware with his quiet wisdom. He didn't continue his thought, but simply drove them northwest across the alfalfa field, in a different direction from the entrance.

They drove over a ridge to find, laid out before them in a small ravine, a brilliant field of white, yellow, blue, and pink flowers.

It took Leah's breath away.

After a few seconds of stunned silence, she whispered, "How did they get here?"

"I figure there had always been some flowers in the bottom, and then one year it didn't get grazed. It allowed the flowers to bloom and seed out. Over the years, with good rainfall, they just kept spreading. Sometimes, during dry years, they lay dormant, but with the good rains this year they seem to have exploded."

Leah was upset with herself for leaving her camera at home this weekend. She had never dreamed that there would be such gorgeous scenery. When she finally took her eyes off the flowers, her gaze continued in a northerly direction, where she caught sight of a windmill on top of a hill.

It struck her as a guardian, keeping watch over the pasture it supplied water to. With every breeze it pumped life, just like blood for the human heart, but it pumped water for the thirsty. Fresh water for a human out of a spigot, or into a tank for the cattle and wild game.

"I just want time to freeze and stay still." She was struggling to find words to describe what she was feeling, so she kept her thoughts to herself, and took a deep breath of fresh country air.

J.P. did not want to move either. "It's been too long since I've enjoyed this land and my animals." He put his arm around Leah and thought to himself, *Life doesn't get any better than this.* There he sat, with his arm around the woman he loved, in the midst of the world that was etched on his heart. They let the wind blow gently over them, and got lost in silence for a few more moments.

After seeing some movement from the cattle in the corner of his eye, J.P. smiled. "Doesn't matter how good the grass is, cattle are going to check out their boundaries." During their quiet moment together, some of the more curious cattle had made their way toward them. He gave them a friendly wave and turned to Leah. "I've got everything done here that I needed to do. You ready to move on?"

She nodded, and he started the engine. They drove back through the dirt road and J.P. stopped the pickup at the gravel road to look both directions. Leah took the moment to put her hand on his knee and said, "Wow, Joseph. It is so beautiful out here."

He replied in a heartbeat, "It is splendid out here. In fact, I think

CHAPTER 19

I'd even call it heavenly."

The corner of her mouth curved up slightly, and she nestled in closer to him. With anyone else, she would have made a joke about such flowery words, but in this moment, she couldn't really disagree with him. It *was* splendid.

They drove on, saying nothing, simply enjoying each other and the experience of the country beauty.

"After a few minutes, they turned into another farmsite."

J.P. said, "This is my son, Daniel's place. I want the two of you to meet."

"Oh! Good!" replied Leah. "You've mentioned Daniel plenty of times, but haven't divulged many details. I'll be nice to put a face to the name."

They stopped in front of a metal building, directly in front of a sign that said *"NO parking. Violators will be towed."* She pointed it out to Joseph with a raised eyebrow.

He only laughed. "You don't need to worry, I know the owner."

Leah let out one of her girlish giggles — a sound that was so new in her own head she, barely recognized it.

When they stepped inside the building, they found Daniel busy inspecting and servicing a hay baler.

"There's someone parked out in that no parking zone out there! Better take care of it!" J.P. called out, as his son's head jerked toward him in surprise.

"Hey, Dad!" Father and son walked up to each other quickly and greeted with an enthusiastic hug. Leah was touched by the show of affection between the two. *Will I ever stop being surprised by this man?* She thought to herself.

J.P. turned to Leah in introduction. "Daniel, I would like you to meet my friend, Leah."

"Happy to meet you, Leah," Daniel stuck out his hand for a handshake. "When dad and I talk he always manages to mention you in some way."

Leah took his hand and smiled. She could see a blush run up Joseph's neck as he cleared his throat. The blush, his posture, everything about Joseph displayed nerves and even a little nervousness. *"Now this might be the most surprising thing of all,"* she thought with glee, as she decided this adorable moment could never be topped.

Daniel and Leah exchanged genuine pleasantries after their handshake, without any awkwardness or discomfort. J.P. noted the change in Leah since their initial meeting. He remembered vividly when she was so locked into herself — out of fear of being hurt — to shake hands or even look at J.P. He was thrilled that she no longer felt the need to hide within herself.

"We just moved the main herd to the middle pasture, and now we're going to check the cattle on Harry's and Doc's places."

"That's great! Thanks, Dad. I'll probably be baling hay at Guy's this afternoon."

Leah took the technical chatter of Daniel and Joseph's conversation as an opportunity to look over the farm equipment. Everything on the farm seemed so much bigger than things in the city. From the wide, open spaces to standing next to the enormous tires on the tractor that the hay baler was hooked to. She thought, *"Maybe this is why Joseph's perspective on everything is so much different."*

The two men talked over several topics concerning everything from the farm in general to corn borers, aphids attacking the beans, and fuel supply and prices. Leah could detect the excitement in their voices when discussing the condition of the crops. After about fifteen minutes of lively conversation, and Leah's comfortable, quiet exploration, it was time to go. They said their goodbyes, and assured one another they'd meet again soon.

J.P. and Leah jumped back into the old pickup and continued on down the road. The Chevy had served him well with its 180,000 miles. It had earned a place of dignity as the truck that got him around the farm, dirt roads, and fields filled with pasture grasses. As they progressed down the road, he stopped frequently to point out objects, animals, and landmarks that were important to him.

CHAPTER 19

Because they came in last night after dark, Leah felt entirely disoriented. She was totally lost as to which way was north, south, east, or west. Luckily, she was snuggled up next to a regional expert, and she trusted that he knew exactly where they were.

J.P. knew everything about everyone and every farm in the area. It gave him pride in himself and his home to have so much knowledge about the history.

They turned a corner where J.P. drove up a short trail to a clearing where only a barn stood. J.P. told her that his father's grandparents moved onto this farm in 1910. HIs grandfather was the second of fifteen children. The farm was lost during the depression in 1928, but they managed to live there until 1935.

Leah was somewhat embarrassed that she didn't know more about her grandparents, let alone the generation before them. She felt that she had nothing to add to this conversation. She was the tourist and Joseph was her guide.

As they continued their journey around J.P.'s rural neighborhood, he informed Leah that their next stop would be his parents' home.

"You ready to meet the parents?"

She smiled at him, although a bit nervously. "Ready as I'll ever be!"

Another half mile, and she could see the beginnings of a vibrant floral display like none she had ever laid eyes on. The variety of colors and types of flowers were so well-arranged that she found it difficult to believe any one person could have been responsible for it. The display of flowers seemed to be bursting with life.

"Well, I see where you got your love of flowers!"

He chuckled quietly, enjoying her reaction. There really were flowers everywhere. They started at the mailbox and cheerfully lined the hundred-foot drive, and could be found all around the outside of the house.

J.P. could see that his father wasn't home, since his pickup was absent from its parking spot in the open metal shed just ahead of them. He figured he was out checking on the crops and cattle and everything else in the neighborhood.

The red pickup that Herb — J.P.'s father — drove looked like it had been through a demolition derby. One by one, scratches, nicks, and dents added up over the years to make it the dismal truck that it was. With two newer trucks in the shed, one would think he'd give the ancient pickup a break, but no. He always chose the old reliable "Red." No matter how many family members tried to talk him into parking Old Red for good, J.P. knew he'd never give it up. He didn't necessarily agree with his dad, but he understood. There was a bond between man and truck here — what happened to one happened to the other. Herb believed that, at seventy-eight, the family would begin to add pressure for him to stop working, and he wasn't about to go down without a fight. So, as long as old Red kept going, he could, too.

J.P. rapped on the door as they entered the house. As soon as they walked in, J.P. knew what was in the oven: his mother's county fair purple ribbon ranger cookies. Leah breathed in the sweet smell and broke out in a grin.

J.P. began to call out to his mom, just as she appeared from the corner of the pantry, a small red headed lady with only a slight hint of gray in her hair. Leah couldn't have known that her hair color came from her Danish heritage, but she *did* finally get the answer to her question about the source of Daniels' reddish hair. His mother gave him a hug.

Quickly J.P. cleared his throat and turned toward Leah. "Mom, this is my friend, Leah. Leah, this is my mom, Kate."

To Leah's surprise, Kate leaned in and gave her a warm hug. The embrace from Joseph's mom triggered a stir of emotion in her — memories of hugs from her own mother flooded her mind. *"It has been a long time since I have been hugged by a mom... of any kind."* thought Leah. She wanted to hang on for a few minutes, but, knowing it would be awkward, refrained.

A tray of freshly baked cookies sat on the kitchen counter.

"Please, come in. Have some cookies! And for drinks you could have a cup of coffee, or I've got milk and iced tea."

CHAPTER 19

"Thank you, Kate. They smell wonderful." Leah was struggling a bit, to fight back the emotions that were building inside of her. First a motherly hug, now warm, just-baked cookies. Memories were streaming through Leah's mind, like old silent movies, making it difficult to focus on the reality in front of her. She shook her head discreetly while Kate and J.P. chatted, trying to shake her sudden sadness and focus on the present.

With a couple of cookies in one hand and a glass of iced tea in the other, they moved to the dining room. Leah was delighting in all of the pictures on the wall, especially Joseph's high school senior picture. She studied it momentarily, then turned to Joseph and commented, "You look the same... except with longer hair and those impressive sideburns!"

J.P. replied with amusement, "I was proud of those sideburns, you know. Not everyone could grow them at age seventeen!" J.P. took a sip of iced tea and reflected, "Back then I wanted to look older and now... well at my age I would like to look a little younger."

She sent him an affectionate smile. "Well, I'm grateful to get a glimpse at a 'youthful' Joseph."

They continued to lazily drink tea and chatter over the pictures of Joseph's siblings, until J.P. called her back to the picture next to his.

"This is my brother Daniel." He reached up and briefly touched the frame. "I've mentioned to you that I lost a brother, right?" Leah nodded without speaking. J.P. continued, "This is his junior picture. We lost him the summer before his senior year."

"Daniel." Leah whispered. "Your Daniel's namesake?"

He nodded, and they stood for a few moments in silence, letting the information and a new piece of their bond settle between them. Soon, though, J.P. continued the introduction of his siblings' pictures to Leah: each of his three sisters and his youngest brother.

Fully aware of what was going on in the other room, Kate remained in the kitchen. When she knew Joseph had completed the photo tour, she decided to join them. The two were now sitting at the table enjoying the cookies.

"So, Leah." She said as she sat down with them. "How do you like the farm?"

Leah responded quickly, with an energy that surprised her, "I love it! It is so beautiful out here." "Thank you," Kate responded with a quiet sense of pride, "We like it. And the rains this year have been such a blessing."

Leah was quickly realizing how important the rain was to this rural community; it seemed that it was always a part of conversation. Some city folks might bring up the weather as small talk, but for rural folks it truly was a huge part of their lives.

Kate continued, "Joseph tells me that you've been working at the garage for a number of years?"

"Yes, I started there when I was in high school, actually. I do the bookkeeping for George's Garage, and three other independent service stations around the city."

Kate, always impressed with a resourceful woman, nodded in approval. "And you have one son, is that right? He graduated from high school this past year?"

"Yes!" She shot a sly look over to J.P., acknowledging the fact that he had clearly been talking about her to his mom. "Nick graduated, and is going to start at Southeast Community College in the fall."

"You must be proud of him," Kate said, smiling.

"I am! I'm very proud of Nick. He's turned into a fine young man, I think."

"I'll vouch for that," J.P. confirmed, putting a hand on her knee and giving it a small squeeze.

Satisfied with the information she'd gleaned, Kate turned her attention to Joseph.

"You getting everything checked out the way you had planned?"

"Working on it." He drained what was left of the tea in his glass. "The cattle are moved at my place and I've met up with Daniel. I need to check cattle on Doc's and Harry's and show Leah around a bit more yet."

Leah could tell by his voice that the visit was wrapping up, and

CHAPTER 19

she couldn't help but feel a little disappointed. She was very anxious to ask Kate more questions, but she knew this was not the time. She enjoyed the last few bites of her cookie and got up from the table.

As they were walking out of the dining room, Leah noticed that Joseph took an extra cookie.

"You know, why not?" she asked no one in particular, and helped herself to another one as well. This fresh country air seemed to be having an effect on her appetite.

Kate cleared the napkins and glasses from the table. "We'll see you two at the rodeo tonight!"

Before leaving the room, Leah turned back to Kate and gratefully added, "It was very nice to meet you! And thank you for the delicious cookies!"

As they stepped out of the house and made their way to the pickup, J.P. and Leah held hands as though they'd been doing so for years.

Leah slid closer to him on the seat and said, "That was nice."

"I hoped introducing you to my mom would go well."

"I think it did."

When they turned out of the driveway, it broke their comfortable daze and brought them back to the task at hand.

Leah remembered something he'd mentioned inside the house and asked, "What did you mean when you said 'Doc's and Harry's?'"

J.P. answered, happy for her questions. "Most of the farms are named after the former owner or renters who lived on the land. Doc's was owned by a doctor from Omaha who bought the land in the 1940s and owned it for nearly fifty years before selling it."

Leah's lips parted in awe. "Fifty years? Wow."

Doc's farm was located a mile north of J.P.s' parents. He briefly stopped and gave the cattle at this location salt and minerals, but he didn't need to move them.

They then drove back toward his parents' and turned west for a half mile into a valley that turned out onto a grass driveway. They drove through a beautiful three-row-tree shelter belt, and found a rustic, abandoned building site. There was a house, barn, granary, and, by the windmill, a small summer house. As they stopped in the yard of the smaller cottage, Leah asked "Does this farm have a name?"

"Yep." He looked at her, relieved to see that she wasn't bored by the tour yet. "This farm we call 'Harry's.'" He turned back to the small house to take it all in. "A fellow by the name of Harry Porter lived here from 1940 till he retired in 1961. So this farm is named Harry."

"Why are there two houses? And why is that one so small?

J.P. explained, "The small house is what they called a summer house. In the summers, they would cook in the smaller one so that the main house could stay cool. If the farm had a hired man, they usually stayed or lived in the summer house."

"Wow. Those sure were different days. I'm not sure I'd survive without air conditioning."

He laughed, then added, "This little house has an unusual story, actually. In 1930, a family named Decker lived here. They had a daughter who got married. Well, the newlyweds lived in that little two-room cottage for a year." J.P. grinned at Leah. "Could you imagine that? No electricity, you have to carry your water from the windmill, and — on top of all that — you live fifty feet from your parents' house. You use the same outhouse, plus the two rooms of the house are smaller than a hotel room today."

Leah tossed her head back and laughed. "No! I cannot even remotely imagine that." She shivered at the thought of herself in that kind of lifestyle. She had to admit, though, that it was kind of fun to imagine like this. She hadn't ever given much thought to history, to what it would have actually been like to live in the past.

J.P. added "The Deckers lost the farm during the depression of the 30s, but lived here until 1940, That's when Harry moved here.

"I can't believe how many details you know about this abandoned farm." She asked, "How do you know all of this history? All of it happened so many years before you were born!"

J.P.'s eyes lit up at the question. "I ask questions, that's all. I was always listening to the stories."

Leah took in a deep breath of sweet air and pulled open the

CHAPTER 19

passenger side door. "Can we look around?"

"Sure."

They got out and walked toward the big house. J.P. opened the yard gate for Leah, and they stepped onto the open porch. Leah tried to peer into a foggy stained window as J.P. simply opened the door and stepped in. Suddenly, it felt like they had taken a step back into 1950, with the wallpaper still colorful on the walls. There was a small, metal, round kitchen table sitting in the middle of the room. The cabinet doors were all open; the inventory displayed a half-dozen empty quart jars and two rusty tin containers — one for soda crackers and the other for tobacco. Plus, there was an empty, mid-sized, round-edged refrigerator sitting along the wall, with the rusty door hanging wide open.

J.P. and Leah simply stood, looking around the room. Even though it was messy, dirty, and abandoned, they could feel the history in the house. They didn't touch a thing, and silently took in the scene.

This was another first for Leah; she had never walked into a deserted house.

After one last look around, they walked out onto the porch and took a few deep breaths. The air inside had been musty, after years of quietly filling the empty rooms. Joseph then led them to the summer house.

"The measurement of the whole house is sixteen by twenty-four feet, and divided evenly into two rooms."

"Wow. It's smaller than a studio apartment!"

The only item in the house was a wood cookstove in the north room.

Grinning from ear to ear, he held his arms out wide and said, "Welcome to the 'honeymoon cabin.'"

She laughed quietly and moved slowly forward, inspecting the cabin. It didn't look like much then, but seven decades ago she bet that it was a cute little place. Then Joseph's words finally reached her mind — *the honeymoon cabin*. For just a moment, Leah let herself imagine a honeymoon with Joseph, and a smile crept over her face. She knew that this weekend could not be titled a honeymoon, but she was learning a lot more about Joseph — and her feelings for him — than she ever thought she would. Before she could stop the thought, another 'honeymoon' possibility popped into her head, and she felt a deep blush creep onto her cheekbones.

J.P. placed his hand on her arm, jolting Leah to the present, "If we're done with the tour of homes, we've got plenty more work to do."

Reluctant to leave, but recognizing there was work to be done, Leah followed him back to the Chevy where, as he did earlier, J.P. began honking the horn repeatedly.

Soon she could see cattle moving toward them in the far distance. They moved over the hill and down toward the farm.

He unloaded some salt and mineral for the cattle and, just like the first herd they had worked with, the leaders came running. The cattle gathered around the pickup like bees to their honeycomb, waiting for him to dump the sack of cubes so they could enjoy their treat.

J.P. got back into the pickup to chat with Leah while they ate. After some of the cattle realized they had run out of cubes, began looking into the windows of the pickup, as though they were begging for more. She didn't want to admit it, but seeing the giant animals moving around them outside the pickup was more than a little frightening.

The cattle were so big, looking straight at Leah through the window. Slobber and foam formed around the cattle's mouths from eating the cubes as they left a mess on the windows and hood.

Finally, after a few minutes that felt more like a few hours, she saw who they were waiting on: the last of the animals to make it to their location.

'There he is. That guy right there is a four-year-old Angus bull that I've raised from a calf." The bull's ear tags read *J.P.D 54*. "He's grown up to be the sire of the twenty purebred cattle that are the foundation and replacements of our whole herd." Abruptly, J.P. got out of the pickup without saying a word.

J.P. gave the cows another sack of cubes, then he opened another sack and walked comfortably up to 54. The big bull stopped what he

CHAPTER 19

was doing and started eating like his only chore was to consume the whole fifty pound bag of cubes.

To Leah's surprise Joseph started petting the beast. With gloves on and such a deliberate motion, it appeared to her that he was giving the bull a rub down. In reality, it was more like a good scratching, and 54 was clearly enjoying it. He went from side to side, giving the big guy a thorough petting.

After the shock wore off from seeing Joseph petting a bull the size of a house, she started paying more attention to the massive creature. He was so huge she could even recognize the muscle definition from her safe perch in the pickup. There were bulges all over his frame, and Leah noticed that the same tattoo-brand that was on the upper part of Joseph's shoulder — and on the barn — was also on 54's left hip.

She began to wonder about this thing... the idea of a brand. She didn't know that a brand is, at the most basic level, simply a cattleman's signature. Joseph would later tell her that it was the same as signing a name; a brand represents who you are.

She marveled over 54 and Joseph who, she thought with a chuckle, both had fine physiques. There seemed to be a friendship between them, like what one usually shares with a dog or a cat. J.P. turned to look at Leah and smiled, then turned back to give 54 one more enthusiastic scratch. She smiled and shook her head in disbelief; it was like J.P. and 54 didn't want to say farewell. It reminded her of friends at an airport, giving each other one more hug before saying goodbye.

J.P. patted 54 with friendly finality, and emptied the rest of the sack for the cattle before returning to the Chevy and Leah.

When he was once again seated next to her, she could feel her motherly instincts kick in. "You know, you could get hurt doing that. He's huge!"

J.P. just shrugged and smiled. "Don't you worry too much, we're old pals."

J.P. stopped at the end of the drive, turned to Leah, and asked, "Do you want to see more of the neighborhood?"

To Leah, a neighborhood was a few city blocks. She was learning that, out here, to J.P., it meant *miles*. Luckily today, she was feeling confident, and up for just about anything. "Sure!" She responded, with excitement in her voice.

He searched her eyes for a moment. "You sure this isn't boring you? All this driving around?"

She looked into his eyes, gave his arm a reassuring squeeze, and said, "I am never bored when I'm with you." J.P. wasn't much of a blusher, but he could feel his cheeks flush at her words. He gave her a quick smile and turned back to the road.

"I mean it." She said, quietly but firmly. "From the very start — bringing M&Ms and flowers to the shop, cleaning the restrooms that first week. It might not sound like much to you, but that was more excitement than I'd had in years!" She laughed. "And your theory about the ants? I've got to admit that, at first, it really pissed me off. I wasn't ready to have my mind changed, about anything then." She could have kept going, but figured by his blush that she'd shared plenty. If she would have gone on, she would have mentioned how good he had been to and for Nick. How surprised she was that their relationship had survived her family's 4th of July. No, it had not been boring having Joseph in her life.

J.P. turned the Chevy onto a gravel road that led up the hill and out of the valley. At the top of the hill, J.P. slowed the Chevy to a crawl and pointed out his drivers window.

"My family has farmed this land since 1948. Now Herb owns it."

All morning, Leah had been hearing the names of different farms and was betting this farm had a name, too. With as serious a face as she could muster, she asked "What is this farm's name?"

It was J.P.'s turn to smile; he could see the little smirk on her lips.

"I get it, I get it. Naming farms must sound pretty comical to city folk." He looked out ahead and gestured at the view. "This farm's name is Eddy. Local fellow by that name married a school teacher and lived here for a long time. When her father retired as a big wheat farmer in northwest Kansas, they moved there to take over his operation."

CHAPTER 19

"Wow." Leah shook her head. "That would be quite the ordeal!"

"Yep. Herb and his brother bought it from him, then Herb purchased his brother's half and now Daniel and I rent it from my parents. All those owners combined, my family's been farming this land for fifty years."

Leah stared out the window, with a little bit of awe. "I'm still amazed at how you can rattle off so much history!"

Soon, they drove down a long hill that hosted yet another old building site. J.P. stopped in the driveway of the vacant place. He said, "When my parents got married in 1953, this is where they lived. It's actually where I spent the first few years of my childhood." He took his hat off for a moment to wipe some sweat off his forehead before it reached his eyes. "We lived here until 1960 and, when I was five, we moved six miles to the south. This one was a pretty small house for our family; just five rooms."

Leah could tell by the heavy tone of Joseph's voice that this stop had significance to him. Knowing this, she turned back to the property in order to soak it all in. The barn was closer to the road on lower ground, and the house was halfway up a little hill. In a lighter-hearted tone, J.P. seemed to read her mind. "Yes, this one also has a name."

With a quizzical look, she waited patiently for the name. He continued "With the house sitting part way up the hill, the name is the Sidehill Ranch."

She giggled and said, "What a fitting name!" He simply smiled with approval.

Slowly, the tour moved on. Normally, Leah would be feeling antsy; like she needed to get something productive accomplished. This morning, though, with the warm air flowing through the windows and her computer a two hour drive away, she was doing her best to simply go along for the ride.

Another mile to the west was a large, well-kept farm. As they rolled slowly by, J.P. said, "My grandparents moved here in 1942, and bought the farm in 1951."

"And it's still in the family now?"

"Yep. When they retired in 1959 and moved into Frankton, their son, Ed, moved onto the farm, followed by his son Bill, who still lives here."

Leah could hear the pride in Joseph's voice as he shared his family's history. He told her more about his grandparents, Paul and Frances, who had survived 13 years of drought during the depression. "We call this the 'Home Place,' and it's got a lot of hard work put into it."

She smiled at him. "Hard work seems to be a theme around here."

"That's for sure. My family has never had anything given to us... other than maybe our work ethic and our faith in God."

"Wow. We had very different childhoods, that's for sure!"

"Well, I don't know too much about that, but I do know my grandparents worked many a day through empty stomachs. Feeding thirteen children was a full-time chore."

Leah looked at Joseph with a stare of astonishment. He couldn't help but laugh at her dropped jaw.

"You heard right. Thirteen, from the first-born Helen in 1922 to their youngest, Larry, in 1945."

"I can't even imagine!"

The Chevy moved up the next quarter-mile-long hill without any struggle. At the top of the hill, a one-room schoolhouse sat alone, next to a gnarled old tree. J.P. pulled in the schoolyard and shut the Chevy off.

"I only went here for half of my kindergarten year, but seventeen of my other family members attended for as long as they could." He let out a wistful sigh as he took in the old building. "I didn't go there for long, but I kind of like being able to say I went to a one room school."

The sign above the school's door read "MOUNT ZION DISTRICT 28."

Leah breathed out a sound of awe as she surveyed the small valley below them. "I know I keep saying it, but it's all so scenic out here. I can see your parents' house!"

"Sure can. See those trees? That's my place, almost six miles a

CHAPTER 19

way. One of my favorite views. I always found it fitting - the word 'mount' means 'to climb,' and here sits Mount Zion, right at the top of the hill."

She nodded silently. The wildflowers, their picnic, these expansive valleys and rising hills — she'd been living in the middle of all this beauty her whole life and simply had never paid attention. It felt new and exciting, but the truth was that it had always been there, and it had taken Joseph to open her eyes to it. She shook her head a bit to bring herself back to the conversation. "Anymore stops on this tour?"

They continued to the south, going over hill after seemingly endless hill, with the radio playing quietly in the background. Leah watched the hills and enjoyed the warm air for so long, she felt almost hypnotized. Then, all at once, the hills ended. Below them was a beautiful valley with the Loup River winding through it. It was the first river that they had crossed going into Frankton last evening, only this time they were about 20 miles up-river.

J.P. grinned "Pretty isn't it?"

Leah answered quietly, "It's beautiful."

As they came to the first intersection down into the valley, there was another schoolhouse. This one was still painted, with a cemetery adjoining the schoolyard. "The iron driveway arch into the cemetery read "Glenwood 1884."

"That's one hundred and twenty years ago!" Although she'd seen plenty of history during her informal tour, the magnitude of the past was finally sinking in. If she was honest, she'd have to admit that she'd never given the past much thought — people, places, or even family. She'd taken history classes and passed her tests, but had never really allowed herself to think too hard about it. She had never *felt* history like this before, like it was swirling all around her.

And it reminded her of yet another difference between her and Joseph; he knew who he was and where he came from. In the last two hours, she had "met" five generations of Joseph's family —

from his great-grandfather to Joseph's son Daniel.

"This whole experience has been incredible... and a little overwhelming, if I'm honest. I feel even closer to you now, knowing so much about your family." She fidgeted with her seatbelt, and turned to look out the window. "I'm also just a little envious. When it comes to knowing *my* family, I probably know less than a fourth of what you know about your own."

"Well, I don't think it's ever too late to learn more about the things you don't know."

"I suppose you're right about that."

Leah was getting a much clearer picture of the man she had so quickly grown to love. He had seemed complicated at first — with the ants and the sudden moments of philosophy — but she knew now that what he really was was *simple*. Simple in the best sense of the word. He saw the whole picture of life, knew where he fit, and accepted it.

She turned back to look at him as he drove, and felt almost dizzy with emotion. Joseph shamelessly showed his love for everything; family, nature, animals, music, dancing, and his God. His silence felt like a promise, not a punishment, and that meant more to Leah than she knew how to express. She moved as close as she could to Joseph as they drove to the east, finishing their tour with eight miles to get back to J.P.'s farm.

Before they pulled into the place, J.P. stopped at his mailbox.

"My farm is a relatively high spot in our area. You can't see as much as you can at Mount Zion, but there's still plenty of things in view." He pointed to some of the places they had been to earlier, including Mount Zion school, high on its hill.

It was now after noon, and as they pulled up to the house, J.P. said, "I'll make dinner."

Leah's stomach growled at the suggestion. She hadn't even realized she was hungry! "That sounds fantastic. I could eat almost anything right now!"

He started the grill while she sat on the front porch and chatted

CHAPTER 19

lazily with him in the balmy air. They had burgers for dinner, and Leah couldn't seem to remember having a nicer day.

After the meal, J.P. gave her a wink. "You better rest, because it is going to be a long day *and* night."

"What? We've been all over the countryside already!"

"Trust me, we're just getting started."

She meant to raise a suspicious eyebrow at him, but let out a surprisingly large yawn instead. Even though she'd mostly ridden around the countryside in a truck all morning, she felt exhausted. Maybe it was being away from home, maybe it was nervousness about meeting Joseph's family... even though meeting Daniel and Kate had ultimately gone well.

She yawned again. "I don't know if it's all this fresh air or all the history, but I think you might be right about getting some rest. Suddenly, I can barely keep my eyes open."

"Well, I've got a few things I'd like to get done around here before we head out, so you might as well get in a nap." He gave her a quick, comfortable kiss and stepped off the porch as she headed into the house.

Before she headed down for a nap, Leah watched out the kitchen window as Joseph climbed up onto a tractor. He had mentioned needing to shred and mow around the farm and roadsides, so she figured that's what he was doing. What she *hadn't* figured was that he'd take his shirt off to do so. She decided she could wait a *little* longer before her nap, and leaned contentedly against the sink as she watched him ride around the farm in the sun. She smiled to herself, recalling J.P. saying how much he missed his farmer's tan.

When he finally rode out of sight, Leah went downstairs to take a quick look around before she closed her eyes. She tip-toed into the bedroom that Joseph had slept in the night before, feeling slightly guilty for sneaking around. Once she saw all the trophies, though, her guilt gave way to curiosity.

A row of tall, gleaming, shiny trophies lined one of his bedroom shelves. Leah looked them over and discovered that they were all from baseball and softball. There were eight trophies, including league runner up and league champions for the baseball teams that Joseph had coached when Daniel had played. There was a "Player of the Year" trophy with J.P.'s name on it, and a medal that boasted "All League Team." She shook her head in amusement. J.P. had never said anything about these — all he had divulged was that he "Played a lot of ball."

To Leah's surprise there was a gun cabinet with seven guns safely nestled inside. Hunting wasn't something he had mentioned, and she made a mental note to ask him about it. She would later find out that Joseph hadn't shot anything but blue rocks, targets, and a few occasional "varmints" in the last twenty years.

After a thorough exploration of his bedroom, Leah went to her own and tried to nap. Her eyes would close, but her brain wouldn't stop spinning. She was thinking about how interesting everything had been since they crossed the Loup river last evening. One thing was for sure: life was different out here in the country. She didn't think she could process all of the things she'd learned and felt over the past 24 hours even if she tried. As she recalled each stop, each smile, each touch of his hand, her eyelids slowly fluttered closed and she drifted off into a deep, pleasant sleep.

CHAPTER 20

Two hours later, Leah awoke feeling slightly disoriented in the unfamiliar bedroom. She smoothed down her hair, made her way up the stairs, and found Joseph having a glass of ice water at the kitchen table.

He grinned "The basement sleeps good, doesn't it?"

Leah moved toward the sink for her own glass of water and answered, "Yes it does," she sighed. "it must be the country."

"It could be." J.P. smiled at her, clearly pleased. "I have a surprise for you. It's what we're going to drive tonight."

"What?" She laughed. "How many secret cars do you have?" She held onto her glass of water and followed him outside. The garage door was open - one she hadn't paid any attention to previously. J.P.'s grin continued to shine as he led her over to a brilliantly beautiful, orange car.

"Oh, wow! It's really pretty!"

J.P. pretended to look offended. "Pretty? That's practically a mint condition 1969 Chevrolet Chevelle Super Sport!"

It was Leah's turn to pretend. "Oh, *really*? Well, in that case, consider me impressed!"

He playfully rolled his eyes at her and put an arm around her shoulder while they took a moment to admire the car. "It was my high school car. It mostly sits covered in here except for special occasions and a routine startup now and then."

"High school, huh? I'll bet this old girl has seen some things."

He gave her a squeeze and reached out to open the door for her.

"What do you say we take it for a drive?"

As Leah settled into the passenger's seat, she noticed Joseph's senior key hanging from the rear view mirror. On the passenger floor was an old, gray carrier box. J.P. said, "Open it."

When she did, she found two dozen eight track cassettes.

She laughed in surprise. "Three Dog Night, Chicago, The Guess Who, Charlie Pride. Haven't listened to any of these in a while!"

"And that's just the start of my collection." His eyes crinkled with amusement as he watched her take in her surroundings. In the back seat were two throw pillows — orange and black — to match the car's orange exterior and its black interior. She turned back to him. "And they say men don't understand the decorative power of throw pillows."

"What can I say? I've got style." J.P. used his best smooth-talker voice, and Leah let out a wave of giggles. "This car was the fastest car around when I was in high school. I just *had* to use our school colors, being the Tigers." He pulled out of the garage and out onto the cement driveway. "With the 396 cubic engine, I can smoke them."

Leah gave him a lost look. "What do you mean, *smoke them*?"

J.P.'s grin expanded even more than she thought possible. "Hang on!"

He hit the gas and let the Chevelle do its thing. The engine roared, the tires screamed, and the acrid air from the burning tires made her nose scrunch up, yet she couldn't help but let out an excited yelp.

J.P. laughed as they pulled out of the driveway and turned slowly onto the gravel road. Leah turned and raised an eyebrow at his suddenly cautious driving. When they reached the highway, however, and stopped at the stop sign, J.P. said, "By the time we reach that first power pole we'll be doing eighty."

Leah's eyebrow dropped and she double-checked her seatbelt, then braced herself for the jump in speed. In a few seconds, they were hurtling at 80 miles per hour down the highway, far past the power pole he mentioned. After a mile or so, he decided to let up and give in to the speed limit. "This beauty will go somewhere around 120 miles per hour." He laughed at her white knuckles. "You doing alright?"

Leah was fighting all of her motherly instincts — the ones that

CHAPTER 20

wanted to tell Joseph to slow down — but she managed to give him a smile instead. She hadn't seen that naughty (Joseph would probably call it "ornery") look on his face before. The car was bringing out the teenager in him, like it had so many years ago.

"Have I told you how I got the Chevelle?"

She gripped her seatbelt, but smiled at him. "No, I don't think so."

"Originally, it belonged to my friend, Glen. Glen Adams." He flexed his fingers a bit, then replaced them on the steering wheel. "He was two years older than me. Grew up a mile and a half from me. He was an only child, so you could kind of say I was like a little brother to him. I sure looked up to him like it."

Leah enjoyed hearing him talk about history, but she could tell by the sound of his voice that this particular story didn't have a happy ending.

"Glen graduated high school in May of '71. Enlisted in the army. By May of next year, he was gone. Vietnam." J.P. flicked his eyes up to the rear view mirror, then quickly brought them back to the road. "Glen's parents knew what he would have wanted them to do with his car. They gave it to me."

"That's... that's quite the honor."

"It sure is. I vowed that day I'd never sell it, and I'd keep it in tip-top condition."

"Well, I'm no expert, but it sure looks like you've kept that promise." She reached over and rested her hand on his shoulder.

"I had planned to enlist myself, after my high school graduation. With the ceasefire and withdrawal from Vietnam in '73, though, I was starting to reconsider. When we lost my brother that same year, I decided not to leave home."

"Do you regret that? Not leaving?"

For just a moment, he turned and studied Leah's face. He hadn't told anyone that he regretted that decision, and here she was, outright asking him.

"Yep, sometimes. I never left home after high school; I just kept farming. Never continued my education, never enlisted, never left."

J.P. could have gone on, could have told her that he'd always felt like he'd cheated himself out of life-changing memories. He could have told her that, deep down, it's probably why he moved to the city… to fill that yearning for experience off of the farm. Or, hell, maybe it was just a midlife crisis. He could have said all those things, but he didn't. Instead, he took a couple of seconds to turn and take in Leah's calm, pretty face as she watched the fields pass by. Whatever the reason was, the move to the city was working out well for J.P., and he was going to leave it at that, for now.

After a couple of miles on the highway, he turned the Chevelle around and they headed back to the farm.

As they drove onto the property, Leah noticed how Joseph had mowed around the farm while she had rested. She was happy that J.P. was getting the things done that he wanted to this weekend. "Looks like you got plenty of work done while I napped!"

"I did. Checked and moved the cattle, looked over the crops, made sure the building site's in order. Usually when I come home, I've got a lot more work to do."

"More than this?"

He chuckled at her surprise. "Yes ma'am. Like spraying crops. But now they're fully grown, so any spraying done now is by airplane"

"You mean you don't fly airplanes, too?"

That got a genuine laugh out of him. "No, believe it or not, I don't. I also usually help with haying," He gave her a meaningful look. "But I've got company this weekend, and that takes priority over other farm matters."

Leah blushed.

He parked the car back in its sacred garage. "Time to get ready for the rodeo. You can have the bathroom upstairs, I will use the one in the basement."

Leah gathered what she needed and went upstairs to shower. It was odd — she couldn't remember the last time she'd showered somewhere other than her own home. Not even a hotel room.

When she finished getting ready, she came out into the kitchen

CHAPTER 20

to wait for J.P. He had emptied his pockets onto the kitchen table before he went to the basement. She was grateful for the quiet moment, and for the little peek into the details of his life. On the table was the usual: his cellphone, chapstick, Rolaids, pocket knife, nail clippers, and coins. And something else.

Leah had noticed that Joseph wore a light chain around his neck, but she never had seen what hung at the end of it. He had always taken it off discreetly when he had taken off his shirt. There, at the kitchen table, she finally got a look. It was a flat, metal crucifix. Tentatively, she picked it up and studied it. On the back side, the engraved words said, *"Christ is Counting on You."* She wasn't quite sure what to think. Joseph had never talked to her directly about God, even though he had made reference to God and heaven a number of times. Yet, here was proof that his spirituality was much stronger than she had realized.

Leah heard Joseph coming up the steps, so she quickly replaced the chain, trying to act as innocently as possible. She knew she hadn't, but couldn't help feeling like she had done something wrong. She had stolen a glimpse of Joseph's faith, before he'd chosen to show her himself.

She tried to shake off the feeling of guilt — he had left it lying on the table, right in plain sight for anyone to happen upon it. It clearly wasn't a secret. She hadn't really thought about her view of God much, and certainly didn't feel comfortable enough to have a crucifix anywhere on her.

J.P. walked into the kitchen whistling, then headed to the table to fill his pockets with everything he wanted. He took off his cowboy hat and put the chain around his neck, slipping the crucifix under his shirt. He acted as if it were as natural as putting his hat on.

Leah didn't feel comfortable asking him about the crucifix, so she acted like she hadn't noticed. Instead, she decided to focus on the fresh, clean, handsome cowboy in front of her.

He was dressed in full cowboy attire tonight: his favorite boots and hat, which she had seen before, as well as a new belt. The initials "J.P." were engraved on the buckle, and she could see the words *"Cowboy Up"* on the back. A small part of her felt a giggle bubbling up; If Leah would have been home in the city, she would have thought twice about Joseph's getup. She had a hunch, though, that she would see many cowboys tonight... and if she was going to be really honest, she didn't mind the view.

As they got into the Chevelle, J.P. said, "You pick out the music." Leah couldn't help but chuckle at the novelty of it all as she looked through the eight-tracks, and pulled one out that was titled *The Best of Rock n Roll.*

"On to the gravel road they went, but slowly. "I don't like to go over forty on dirt in this one."

Leah tried her best to nod sagely, as though she knew just as much about cars as he did. Once they made it to the highway, though, he didn't hit the gas like last time. She gave him a questioning look.

"I'll go fast some other time. I want tonight to last as long as possible."

The rodeo was in Washburn, eighteen miles west on the highway. As they came over a hill, the neighboring village spread out below them. The sign read "Washburn, Pop. 280." Leah marveled at it.

"I still can't get over that! I'm more used to seeing 'population 220,000!'"

They went to the community center for supper, which was a foreign concept to her in and of itself. Among laughing, chattering locals, they sat down to eat their meal of deep-pit-cooked roast beef. The tender beef and the savory flavors ignited Leah's memory. She had tasted this before, under a dark, starry sky in silence with the man she loved.

Leah whispered to Joseph, "It tastes just like our picnic roast." J.P. winked at her. They finished their meal, disposed of their plates, and headed out the door toward the main event of the night: the rodeo.

As they walked toward the arena, three blocks away, Leah began to get a little nervous. She wondered how many people could possibly be at the rodeo with only 280 people in the town. To Leah's surprise, she

CHAPTER 20

could see vehicles *everywhere* as they got closer to their destination.

She turned to ask Joseph, "How many people come to this rodeo?"

"I think it averages somewhere around a thousand people."

Her jaw dropped. "How can that be? With only 280 people in the town?"

J.P. laughed as he surveyed the area. "There will be people from fifty miles in every direction here tonight!"

"Well, consider me impressed. I've never been to a rodeo, and I'm anxious to see what could possibly draw people from far and near."

As they sat in the bleachers, Leah noticed at least one third of every man, woman, and child wore a cowboy hat. She had been right to assume Joseph would blend right in.

"I have no idea what to expect from this. You'll have to help me out."

"Don't you worry. The first event is ladies barrel racing."

Leah watched in awe as the women, decked out in their best western wear, navigated their horses around barrels in an intricate pattern. She couldn't believe anyone could stay on such a rough looking ride, then make turns around barrels that looked almost impossible.

"That's incredible!" Leah breathed, and then added, "Especially for a gal!"

J.P. clucked his tongue. "Don't say that out loud. These cowgirls don't wear boots, spurs, buckles, and hats for nothing." He watched for a few more seconds. "They're tough."

She whistled. "I believe that!"

The events continued, one after another. Next there was calf roping; two different events. The first one was to rope a small calf that was running from a moving horse. After roping the calf around the neck, the rider would jump off of his house, flip the calf on its side, and wrap at least three of its legs.

J.P. couldn't help but enjoy the gasps of concern and excitement coming from Leah, and he scooted a little closer to her on the bleachers with a grin on his face.

The second roping event began, but this time it was for teams of two people. One would rope the head of the calf, then the other would try to rope its back legs.

"I've got to be honest," she said skeptically. "This looks more like luck than anything else."

"These people have been practicing their whole lives." He added, "Doing these events takes skill, will, and patience." He watched intently for a few more seconds. "Just like all athletes, it takes practice, practice, and more practice."

"Huh. I guess I hadn't really thought of them as athletes, but you're right. I've got no desire to even try to sit on a *standing* horse, let alone travel twenty miles per hour on a galloping one!" The more she watched, the more she started noticing the cowboys, cowgirls, and their horses working together. She thought back to the barrel racing, the way the women and the horses would lean together around the turns. During the roping, if the calf veered off in a direction, the horse would automatically follow. Leah had never seen people and animals work together like this before.

J.P. winked at her. "The next event is bareback bronc riding."

"Bareback bronc? As in 'bucking bronco?'"

He grinned at her surprised look. "Yep. You're in for some excitement."

And he was right. This was different than the previous events; there was no working together. It was man and animal, pitted against each other. The bronc was jumping, kicking, and bucking trying to get the cowboy off its back. Leah's pulse sped up as though she were watching some blockbuster movie, full of explosions and peril. The cowboy was working hard at balancing himself and riding the bronc for as long as he could, and by the end of the event, Leah felt as exhausted as if she had been riding the bronc herself.

"Think you can handle bull riding now?"

She looked properly shocked. "You mean there's more?"

"Yeah, but it's the final event of the night."

The truth was, there wasn't much "riding" happening during this last portion of the rodeo. Only three out of fifteen riders rode the bull for the full eight-second ride. Leah clung to Joseph's arm throughout the whole event.

"This is so *dangerous!*" She whispered urgently in his ear. It felt

CHAPTER 20

completely different than Joseph petting Bull 54 this morning. Then, it seemed that there was a friendship and trust between him and the herd bull. Tonight, however, there was no friendship. You could surely say there was a healthy respect for the bulls by the cowboys — their lives depended on it. The bulls were a different story. They showed no respect toward their riders; in fact Leah could have sworn the bulls had a look of hatred in their eyes. After a rider was thrown off, many of the beasts would look frantically for whoever had dared to hop on their backs, in order to do them more harm.

It was the clown's job to protect the thrown cowboys. In their silly clothing, they were risking bodily harm to themselves, in order to protect another human.

"You know, I've never thought much about rodeo clowns... but you might almost say they're... heroic."

J.P. chuckled and put his arm around her. "Yeah, there's a lot riding on them, that's for sure." Leah sighed. She was realizing that just about everything had a different way about it, out here in the country.

When the rodeo was over, they walked uptown together, hand-in-hand in the late summer air. They had left the Chevelle closer to the street dance than the rodeo, to make it easier to leave later on.

"Hope you don't mind the walk," he said, as he swung their clasped hands like a giddy kid. She laughed. The whole village was only eight blocks long, so a walk from one end to the other wasn't a big ordeal for anyone who could handle a little exercise.

"I've got to say, I'm awfully excited to bring you to the street dance." He squeezed her hand. "Tonight's dance is what people around here call a 'big one.'"

"Oh really?"

"Yep. There could be five, maybe six hundred people at this dance tonight." She turned and stared at him, jaw dropped. He laughed. "They fence off all of main street, just so we can cut a rug." As they approached the dance, Leah couldn't believe the size of the crowd. Just like the rodeo, lots of people had cowboy hats on. J.P. was visiting with more people than she could imagine talking to in one day. With her head spinning, she linked her arm in his, and leaned into him slightly as they walked, just to be close to something she was sure of.

J.P. leaned in and asked Leah, "Remember when we went to the Starbrite?"

Leah hung tight to his arm and she said, "I will never forget."

He liked that answer, and gave her a smile, but shook his head. "No, I mean the crowd. Remember when I asked you if you knew any of the people? You said you didn't, but that you recognized a few people."

"Oh! Yes, I remember."

J.P.'s eyes developed a knowing twinkle. "Well, welcome to *my* dance."

"What do you mean?"

"I can tell you the first or last name of half the people here." He looked around and gestured at the chattering crowds around them. "I'd say I recognize another fourth of them without knowing their names right away."

Leah said, "No way."

His grin couldn't have gotten much bigger. "Go ahead and ask me."

She tried not to be obvious, but she *did* ask Joseph about certain people, and his percentages were right on.

"See?"

"Yeah, well, you could still be fibbing... but I'm not about to go up to someone and ask them if they know a guy by the name of J.P. Dreul."

Suddenly, the music started, and the DJ knew exactly what to play to get the crowd moving. Cowboy hats bobbed to the beat, hair bounced around and twirled, and the laughter and chatter of hundreds of people rang out into the night. At one point, Leah thought the entire street full of people was moving as one, big, ocean of happy bodies. Between the raucous sounds, the beat of the music, and the intoxicating feeling of a summer night quickly cooling off, Leah could have sworn she was half drunk... but she hadn't had time for even a sip. Everyone seemed to be having a fantastic night, and Leah couldn't help but agree with them. She was starting to feel the

CHAPTER 20

effects of dancing on the street all night — it felt like a real workout. Nothing like dancing on a well-cared-for dance floor.

It seemed that midnight was *their* time, and with aching feet and racing hearts, they decided to head back to the farm.

When J.P. started the Chevelle, he revved it up and enjoyed the roaring motor. There was that ornery boy, twinkling out of J.P.'s eyes, just like the night of their first dance. Leah scooted closer to Joseph and closed her eyes for a few seconds, taking stock of all her senses before opening them back up again.

She was feeling something she'd never felt before in her life.

"I can't believe I'm sitting here, next to the guy I love, in his cool high school car."

"You think it's cool, huh?"

"Definitely."

Never once in high school did she ride in a car like that, and if she *would* have, she certainly wouldn't have sat on the console next to the guy driving. But here she was, thirty years later, doing exactly that.

And it felt great.

Leah couldn't keep her hands off of her guy, and Joseph was enjoying it.

This was bringing to life some of the most distinct memories that a man has in his mind; his favorite vehicle and a special gal.

He hadn't realized until after the dance where this ride home was going to lead to, but he was sure of it now. They were going to stop somewhere in the country for some good, old-fashioned parking. By the time they reached their destination, their pulses were racing.

When Leah realized they were pulling into the Mount Zion schoolyard, she raised an eyebrow at him in the dark.

She knew full well what was going on, but between rubbing Joseph's chest and nibbling on his right ear lobe, she innocently asked, "What are we doing here?"

J.P. turned off the Chevelle's engine and turned toward her with a lazy smile. He leaned into her, but before their lips met, he whispered, "Did you ever want to go to country school?"

That upward curve of his lips, the purr in his voice; she could barely control herself. Somewhere deep inside of her, an animal eagerness — one that she had kept subdued almost her whole life — began to emerge. It had started as a slow burn, and now there was no chance of controlling this blaze.

After they parted from a kiss filled with passion, Leah let out an excited sigh. J.P. couldn't wait any longer.

"Let's get into the back seat." His cowboy hat and billfold went to the dashboard, and he struggled to get his boots off in the limited space of the driver's floor board. If she hadn't been overwhelmed with such urgency, Leah probably would have giggled at him. She, however, was already in the back seat, shoes off and, when Joseph glimpsed into the rear view mirror, he saw that her shirt was coming off over her head. He stopped what he was doing and simply watched, his pulse racing and fog growing on the windows.

As she stacked the two little pillows for her head to rest on, she finally came to a realization. "These pillows don't have anything to do with decoration, do they?"

He smiled at her and held his hands up, as if surrendering. "Well they *do* match the paint job." Joseph surveyed the scene in the back seat just as Leah had rested her head. There was just enough light from the half moon that he could genuinely focus on the view, and he was awestruck.

After giving him a moment, Leah extended a hand and said, "Care to join me?"

As Joseph carefully climbed into the back seat, he tried to quell the tug of war that was beginning to happen inside of him. He desperately wanted to take the time to appreciate the view, but the feelings flooding his mind were becoming distracting.

The thought of how lucky he was to have Leah with him that night, at the rodeo that he had been to so many times alone. The feelings of past loneliness that he kept away from the surface, but were always there, hovering over his heart.

Even though he was incredibly happy at the present, he wondered

CHAPTER 20

why he couldn't have had someone like Leah in his life for years. The happiness he felt was overwhelming — he couldn't imagine what his life would have been like if he had been allowed just a fraction of this feeling before.

Then, of course, there was guilt. He was a married man.

Leah, who had noticed the look of quiet distance in his eyes, got his attention.

"Hurry." She whispered, frantically. For her, an experience in the back seat of a car was something the cool kids did in the movies — not regular old Leah who works at George's Garage. In the moonlight, she watched like a hungry wolf as Joseph removed his shirt slowly. The movement of his strong arms, shoulders, and chest was stirring, to say the least. She couldn't wait, and that was an obvious fact.

"Though it had been a decade or two," Joseph was no stranger to hormonally-charged, late-night country drives, and wasn't quite as overcome by the novelty. He *was* overcome by Leah's ethereal beauty, and wasn't in a hurry for the night to be over.

He was willing to simply put a *hold* on this scene. He wanted this feeling to last and last. This was what he had been missing in his past: joy, affection, communication, someone to share his life with.
They may not have been in his past, but he was hoping that the future held all of these promises for him.

He touched her face, stroked her hair, kissed her tenderly. And, although the urgency was still there, Leah was enjoying the effect that his slow pace had on her. Joseph's hands, lips, and breath were all over her. She sighed desperately and surrendered.

On the giddy ride back to the farm in the moonlight, Joseph wore only his jeans and Leah comfortably snuggled up to him, wearing nothing but his shirt.

They practically tumbled out of the Chevelle and onto the driveway, and in their short twenty foot distance to the house, the two were giggling like a couple of kids tip-toeing through a lawn sprinkler.

Unlike the night before, they slept together just as they were — jeans, oversized shirt, and all.

CHAPTER 21

Just like every other day, J.P. was awake at 6 am. Only this time, he took a long look at Leah and smiled. In the dim, morning sunlight, he knew life was good.

He drove the Chevy pickup back to the flower pasture to make sure the cattle had stayed in their boundaries. With the morning sun casting its first rays from the eastern glow, everything looked innocent. He decided to stop the pickup and take in the magnificence of the sights around him, which he hadn't done in a while.

The cattle were content, either laying down, chewing their cud, or happily standing in the belly-tall grass, eating. The flower patch was still in full beauty. The cattle wouldn't eat the flowers — when they had eaten their fill of the pasture grass, they would simply walk through the flower bed looking for more fresh, green blades.

He smiled at the windmill across the canyon, standing at attention, as if watching over everything within view. There was a shadow from the sun of its thirty foot height. J.P. had never noticed it before, but the shadow of its slowly-moving wheel reminded him of the flicker of an old movie projector. For sixty years the windmill had been a mainstay, and it felt comforting. Familiar.

J.P. enjoyed this view, perhaps a little more than usual, since it had been so long since he'd seen it daily. Being in the city for these three short months had him missing the farm, the landscape, and the feeling of belonging.

But he wasn't frowning; in fact, a grin crept onto his face. He may have missed the farm, but he certainly wasn't sad. J.P. thought

CHAPTER 21

back to the view of Leah in the moonlight last night, and waking next to her this morning. His grin softened into a gentle smile as he felt a quiet joy fill his heart. He had always appreciated, respected, and loved the beauty that he found in nature... and now he felt he had a new perspective on it. Seeing Leah in the cool moonlight and then this morning in the rising sun — he didn't think nature could get more beautiful, but those sights proved him wrong. J.P. stayed parked there for a few minutes as he contemplated his past, present, and future. Frozen for a moment in the middle of the world he loved, his mind wandered its way through many thoughts, swaying like the tall grass in a prairie wind. This farm was, of course, his past, and he fully planned for it to be his future as well. The land hadn't changed, not really, but many other things had. Claire was in his past and, nestled contently in his own basement was Leah — his future.

Finally, he brushed his hands on his jeans, an absentminded signal that it was time to get back to work. He got back in the pickup and headed through a path in the cornfield, then back onto the gravel road.

J.P. decided to stop by his parents' house. He tapped on the door and, as was normal, didn't wait for a response before walking in. The scene before him gave him pause, and brought a wistful smile to his lips. Because he'd been absent for three months, he hadn't realized until now that he had taken this setting for granted. Everytime a person walked into Kate's kitchen, it was filled with aromas that gave you a big hug and simply said "home."

This morning he could make out the scent of eggs and sausage. Other regular appearances in the kitchen were fresh-baked cookies, pies, and bread.

And he knew that, when you didn't smell cooking in Kate's home, there was surely to be the smell of freshly-cut flowers.

He greeted his parents, sat down at the kitchen table, and, just as he knew there would be, there was a plate of scrambled eggs and a plate of sausage placed in front of him.

Herb was enjoying his as-is with toast and coffee. Kate and J.P.

had turned their eggs and sausage into breakfast burritos.

Kate took a sip of coffee and asked, "What did Leah think of the rodeo?"

"The bull riding scared her, and the cowgirls impressed her. You know how it is — their ability to stay on the horses going around those barrels always turns some heads."

She chuckled. "That's the truth. We went home early — no street dancing for us! How did it go?"

J.P. smiled and said, "As big as ever. The whole block was full of people, and Leah had never seen anything like it! Hundreds of people crowding the streets and dancing to a DJ." He finished a bite of burrito and continued, "We had a great time. Stayed til midnight."

Bored with the topic, as usual, Herb stabbed some eggs with his fork and interrupted, "Are you going to church? Is she going with you?"

Kate shot her husband a glare, embarrassed by Herb's typical forwardness. J.P. had realized long ago that his dad was never going to change. He had grown up with it, that unwavering abrasiveness.

Trying to keep the tone casual, he answered, "Yes, I am going to church. I haven't asked Leah yet, but I plan on seeing if she wants to go with me."

Herb grunted in response, and J.P scrambled to lighten up the mood. "It sure was great to take the Chevelle out last night!" He thought for a moment, then added, "I can't remember the last time I took it out."

What he thought, but didn't say out loud, was, "It's been a long time since the Chevelle's seen such a pretty date."

His mother smiled, and his dad paid no mind to what he said.

With discussion of last night's events out of the way, they all continued with their breakfast, Kate and J.P. chatting about various things, Herb silently cleaning his plate. After taking his plate to the sink, Herb reminded him, "See you in church."

J.P. stifled an exasperated sigh and instead answered with, "Yup."

Before he left, he made up a breakfast burrito for Leah.

CHAPTER 21

As J.P. drove back to his place, he wondered why he hadn't mentioned church to Leah. He considered the time he had spent with her. Most of it had been at the garage, but deep, personal beliefs weren't typically what you talked about at work. The first time he was at her home, they had watched a movie, talked about their families, and she had played the piano for him. All of their other time spent together — baseball games, dancing, and certainly not the fourth of July, were full of lighthearted conversation. Considering the direction in which their relationship was headed, he decided it was probably time to add a little more meaning to the equation.

J.P. parked the work pickup, his heart beginning to flutter. He felt nervous, he couldn't help it. This was going to be a very sudden question for him to ask, and it required a fairly quick answer from Leah.

He put the burrito in the refrigerator and quietly stepped down stairs. He took a moment to simply look upon Leah before he had to jar her from such a hard sleep. He brushed some hair from her ear and whispered to her. She stirred, then slowly opened her eyes.

"Good morning." The corners of his eyes crinkled with his smile.

From under a pile of unruly hair and a mountain of pillows came a mumbled, "Hello."

J.P. said, "I brought you a breakfast burrito from Mom's."

Leah propped herself up on her elbows and said, "Thank you." She rubbed her eyes. "After dancing all night I feel like I could eat an elephant." She stretched her legs and groaned. "And my legs feel like I ran a marathon!"

He chuckled. "Ah, I think you'll live. You ready for the day?"

"I suppose you've been 'out and about on a drive around?'"

He grinned. "Now where did you learn such local language?"

She gave him a sneaky smile and answered, "Well, I've been hanging around this country boy a lot lately. He seems to be influencing me."

J.P. was still grinning, and figured he may as well just get it over with. "Do you want to go to church with me?"

Leah sobered up immediately.

She pulled the blanket up tighter around her as her thoughts swirled. Here she was, lying in a strange bed, wearing only Joseph's shirt, and being asked to go to church. She swallowed, her appetite for the breakfast waiting for her in the kitchen had disappeared into thin air.

She studied him for a moment, and gave in. "Okay, sure. I'll take a quick shower."

As they left the house, Leah was relieved that Joseph was driving the Dodge to church. She would have felt all the more uncomfortable riding there in the Chevelle after the activity that she was involved in the backseat just eight hours earlier.

Really, she didn't know how to feel about going to church in general. It's something she never did; getting dressed up, going every Sunday, singing with everyone surrounding her. A feeling of guilt was surfacing with each mile they drove, her chest constricting a bit more with every minute. She rolled down the window a crack for some fresh air and thought, *Why would people go to church if this is what they feel?* As far as she could tell, Joseph seemed as happy and cheerful as ever.

J.P.'s outlook on the topic was completely different. For him, it was like going to visit his partner in life. His God is who he shared all of his joy and happiness with. He didn't assign blame when something unfortunate or bad happened to him or others, he simply went forward in trust.

The church was big, as large as any in most cities. Wanting to break up the uncomfortable silence, J.P. switched back into tour guide mode. "It was built in 1920. They gave it an interior renovation about five years ago."

"The cream and blue colors are beautiful," Leah murmured, happy to have something to talk about. This morning the church was about 50% full with two hundred people and, to her dismay, they walked three-fourths of the way up the center aisle. She wished

CHAPTER 21

they could have sat in the back, but this was Joseph's call, so she just followed.

Once she sat and got settled, she realized she felt more at ease than she thought she would. With the church's soothing colors and the murmuring crowd, she didn't think she stuck out like she had been afraid she would. She had to admit, she actually felt kind of comfortable.

"Today's Gospel reading is from John," Monsignor Mike began. His voice was surprisingly warm, almost comforting. "A large crowd had been following Jesus, because they saw the miracles he was performing on the sick. Jesus went up the mountain and sat down there with his disciples.

When he looked up and saw a large crowd coming toward him, Jesus said to Philip, 'How are we to buy bread for these people to eat?' Philip answered him, 'Six months' wages would not buy enough bread for each of them to get even a little.'

One of his other disciples, Andrew, said to him, 'There is a boy here who has five barley loaves and two fish. But what are they among so many people?'

Jesus said, 'Make the people sit down.' Now there was a great deal of grass in the place, so they sat down, about five thousand in all.

Jesus then took the loaves and, when he had given thanks, distributed them to those who were seated. He also shared the fish, as much as they wanted. When they were satisfied, he told his disciples, 'Gather up the fragments left over, so that nothing may be lost.'

So they gathered them up, and from the fragments of the five barley loaves left by those who had eaten, they filled twelve baskets." Monsignor Mike paused for a moment, then smiled at his congregation.

"When the people saw the sign, they began to say, 'This is indeed the prophet who is to come into the world!'

The next day the crowd looked for and found Jesus, and Jesus said to them, 'Very truly, I tell you, you are looking for me — not because you saw signs, but because you ate your fill of the loaves. Do not work for the food that perishes, but for the food that endures for eternal life, which the Son of Man will give you.'" The priest held his hands out in demonstration.

"Jesus continued, 'I am the bread of life. Whoever comes to me will never be thirsty. For I have come down from Heaven, not to do my own will, but the will of my Father who sent me.

This is indeed the will of my Father, that all who see the Son and believe in him may have eternal life, and I will raise them up on the last day.'"

Monsignor Mike stepped down from the pulpit and took a few steps down the aisle.

He said, "We have approximately 200 people here today. So, 5,000 people would be 25 times as many as we have, sitting here comfortably." He gestured to the west.

"To make room for 5,000 to sit on the grass and ground, well, picture both ball fields *and* the park across the streets crowded with people."

Monsignor continued "Then the word had come from Jesus to be seated. Now, it's more than likely you wouldn't know the people around you."

Leah moved her eyes slowly from side to side, trying not to make it obvious that she was looking around. She did not know anyone but Joseph.

Monsignor said, "I am sure that only those immediately near Jesus heard or knew that he had given thanks, but word had spread, and the crowd was there to see miracles. Picture with me, people with baskets and blankets going around, handing out bread and fish to eat."

At that exact moment, Leah's stomach growled. Not that barley bread and fish were what she had in mind, but she suddenly realized that she hadn't eaten since last evening at the barbecue. At the very least, she was thinking that coffee, toast, and maybe some of Joseph's perfectly-fried bacon would be satisfying.

Monsignor added, "Some of these people had not had a full meal for days. Some were wanderers, and some had traveled far distances to see the works of Jesus. They did not realize that the true miracle was Jesus, the walking, talking Son of God, here on earth."

CHAPTER 21

The gentle priest continued, "Picture that walking, talking Jesus here. In the aisle, maybe taking a seat next to you, offering you something to eat out of his basket. Maybe it's coffee, juice, milk, and a donut."

Then Monsignor Mike took a step forward, turned partially, and lifted one hand to his ear. "Let us listen for our Heavenly Father to say, 'Come sit at my table, for you will never hunger or thirst again.'" You could hear a pin drop, even with the 200 men, women, and children in attendance.

Monsignor Mike stood for a few more moments with his hand to his ear, gave everyone a smile, and turned back up toward the pulpit.

In the echoing quiet, Leah suddenly felt that her body was heavy, while her head felt inexplicably light. She listened for the invitation in the silence, and was shocked by the words that came to her. Words that she had seen for years on a church marquee, just four blocks from her home: *"Blessed are they who hunger and thirst for justice, for they shall be satisfied."*

All weekend, Leah had been learning about Joseph's family, farm, and history. She knew she was not a part of that past. But, all at once, she felt it. Was it a piece of Joseph's life, or was it a piece of hers that she had been missing? Right then, she was feeling something she hadn't felt before. Did it have a name? Was it real? Was it all in her head?

Then, she realized, she already knew what it was. It was the warm welcome and embrace she had received from Joseph's mother; a genuine touch of love. That sums it up: *love*. The love Leah felt for her son and her piano had been expanded with her meeting, knowing, and loving Joseph. Now, somehow, sitting next to him in church — a place that rarely elicited any feeling from her — she felt like she had been re-introduced to God. Seeing Him reflected with such fondness in the eyes of the man she loved was a shock to her system. The guilt she had anticipated had faded away, and was replaced by a surprising happiness.

She took another secret glance at Joseph, and could see he was deep in thought after hearing the homily. He looked recharged; full of joy and peace at the same time. His lips moved silently in a quick prayer.

As J.P. and Leah walked out of church, she was baffled by the fact that the congregation simply moved outside and stopped. Everyone was visiting with one another; Leah heard time and time again, "Good to see you, J.P!" or "Glad you're back in town, Dreuel." Even though they were mostly greeting the man by her side, she warmed with the feeling of belonging. It was the true meaning of community, one she hadn't known in her neighborhood. Here, people in pickups and cars waved at each other when they passed on Main Street. They knew virtually everyone at the neighboring town's street dance. At this small community, there was no such thing as a stranger.

Right then and there, Leah decided that she wanted this... whatever *this* was. It was a feeling she had craved, but hadn't realized it until she had gotten a taste of it. If it was a sip of water, she wanted a whole pitcher. If this was a bite, she wanted the whole pie. Leah was finally getting the whole picture; this was the finishing stroke that she needed to see who Joseph really was.

That first week at the garage, she had wondered if he was a country hick, or just plain weird. She realized now that he was simply Joseph, the missing piece to her puzzle.

She was jarred from her thoughts when she realized that Joseph was shaking the hand of Monsignor MIke. The kind man was saying, "Good to see you J.P.! We miss having you here weekly."

"Thank you, Monsignor, it feels good to be back. I'd like to introduce you to a friend of mine." He stepped to the side to give Leah more room. "Monsignor, this is Leah. We work together in the city."

She could feel an anxious flush traveling up her neck as she held out her hand in greeting. Thirty minutes before, when the Monsignor was giving his homily, was the closest Leah had ever been to a priest. Now she was shaking his hand. She braced herself for questions about her relationship with Joseph, but Monsignor Mike simply said, "We are so glad to have you visiting us, Leah." He placed his other hand on top of hers. "Please come back again."

CHAPTER 21

With relief, Leah let out a breath she hadn't realized she'd been holding, and answered, "Thank you. I hope to be back."

As they were leaving town, heading back to the farm, Leah said to Joseph, "Thank you." J.P. didn't have to ask what for; he knew. By the smile on her face, the happiness in her voice, and a sort of glow about her, he understood what she was feeling.

Leah wasn't the only person overcome with relief. He was more than glad that going to church had been a positive experience for Leah. He made sure to never push his God on anyone, but he was willing to share his beliefs with anyone who was interested. Because it was such an important part of his life, he was overjoyed at the discovery that Leah may have just become interested.

They were quiet on the drive back to the farm.

For J.P., it had been a dream come true. To share who he was with Leah was a great satisfaction to him. He rejoiced at the opportunity to share with her his family's property, the crops, the cattle, the beauty of the landscapes he loved. He took pride in introducing her to Daniel, his mother, and his family history. Adding in their trip to the rodeo and street dance in the Chevelle, and their memorable appearance in church, J.P.'s chest was about to burst with feelings he never thought he'd get to experience.

While Leah was certainly happy, she was utterly exhausted — mentally, physically, and spiritually. For her, the weekend had been a comprehensive historical tour, a full-body workout, and a spiritual revelation all rolled into one. Her overtired mind reached for a good word for it, and the best thing she could come up with was "overwhelmed." Happy, a little scared, and hopeful all at the same time.

When they finally got back to the farm, J.P. and Leah sat at the kitchen table, grinned at each other, and blurted out at the same time, "I'm tired." They laughed, and he reached across the table to hold her hands in his.

"I'd say we've had a pretty full weekend. Should we head back to the city?"

Leah awoke Monday in her own bed, and by herself. She stretched and smiled lazily as flashbacks from the weekend replayed in her mind. As she recalled all the beauty of the area that Joseph had shown her, meeting Daniel and Kate, and spending so much time with this man she loved so much, she wondered if she could possibly be happier. As she headed to the bathroom for a shower, she actually found herself giggling at her luck.

When Leah showed up to work at the garage, she still had a smile on her face. George could already tell that the weekend had gone well, but he asked anyway. "How'd the weekend go?" Leah answered with her face beaming, "Fantastic."

That is exactly what George had been hoping to hear.

J.P. had come to work early, which was his usual way to start the day. When George came to the garage, he found his newest employee busy at work replacing a fuel pump on an older Chevy pickup that reminded J.P. of his work truck on the farm. George greeted him with a cheerful, "How was your weekend?" J.P. looked up with a grin, but he tried to play it cool. "Mornin', George. It was a fine weekend. A lot of fun."

When J.P. noticed that Leah had arrived at the garage, he couldn't help himself — he had to say hello. He slipped into the office and closed the door quietly behind him.

"Good morning," he greeted her. For a few seconds, they both smiled quietly at each other. Finally, neither one of them could contain themselves, and they quickly closed the space between them with an excited, lingering embrace.

George stayed back in the work area, watching J.P. and Leah. From what it seemed to George, however, they would have been oblivious even if he'd been standing right there in the office. George's heart was warmed by the scene, and any remaining worry he had evaporated in the cool air of the garage.

At morning break, George, Pete, and Fred were eager to hear about the weekend. Leah was pleased, and ready to give them the details of the trip. From the area's beauty, to meeting J.P.'s family, all the

CHAPTER 21

way to the history she learned on each individual farm. Seeing that the guys were entranced by her stories, J.P. slipped out of the office, figuring his absence would go unnoticed.

He went back to his job of putting the brakes on a Buick as Leah continued with details of the rodeo and street dance, as well as Joseph's cherished Chevelle. George whistled. "I'm mighty interested in hearing more about that Chevelle. Maybe I'll get to see it someday," he winked. No one in the room knew, of course, but she deliberately left out their trip to church.

Later that day, at his request, J.P. filled George in on the Chevelle, including the tragic past behind it. Standing as if at attention, George paid his respects to Glen by listening intently. In awe of both the Adams family for their generosity and J.P. for his dedication, George realized how happy he was for the relationship growing between him and Leah. His respect grew to an even higher level for his newest employee.

CHAPTER 22

The bond between Leah and Nick had always been strong and special to each of them. Even as a teenager, Nick kept his mother in the forefront of his mind, being careful not to hurt or disappoint her. He seemed to have always been a man above his years.

When Nick started his senior year the fall before, Leah had struggled. Nick would be moving on with his life in a year. What would it be like, alone in the house? When Nick mentioned the "future," Leah wanted to shudder in fear — not for *Nick's* future, of course, but for her own.

It was hard not to enjoy his enthusiasm, though. The joy and pride that Nick had taken restoring his grandfather's pickup had stuck with him, and he had decided to go into that field of study at a community college. His days would be filled with mechanic and vehicle restoration classes, and he was looking forward to it.

The day of Nick's high school graduation, the full realization of him moving away finally struck Leah. She was determined that the coming summer would be special. As it turned out, it was a monumental summer, but neither one of them realized it wasn't going to just be for the two of them.

Nick had liked J.P. from their first handshake. While he had purposely avoided talking to his mother about her personal life, Nick had been secretly hoping for her to find a new, positive relationship. Thankfully, J.P. was just what he had in mind. Nick could see the difference in Leah, and felt significant relief because of it. She had always been pleasant and kind to Nick, but now she seemed to be

CHAPTER 22

smiling more often than not. For people like him and George, people who saw her every day, this was a dramatic change.

With Joseph in their lives, Nick's transition to college became much easier. The dread and concern that Leah had held in her heart was losing its grip, thanks to this new, important man in her life. Rather than three months of anxiety and despair, they were able to fully enjoy a summer like no other; one full of positive surprises and romance.

As the summer came to a close, Leah was surprised by the peace she felt. She hadn't pondered too much about God since they had come back from the farm, but every once in a while, the thought crept into her mind: is this peace a gift from Him? Monday, August 20th was the day Nick to moved to tech school. The campus was located in Milborn, 25 miles south of the city. Rather than waking up with a feeling of doom, Leah rose from bed feeling nervous, but hopeful.

George had been preparing for this day since Nick's high school graduation. It was a bittersweet day for him, too. He and Martha had been concerned for Leah, with Nick leaving the house. J.P.'s presence, however, seemed to be alleviating that concern. George had always hoped for happiness for Leah, and had to admit he was rather proud that his new employee was making that possible.

Leah, Nick, and even Grandpa Charlie had come over to help. Charlie was proud of Nick, not only because he had grown into a fine young man, but also because of how the teenager had transformed his old pickup. In his mind, it had become a completely new vehicle. He clapped Nick on the back. "Nowadays people don't use their hands and back to do fine work. Yes, sir, Nick you have a gift, to be able to do such good work." His grandson's eyes practically glittered at the praise.

It worked out perfectly to have two pickups for this move. Nick had some tools and equipment that he was allowed to bring to school, and the Dodge was loaded with his personal belongings and a dresser.

Once everything was loaded, it was time to leave. Grandpa Charlie gave Nick a hug and told him one more time, "Proud of you."

Nick responded, "Thanks Grandpa." He pulled back, but didn't quite let go. "This is all happening because you gave me that pickup."

Though he was bursting with pride, Charlie shrugged. "Ah, it was just old junk when you started. Now it's a dandy."

Knowing it was time to leave, the enthusiastic atmosphere took on a somber tone. Leah gave her dad a hug. "Bye, dad. Thanks for helping." Charlie met J.P. for a handshake, finishing it with a pat on top of their hands, as if to silently say, "Thank you." He had kept quiet throughout the summer about the growing relationship between J.P. and Leah, but not because of disapproval. The truth was, the thought of Leah's increasing happiness had brought tears to his eyes many times, and he wasn't the kind of person who openly shared his feelings.

They took Highway 77 to the campus. Nick had visited earlier that month for registration and knew exactly where to park to unload the pickups. "I'm in Pioneer Hall," he explained, "it's the west building on campus."

The 102° temperature was par for the course when moving into a college dorm in August in Nebraska. With the main doors wide open, and a steady stream of people carrying furniture, clothes, boxes, and music equipment, it was just as hot inside the dorms. There were a lot of students introducing themselves, pitching in, and helping one another. Seeing this instant camaraderie helped ease Leah's nervous mind.

When Nick had everything unloaded and somewhat organized, it was time for J.P. and Leah to leave. Leah looked around his dorm room - at his photos, his unopened suitcase — and knew he'd turn it into a home away from home. When Nick hugged his mom, there seemed no need for words. She looked around his dorm room — at his photos, his unopened suitcase — and knew he'd turn it into a home away from home. When they released each other, Nick turned to J.P., shook his hand and said, "Thanks for your help today, J.P." He paused, then added, "And for everything." Nick did not need to go into detail; J.P. smiled at the memories of baseball, discussing

CHAPTER 22

the 1967 Chevy Pickup, and having pizza after baseball games with him and his mom. It had been a good summer, and they were closer because of it.

As Leah left the dorm room, both she and Nick were feeling grateful to have Joseph there. He'd brought a sense of calm to the summer, and knew this situation would be much different without him. She wondered if he realized that. She smiled. *Probably not*, she thought. He was too humble for that kind of thinking.

The three of them made their way to the front doors, noticing that the stream of people going in and out had slowed. Leah turned to Nick and said, "You know what this reminds me of?" Caught off-guard, Nick laughed, and said, "No."

Leah gave him a sad smile. "This reminds me of your first day of kindergarten. Remember your Superman backpack, and how brave you were?" He smiled and blushed. "Yes, Mom, I remember that first day." She didn't finish the story; just the start of it was enough to relax them both. They giggled quietly and gave each other a final hug.

"Love you," she whispered.

"Love you, too, Mom."

When Joseph and Leah got into the Dodge, she finished the story of Nick's first day of kindergarten, how they had held hands going through the doors.

"Once Nick saw other children playing at a table across the room, he immediately let go of my hand to join them." She turned to J.P. and said, "He was ready to move on then, just like he is now."

Joseph smiled. "That's right."

As they sat in the Dodge, J.P. decided to change the tone. "How about we drive the gravel roads back to the city? It will give me a chance to look at the countryside and you can unwind. It's been a big day." Leah moved over to sit next to Joseph in her favorite spot and said, "I think that would be just fine."

This was different than most of the other times she had slid closer to Joseph in the pickup. Before, it had almost always been out

193

of excitement, but this time was for comfort. She sighed in relief: Joseph had proved himself again as a stable force in her life.

As she watched the fields unfold like fans to her right, she let her mind wander. For the last five years, it had simply been her and Nick, caring for and depending on each other. With him at college, her daily routine and motherly duties would certainly change. She had been thinking of this every once in a while, but now it was official: her thoughts and desires had been drifting beyond Nick's departure to college.

Leah couldn't believe it, but her life was actually moving forward. She was no longer lost, sitting in neutral. Her love for Joseph had seemed to enrich every corner of her life.

As they entered the city, J.P. asked, "Should we get something to eat?"

Leah answered, "Sure."

"Where should we go?"

She paused for a moment. "Have you ever been to Fast Freddy's?"

"Sure haven't."

"It's the best burger place in the city!"

He gave her a little nudge. "I think you've learned by now that I'd be satisfied with cheeseburgers at every meal. Let's do it."

Fast Freddy's was an old brick building on ninth street. At each booth and table sat a little book with the building's history. It was built in 1880, and had started as a general store.

J.P. smiled when he opened the menu. Freddy's featured six different burgers, one flavor of soup a day, and one salad. He looked up at Leah over the menu. "This is my kind of place. Simple choices."

Leah giggled at that, and he looked at her curiously. Again, she thought back to her first impression of him, flowers in hand, smiling earnestly. She had wondered if he was good, bad, or just different. She now knew that he was simply... simple. In the best sense of the word. To hear him say it filled her with amusement.

They chatted easily as Joseph polished off his double cheeseburger, and Leah finished her regular one. "So," he said as wiped his hands on a napkin. "Do you have any plans other than going back home?

CHAPTER 22

What's next?"

To his surprise, Leah relaxed her shoulders and sighed, "You know, I think I'd like to just go home. There's cleaning to do."

J.P. knew she meant Nick's room. They'd moved his dresser out, among a few other things. There was vacuuming and rearranging to do.

The work went quickly with Joseph helping. Once the furniture had been moved around and Nick's absence didn't seem *quite* so obvious, they finally sat down together on the couch. Leah's head was spinning — it had been all day. Today was one of the biggest steps she'd ever taken in her life, and she figured she might as well take another one. She had a hard time believing the words she was about to say, but she turned to Joseph and took his hand. Startled by her sudden, definitive movement, he sat up at attention.

"Joseph, you have been here for four months." She took a deep breath. "What are your plans?"

This shouldn't have caught Joseph off guard — as Leah's demeanor had surprised Joseph all day — but it still shocked him. Initially, he had expected Leah to be a mess, but instead she had been calm, confident, and pleasant all day. Her body language had been relaxed, and she didn't seem to be stressed out in any way. He had been relieved and glad for both Leah and Nick that today went so smoothly.

But this bold question on such a day of change was a jolt for J.P.

After a moment of thought, he very matter-of-factly said, "It looks to be a pretty good year on the farm, I mean income-wise." He took her hands. "The job at the service station has worked out well and I enjoy it. I think you know that the best thing about the move has been meeting you." Her eyes glistened, but she smiled.

J.P. continued, "So far Daniel has been getting along with me being gone. Honestly, Leah, I don't know about next spring." He swallowed. "I don't know if that means I go back to the farm, or what." At that answer, Leah's heart cringed.

Deep down, he knew that his move to the city had created more questions than answers. First, he was still married. It was a failed marriage, yes, but he was married nonetheless. Now he was in love with another woman. Secondly, he had told himself that he was getting a job because of the drought and low farm income. Now in late August, it looked as if it was going to be a bin-busting crop. His reasons for leaving were becoming irrelevant. He stroked the top of her hand with his thumb, struggling for words.

Today had been one of the biggest days in the past five years for Leah. She had to admit she was rather proud of the way she had handled it. She knew a part of that strength had come from Joseph, and that the woman he met four months ago would not have handled Nick's leaving as she did today.

CHAPTER 23

With the long Labor Day weekend coming up, J.P. and Leah talked about possible plans. J.P. wanted to get back to the farm to do the jobs that needed to be done. Leah wanted to spend time with Nick and catch up with Julie. It was decided that J.P. was going to head home after work on Friday, and Leah would visit the farm Saturday evening after spending the day with Nick.

He got back to Frankton Friday evening to see most of the high school football game. J.P. loved being back home for the game, for more than a few reasons. His nephew, Andy, was a senior on the team, and, if you asked J.P., nothing brought a community together better than sports. He stopped at the Cage afterwards, where, between the football game and the local gathering hole, it felt like he had talked to a hundred people. At the end of the night, he took a long sip of iced tea and smiled. Nothing was better than being home, and he was glad to be there.

Leah and Nick had their day planned. She made breakfast for him and they spent the morning shopping for things Nick needed at college.

She and Julie went for a walk. It was good to see Julie and talk, but it was also different. They had been friends for so many years — and that would never change — but it was Joseph she was intimate with now. He was now on her list of important people. It was like Joseph was a piece of the puzzle she hadn't realized was missing.

Julie could see that Leah's outlook on life had changed. Never before had she seen Leah's relationship with a man so important to her. She knew this was bigger than the feelings in her marriage to Heath. It had been an unpredictable soap opera and Leah just played a part. This new relationship was an orchestra making beautiful music, and her friend was one of the lead musicians.

They walked and laughed, got some iced tea, and finally parted later in the afternoon. Julie winked at her after giving her a big hug. "Have fun on the farm!"

J.P. was putting in a full day. He wanted to get a start on moving in the year's hay bales. He worked busily and happily, thinking of Leah often. His friendship with Leah was not only exciting, it was also fulfilling. He felt lucky that he could love her, but also was happy to help her in any way she needed. Seeing her smiling was the ultimate reward.

Leah and J.P. met in town Saturday evening in front of the Cage. They were happy to see each other, and stole a quick hug between their vehicles. They stood there, talking for a couple of minutes, then went into the Cage holding hands.

They walked in all smiles, but that changed quickly.

As soon as they stepped through the doors, they found themselves face-to-face with J.P.'s estranged wife, Claire. It was clear she had seen them greet each other outside.

He hadn't seen her since February, and he was kicking himself for not thinking ahead. It made sense that she was back in town to visit her parents on this long weekend. By the look on her face and the glare in her eyes, J.P. knew this was not going to be good. The glazed, angry look in her eyes was one he recognized well — Claire had been hitting the white wine.

Her first, slurred words were, "Hey, J.P., you son of a bitch."

Leah's spine froze in place, and J.P. held up a hand to keep some distance between them. "Claire, that's enough."

Most everyone had noticed what was going on at the front door by now. The chatter died down, and people were craning their necks to get a better look.

Her eyes widened, and she took a step closer. Claire shouted,

CHAPTER 23

"Screw you, J.P.! You didn't even *try* to talk to me!"

He'd managed to keep it under control so far, but at those words his temper roared to life. "We've already had *our talk*, Claire. Remember? Remember when you told me how much you hated the *damned farm*?"

Her eyes stretched even wider and she opened her sneering mouth, but J.P. cut her off. "And then you left!"

He was yelling now, and he didn't like it, but it was all finally pouring out. "You left me, and you left the farm, and you took whatever you decided was important out of the house — and it wasn't much. You left." He took a small-but-deliberate step toward her, which elicited a quiet gasp from Leah behind him. "So what the *hell* would we have to talk about, Claire?" After an ominous pause, J.P. stepped back away from his estranged wife and took a slow, deep breath. "You know, I was having a really great day, Claire. I was having a great day and a great life until I ran into you. So, there. There's *our talk*. Is that good enough for you?"

As soon as he finished his question, her angry lips closed and turned up at the corner, in just a hint of that vindictive smile he had come to know so well in their last year together. She reached up and fixed a piece of hair that had fallen across her eyes, and added, "I hear you went and got yourself an off-the-farm job." The hint of smile disappeared. "You just couldn't get it to rain, could you?"

This time, it was J.P.'s turn to open his mouth without having a chance to say anything. Belligerent again, Claire jutted out her chin. "I filed divorce papers yesterday," she spat out, the words clouding the air like poison gas.

She'd caught him off guard, but it only took a beat for him to reply with, "That's the best news I've heard in years."

Turning her attention back to Leah, Claire looked her up and down before whipping her gaze back to J.P. "I hope you and your whore are happy."

"Claire, that is *enough!*" J.P stepped in front of Leah, putting himself between the two women. He leaned into Leah's ear and said, "I think the best thing we can do is leave. Let's go." She nodded eagerly, and took his hand. He turned around to keep an eye on Claire as they left, but she had other plans. When he had taken his eyes off her, she had drawn back her open, angry hand, and slapped J.P. fully across the face.

It was as loud as a shotgun blast.

Everything came to a standstill; time froze. The left side of J.P.'s face burned with the sting of it. When J.P.'s awareness came back to him, he simply grabbed Leah's hand and exited without adding a word.

Even though Leah's Blazer was there, they scrambled into the Dodge. J.P. peeled out of the parking lot and into the night.

J.P.'s adrenaline was still pumping through his veins like hot oil as he slammed the Dodge into park. He had driven straight to the city park to stop and find a place to regain his composure. His cheek burned from Claire's fingertips, but he knew most of the heat in his face came from shame.

That night was different from the fourth of July. That slap had come out of nowhere — even though he had been concerned about the allegations against him, he had known, deep down, that he wasn't at fault. He couldn't say the same about Claire's slap. How many times had she begged him for a change? And how many times had he ignored her?

And he'd yelled tonight. He hadn't yelled at someone in two years. He'd taken a step toward his wife — whether he wanted to admit it to himself or not, she was still his wife — and Leah had seen the whole thing. He took a few deep breaths and turned to Leah.

"I'm sorry you had to see that." Before she could respond, he continued, "I'd like to apologize for losing my temper. And, well, I'd like to apologize for the name that Claire called you."

Leah shook her head quickly and looked into J.P.'s eyes. "It wasn't you. She'd had too much to drink." She wanted to touch his face, but stopped herself. She had watched him get slapped twice, now, and she hated it.

CHAPTER 23

"I shouldn't be surprised. That's the way things go in life." He stared down at his hands, but continued. "We hope that, by not talking about things, they'll disappear or correct on their own." He let out a sad chuckle. "They seldom, if ever, do."

Leah nodded. "It's just like the 4th of July. With Heather. We ignored the signs, and the problems… and I didn't warn you, either."

"I've been having such a wonderful time this summer. It's been easy to pretend there was nothing unfinished in my past, but there is, and I have to confront that. I've been avoiding my broken marriage for too long, and it finally showed up and slapped me across the face."

Leah started to contradict him, but stopped herself. She certainly didn't like the woman, but she had to admit that she'd found herself agreeing with some of the points Claire had made. So, instead of saying anything, she decided to simply listen.

"No, this whole mess should have been taken care of. I know now that part of the reason I moved was that I was running away from it. And tonight it caught up with me." He shook his head but couldn't bring himself to look at her. "It wasn't fair for you to be a part of it."

Suddenly, Leah noticed tears on Joseph's cheeks. He may have been slapped tonight, but it was clear to her that the worst pain was from his guilt.

He had been ashamed of his loveless marriage for years, and now, adding even more to the suffering, he had fallen in love with Leah. "I don't want to feel this way, Leah, because being with you is incredible. But it…" He wiped the back of his hand across his cheek. "It only makes the load heavier to carry."

Leah scooted closer to him. "Well, I hope what she said was true. I hope Claire filed for divorce. We'll find out soon enough, and when we do, you can let go of this guilt."

Her words rang out like a bell on a clear night to him. Finally, he couldn't hold it any longer; he started to cry. His shoulders shaking, he slumped over the Dodge's steering wheel and wept.

Stunned, Leah laid her arm over Joseph's shoulder and did her best to let him know she was there for him. She certainly wasn't used to crying men, let alone one who needed comfort from her. But, she knew he was the most caring and kind man she had ever known, and that he had been nothing short of a miracle for her. He brought her out of her shell, helped her feel life again, and here he was, shattered in front of her. She leaned into him and added her own tears.

After a couple of minutes J.P. began to calm down, gathered his thoughts, and regained his composure. "I know I said this already," he whispered, "but I'm sorry you had to be there. I'm sorry for what she called you."

She smiled, trying to cheer him up, if she could. "That's just like my Joseph. You're the one hurting and somehow you're also the one apologizing." Leah then gently rubbed Joseph's face where it had been slapped.

He sat up, tried to shake himself out of his funk, and said, "Let's go to the farm. We'll leave your car until tomorrow." He turned the key, the Dodge rumbling back to life. "Do you need your bag or anything?"

"Yes, please."

They grabbed Leah's bag, locked her car, and headed for the farm. As they drove, they decided on a safe topic, and told each other about their days. Both had been good overall, and contained nothing out of the ordinary until that night.

"I thought about you, quite a bit." He smiled at her, the first time since the Cage.

"Me, too."

When they got to the farm, J.P. made burgers, the old stand-by meal. After some pleasant small talk, and filling up the dishwasher, J.P. steered the conversation to an old topic. "Remember the other evening, when you asked me my plans?"

Nervous, Leah answered, "Yes."

"I've been thinking about your question, an awful lot. You've been constantly on my mind." He reached up to his shirt pocket, having forgotten that he hadn't needed a Rolaid in weeks. "I've been thinking about my options. One is to keep the job at the service station and

CHAPTER 23

keep coming back to the farm as much as I can." He looked her in the eyes again. "Another possibility is that we — you and I — come back to the farm. You could keep your bookkeeping accounts out here. I've got internet at the house, we could make it work."

Leah couldn't believe what she was hearing. She'd never thought about that option. *Her* on the *farm*! Leave the city! She loved the beauty of the farm and the area, but had never pictured herself *living* there. .

He went on to add, "If Claire really didn't file for divorce, I will. It's time for that to be done. It's been over for a long time."

J.P. and Leah went to bed together that night. And just like their drive away from the college campus, they went to each other for comfort. Tonight they went to sleep in each other's arms, for the security, and knowing everything will be alright, in time.

In the morning, J.P. gently shook Leah awake. "Are you going to Mass with me?" Leah had been planning on it, got quickly out of bed, and ready for church. The creatures of habits that humans are, they sat in the same pew as the first time Leah had visited. What she heard from Monsignor MIke was not sugar-coated; it made her think, but it also gave her hope.

In retrospect, it was similar to the dramatic events of the previous night. Joseph and Claire's confrontation, the slap — those were real and certainly not sugar-coated. Joseph's crying, and his long-harbored pain had her thinking about hope. How their late-night talk gave her hope for them and their future together. She was surprised to find that she could relate real life to what she heard in church.

After Mass, as people gathered, J.P. told Leah that he wanted to introduce her to a friend. He found his friend, Rich, and introduced them. "We've been friends since high school," J.P. said, and went on to tell her that Rich was a cattle man who raised and sold purebred cattle. J.P. also introduced Rich's five sons, ranging in age between 5 and 21. "These guys are like my second family. Fine boys, all around."

Rich beamed, but went on to say, "We sure miss seeing you

around, J.P. How are you doing?"

"It's different in the city, but I like the job. Leah works in the office of the service station that I work at." He flashed Leah a small smile.

Rich turned to her and added, "We sure miss him! You're lucky to have him around."

Leah grabbed J.P.'s arm quickly. "I know I am." To Rich's surprise, he realized Leah had taken the statement more personally than he intended. But, he let it go. He was glad for J.P. and Leah, and delighted in the big smiles on both their faces.

As they left the church, J.P. took a deep breath of fresh air, and took her hand. "I want to show you the Veterans' Park, and the memorial walls." She happily agreed, and they made their way to the park, feeling a freedom they hadn't expected that morning. As they got out of the Dodge and started the walk up the hill to the walls, Leah looked up at the flags flowing in the breeze. Halfway up the walk was the American flag and, in a row in front of the walls, seven flags of service. To the far left, Leah could see the Pawnee Nation flag, because of their prevalence in local history, and the invaluable scouting help they provided.

When they reached the walls, J.P. said "You won't believe all of the names of my relatives." He showed Leah his grandfather Dreul's name, five uncles, nine cousins, and a niece etched on the wall. Then he showed her his friend Glen's name. She stayed quiet as they sat on a bench, and J.P. again told Leah the story of Glen. How they grew up together, and were like brothers. How Glen lost his life in Vietnam, and how his parents gave him Glen's Chevelle, and that he never plans on parting with it. She had heard the story before, but hearing it here, in this place, felt like the first time.

They simply sat there, taking in the history around them. J.P. became increasingly aware of the sadness in the air as they sat on the bench, and knew Glen would not want that. So he let pride take over his feelings, and focused on the fact that his family represented WWI, WWII, the Korean War, Vietnam War, Desert Storm, and that his niece was currently full-time National Guard.

CHAPTER 23

They paid respect in comfortable silence, the only sound coming from the flags, playing their tune of honor, rifling in the breeze.

When they returned to the Dodge, J.P. opened Leah's door. He walked around, sat in the driver's seat, and smiled realizing that, once again, Leah was sitting right next to him. As they drove by the wall looking down from the highway, they knew this visit would never be forgotten.

They were halfway back to the farm before somebody broke the silence.

"Joseph, last night you mentioned the possibility of moving back to the farm... and me being a part of that."

"Yes."

"I think I really want that." She turned to face him. "I love you and who you are, and I've come to realize a big part of that is here. Frankton, the countryside — where you come from and the lifestyle you live." J.P. felt his heart begin to race as she placed her hand on his knee. "I know it's not that simple. There's a lot to navigate, a lot to figure out, but I think we can do that, together."

He didn't want to interrupt, but he couldn't stop himself from grinning. Encouraged by the smile, she continued. "I've only been out here twice, but nothing has ever been so inspiring in my life." She laughed, embarrassed. "This may sound silly, but I feel like it's calling me."

He leaned into her, just a little. "It's not silly. I know exactly what you mean."

As they pulled into the farm, they realized they had forgotten Leah's Blazer in town. He surreptitiously popped a Rolaid in his mouth, hoping to ease some stress. It was an unwelcome reminder of the unpleasant run-in with Claire. J.P. put the pickup in park, and took Leah's hands in his own. "Before we go any further, I need to tell you something. When I bought this farm it was on a 20 year payment plan. This December 1st will be the 18th year. With the settlement to come with Claire, I figure I'll have to add another ten years on a new loan or remortgage the land." He swallowed. "I've known for a long time, that this is what it was going to be, when the time finally came. So I just wanted to be honest, and tell you what was going to happen here."

Leah gave his hands a squeeze, and said, "Thank you. I understand, and I appreciate you telling me, but I guess that wasn't really a concern. I want you, and if that's the price, I know we can handle it."

Both of them were exhausted. It seemed like the last 30 hours had used up a lifetime of emotion, so they decided the best course of action was to go downstairs for a nap.

Before they went to sleep, they made love. It was the simplest thing that had happened over the whole weekend. Just as they had held each other on the cement bench, they held each other in bed and it washed away their worries.

When Leah awoke, Joseph wasn't in bed, but she could hear the lawnmower above her. After groggily making her way upstairs, she looked out the window to see Joseph mowing the the patch of grass along the drive. As she watched him, she thought he made the perfect picture for the word "content." Just like a lady cleaning her house, Joseph was cleaning his home, the farm. She wondered, *Could she someday be a part of all of this?*

This was the best gift she had ever received. Joseph had finally brought hope back into her life. As her heart swelled at the thought, he noticed her looking out the picture window and waved with a grin. She shook her head, amused. *There's that waving thing that everyone around here does.* That was probably just part of the package out here. If she really wanted this life, she'd better practice it. She smiled and waved back at Joseph.

After he finished mowing, Joseph came in the house and wrapped his sweaty arms around her at the sink. She pretended to be disgusted, but didn't make any moves to escape.

"Did you have a good nap?"

She didn't know if anyone had ever asked her if she'd had a good nap before, but she did feel rested. "Yes I did, Joseph." Her lips curved mischievously. "Do you think it was the basement... or the way I was tucked in?"

With a surge of triumph, she realized that was the first time she had ever made Joseph blush. The roles had been reversed and she loved it. Leah tossed her head back in an earthy laugh as Joseph sheepishly smiled.

He cleared his throat, trying to change the subject and cool his cheeks. "I forgot to mention that there's a supper at my parents this evening."

Knocking her back to reality, the first thought that overtook Leah was Joseph's experience meeting her family on the 4th of July. She let herself relax, though, after a few moments. She had already met Joseph's mother, and that had gone very well.

As they drove into Joseph's parents farm, Leah noticed that the flower garden was getting past its prime, compared to five weeks earlier when Leah had visited.

Kate gave her another warm welcome to her home. J.P. introduced her to his dad, Herb, and a few other family members. "This is my sister, Ranee, her husband, Ken, and my nephew, Andy, who's a senior. And this is Jo Jo, who's a sophomore this year."

She could certainly tell that Ranee and Joseph were siblings, as they strikingly resembled each other. The night was full of laughter, stories, and the revelation that Joseph had another name. "Don't be embarrassed, *Uncle Joey!*" His nephew and niece good naturedly taunted him as he blushed for the second time that day. The conversation stayed light, despite the fact that the whole family had learned about the incident with Claire. To their credit, no one mentioned it.

After their slim lunch of quickly-thrown-together sandwiches, Leah was hungry. The spread of roast beef, mashed potatoes, corn casserole, and homemade bread was a meal that was both delicious and fulfilling. After supper she and Ranee visited like they were old friends, talking about their children, their families, and about Joseph.

She told his sister about the first day of work at the station, when Joseph brought M&Ms and a rose. "We've gone dancing, and golfing, and you're probably not surprised to know that he's an expert in both!" Ranee just smiled. She knew it all about Joseph. She also knew that he had been lonely and the family had been concerned. She knew that Joseph would not have brought just any gal home if she wasn't truly important to him. "We're so glad you came for a visit." Her eyes crinkled with warmth. "I hope you've enjoy it here, in our little corner of the country."

Leah nodded enthusiastically. "I love it here."

Ranee gave her hand a squeeze. She could tell that Leah also loved J.P.

Later that evening J.P. and Leah went to Frankton to get her car. The Cage was closed and dark. They both glanced in that direction, without saying a word. It was a relief to know that the weekend was settling down and their emotions were calming.

When they got back to the farm, they sat out on the deck with a couple glasses of iced tea and no real agenda. They were determined to simply enjoy each other and everything around. This was so different for Leah. If you sat at the front of her house in the city, you would have to fight the consistent sound of traffic to get more than a word of conversation in.

This evening on the farm, the quiet was punctuated with brief bursts of sounds. In the distance was a mother cow bawling for her calf to come back to her. There was the hoot of a barn owl, followed by a lonely coyote barking a warning, then finishing with a loud, haunting howl. Leah grabbed Joseph's hand out of instinct, then relaxed with a smile, as it reminded her of their picnic, when the doe and fawn surprised them.

Soon after, a dozen coyotes added their voices to the chorus. She looked at him in disbelief of the long, wailing cries. After a few minutes of frantic howling, they finally came to a stop, leaving the silence louder than it was before. "How far away are they?" She asked, still a little shaken.

CHAPTER 23

"Probably a mile or two away. Nothing to worry about."

Leah had never heard such an astounding display of nature. Again, she felt a pull toward God. A quiet reminder that there was a lot out there she hadn't yet experienced. They sat contentedly, looking up at the stars. Silently, she asked the heavens, *Can things really be this comfortable, this simple?*

They were there for another hour, enjoying all of nature and life.

The next morning, Leah awoke again to the smell of bacon. As she lay in the warm, snug bed in the basement, she thought a prayer. *Thank you, God, for Joseph. For all of these gifts.*

Even though she was alone, she felt a blush creep onto her cheeks. She had surprised herself. She had asked God for things in the past — out of desperation — but to simply thank Him with sincerity... it was surely a first for her.

As she entered the kitchen, she found Joseph busy putting the finishing touches to a breakfast for her. She snuck up behind him and slipped her arms around his waist, resting her face on his strong, broad shoulders. "You spoil me. I've never made breakfast for you." J.P. rumbled a low chuckle and turned to plant a kiss on her forehead. On the table was a bouquet of over-mature white aster, an apple and banana, and a box of Cheerios waiting to be paired with his signature bacon and toast.

When they finished, she raised an eyebrow and placed her hand on his knee under the table. "What's for dessert?" And without another word, she grabbed his hand and hustled him back down to the basement.

Leah was going to leave for her drive back to the city later that morning. She didn't want to use the word "sad," to describe how she felt about leaving. Sad was the crying after the slap on Saturday night, after the drama on the fourth of July. Maybe "heaving of the heart" was more appropriate.

The couple didn't even try to put their feelings into words when it was time for her to leave. They hugged for a long minute, and exchanged a "See you at work tomorrow."

This weekend had been a whirlwind lesson of *real life*. It had laid a foundation for their future. As she drove back to her home, she thought about her planned walk with Julie later that evening. Sure, she could *tell* her about the weekend, but doubted if she could paint the whole picture.

CHAPTER 24

J.P. and George had agreed that he could have a week off from the station in the fall to go home for harvest. He and Daniel had decided that the third week of October was the optimal time, as harvest would be in full swing by then.

Leah was excited about visiting the farm as well. Plus it was going to be J.P.'s birthday on Thursday, October 20th. She wouldn't be there for the *exact* day, but thought that they could start celebrating the weekend before. She was excited to take a day off from the station on Monday so it could be a long weekend for them together.

She was about to find out that working together at the garage and working together on the farm were two very different things.

They had planned to leave an hour early from work so they could make it back to the high school football game. J.P.'s nephew Andy played on the team, and he wanted to watch another game. When Leah came home on Monday she was going to bring the Chevelle back to the city. J.P. had a couple of maintenance jobs he wanted to take care of on the Chevelle, plus George said he could store it in the back room at the station.

As they drove toward Frankton, J.P. got excited every time he saw harvest going on in a field. "Harvest is... well it's like receiving your only paycheck of the year."

"What? Only one per year? That seems absolutely crazy. I can't imagine having that much faith and trust in something like that!." To wait a year for your income seemed crazy.

Joseph smiled. "You're not totally wrong... it might be a *little* crazy.

I call it my 'plant and pray' job.'"

She shook her head in disbelief. She was starting to understand the special person it took to live such a life, by learning more from Joseph all the time.

At the football game, they sat by and visited with Ranee in the stands. Just like the first time they met Labor Day weekend, she and Leah chatted like old friends. It was a nice feeling — that instant comfort.

The Tigers fans went wild with the night's victory, as it guaranteed the team a spot in the state playoffs. After the game, Ranee carefully asked, "Are you two going to stop at the Cage?"

Leah looked back and forth between the two of them, her pulse quickening with growing anxiety. To her surprise, J.P. simply said, "Yup. See you there."

They hadn't been there since "The Slap," but J.P. and Leah marched confidently into the Cage as if there had never been any history made at the door.

Tonight was different for them at the town watering hole. It was all comradery tonight, with everyone celebrating the successful football season. The night's festivities were a good start for J.P.'s week back home. He certainly hadn't planned on staying late, because the next day harvest would be in full swing.

For some reason, though, he decided to have his "one drink" as a kickoff for his birthday week. The locals were having a great time, with the music blasting and all of the pool tables busy.

When the magical midnight came, it was time to head to the farm. Out the door, hand-in-hand, J.P. and Leah headed out to the Dodge. How different the exit was than the last time they had left the Cage. Tonight was footloose and fancy free. They were in love and didn't care if the world knew.

Tonight, they practically fell into the Dodge through the driver's door and embraced with a long kiss, right there while parked on main street.

As they headed for the farm, it felt to them both like they were

CHAPTER 24

going home. "Football, a fun night at the Cage, a good harvest on the horizon, and my gal sitting next to me." He grinned. "Isn't life great?"

Leah snuggled tighter to Joseph. She felt it, too. "Yes, it is." As they pulled into the farmyard, she glanced up at that smile on the barn, welcoming her home. *What a fitting symbol for Joseph's farm*, she thought. *A smile.*

Laughing and pawing at each other all the way down the staircase, J.P. and Leah headed straight for the basement, with no plans to come up for air until morning.

When Leah awoke, it was 10.00 AM. She jumped up as if she had just realized she was late for work and took the stairs two at a time. There was an envelope with *"Leah"* written on it, lying on the kitchen table. Inside she found a note and cash. The note seemed to sing out at her as she read it.

Good Morning, Leah!

Would you please go to the grocery store and buy supplies for lunches for Daniel and me? A lot of cold cuts for our meals on the go would be perfect. You can drive either the Dodge or Chevelle. Call me if you need something.
    Thank you!
    J.P.

A sense of urgency overcame Leah — she had been asked to do a job. She was actually going to be able to be of use during harvest. She quickly called Joseph, blurting out "I just woke up!"

She heard a rumble of laughter through the phone. "There's something about that basement, isn't there? Or maybe it has to do with who tucked you in."

Flustered, Leah ignored that, and said "I'm late."

"For what?"

"To go to the grocery store!" She raked her fingers anxiously through her morning hair. She had been asked to help, and she overslept.

"Now, I don't think you had a 10:00 am appointment at the grocery store, did you?"

"Joseph! I just want to help!" She didn't think his joke was all that funny, but it *did* manage to chase the nervousness away from her heart. After discussing the grocery list, J.P. added, "I'm on my third trip to the elevator already with the truck. Busy morning!" That just added to Leah's urgency, so she bounded to the bathroom to get ready for the day.

When she walked out the front door, she noticed something that she had missed last night. There, in the small flower bed, were a dozen pumpkins arranged around the border. She smiled. Kate must have put them out as a "welcome home" gesture. *What a fitting display*, Leah thought, *for my Country Pumpkin*. She shook her head in amusement as she made her way to the garage. Joseph would turn 30 shades of red if he ever heard her call him that.

"She decided to drive the Dodge to town. As she crunched carefully down the dirt road, listening to the local weather report on the radio," a feeling of warmth overcame her. It wasn't so much the feeling of importance, but the feeling of being a part of something. It was the first job that she'd been asked to do on the farm. Was she helping? Was she part of the harvest crew? She took satisfaction in believing so. With her concentration on the task at hand, she didn't realize that the truck coming from the other direction was Joseph, waving excitedly from the driver's seat. When he blew the air horn, she shrieked in surprise, but stuck her arm out the window and waved frantically, hoping he'd see it in the mirror.

She had been grocery shopping virtually every week since the death of her mother. What was different this time? As she walked through the automatic door of the small grocery store, she knew that this was more than just shopping for groceries. This was a new chapter in her life. Leah was going to care for Joseph in a way that she had not yet: by buying supplies and stocking his kitchen with nourishment and the hope that, someday, it will be *their* kitchen.

That's what the butterflies were all about — the excitement for the future.

CHAPTER 24

As Leah stood at the meat counter, the man behind it said, "You're J.P.'s friend."

She flashed him a nervous smile. "Yes."

"I saw you last night at the football game. Good game wasn't it?" Before Leah could reply, he asked, "J.P. busy harvesting?"

She again answered, "Yes."

When Leah went shopping in the city, the store employees didn't really care if they recognized you or not. She was beginning to suspect that he — and most of Frankton — probably already knew who she was, what her name was, and that she and J.P. worked together.

"I'm Steve." He placed her wrapped cold cuts on the counter and snapped off his latex gloves. "Thanks for stopping in, and good luck with harvest!"

"I'm Leah. Thanks!"

There, she thought. *That proves it.* She was a part of the harvest crew. As she pushed the grocery cart away from the meat counter, she decided she *was* important. This task and purpose was an important part of harvest — farmers can't farm on an empty stomach. As she explored the aisles, three different ladies startled her, simply by saying "Hello."

As Leah left the grocery store, she stopped when she saw the floral shop across the street. Joseph had given her flowers so many times, and it was a perfect day to return the favor. With two red roses gently packed next to her in the Dodge, she headed back to the farm.

Shopping here was different; there was no window shopping, no wasting of time. You simply bought what you needed and kept moving.

When she got back to the farm, she put the groceries away. She didn't know where everything belonged, but she did the job as best she could. Once they were put away, she decided to give Joseph a quick call.

"Can I make sandwiches for you two?" She asked, speaking loudly over the din of farm machinery in the background.

"That'd be nice. You can bring them up to Doc's, a mile north of my parents."

Leah found the guys without trouble. She could see it was Joseph in the tractor, unloading corn into the truck from a grain cart. She sat on the road watching the machinery, and watched Daniel coming toward them with the combine harvesting the corn. At the top of the combine, Leah noticed that corn was starting to pile up. As Daniel got closer, the small hill of corn began to grow into a mountain of golden kernels on the top of the combine.

When both Daniel and Joseph were unloading corn into the truck, it looked like two flowing rivers of corn. As the corn levels lowered in the cart and combine, a peak of it was rising in the truck. Finally, when the grain stopped moving and the machinery quieted down, Joseph made his way over to Leah, wrapping her up in a quick hug and giving her a small kiss.

To her surprise, they all ate their sandwiches standing, chatting in between bites.

"I don't think I've ever spent an entire meal standing!" She brushed crumbs off her hands and began collecting sandwich bags to put in the trash at home.

Daniel's eyes crinkled with amusement. "Well, if you spend your whole morning sitting in a combine, it feels awfully good to stretch your legs."

Daniel and Joseph were talking about harvest, but it was all foreign to Leah. Words like "grain moisture," "grain weight," and the apparently very important "yield," didn't really mean much to her. Father and son, however, seemed happy and excited about it all. She tried to be cheerful, even though she didn't understand why everyone was so excited. As they finished eating, Daniel took a final swig of his soda, and handed the can to Leah, who was collecting trash.

"Thanks for lunch, Leah!"

Leah couldn't help it; she beamed with pride. "I'm glad to help!"

Joseph nudged her with his elbow. "Want to ride along in the truck, take a load to the elevator?"

"Sure!"

As Joseph helped her up into the truck, excitement bubbled up

CHAPTER 24

inside her like she was a bottle of Coke. She'd never sat in an eighteen wheeler before. It reminded her of when she was a small kid, climbing up a slide and looking down to the bottom. Things looked different and smaller from such a high vantage point.

The truck rumbled to life with a roar of the engine. She quickly looked into the rear-view mirror in awe. "I can't imagine driving a vehicle so *long!*"

When they turned onto the highway, Joseph made a wide swing, giving Leah a sudden understanding of the signs that announce: THIS VEHICLE MAKES WIDE TURNS.

"How did the trip to the grocery store go this morning?" He asked.

Leah told him about Steve and their conversation."It felt like everyone knew who I was!"

"They probably do. You've been to church *and* the Cage twice, a football game, and the grocery store." He chuckled. "When I moved to the city no one noticed, but when you visit Frankton, everyone knows."

When they got to the elevator, they drove onto the scale. Joseph explained, "You weigh when you're loaded, and you weigh when you're unloaded." Leah watched in the mirror as a mechanical spear stabbed into the trailer of corn. "They test a sample of every load for moisture and weight to know the quality of the grain."

They drove up to the cement tower and waited their turn. As the truck before them was emptying into the pit, the corn was disappearing. Leah watched intently. "It looks like we're feeding corn to a concrete monster!"

After making two trips with him in the truck, she was ready for a change of scenery. "I'd like to visit your mother now, if that's alright."

Knowing she wanted to spend time with Kate brought a smile to his lips. "That's great. Daniel says the plan is that we'll work until dark, and then to go to the Korner Bar in Washburn for supper."

"Okay! I'll visit your mother, then go to the house, and I'll be ready to go out."

Kate met Leah at her door and welcomed her in. "How are the guys doing out there?"

Leah said, "Real good, I think. They seemed very pleased about everything, and I believe Joseph is on his seventh load to the elevator."

"That is good." Kate said, while finishing up at the sink. "How are *you*, Leah?"

"I'm fine! I truly enjoy it when I visit the farm." She leaned against the door frame as she watched J.P.'s mom bustle around the kitchen. They made small talk about the high school game, flowers, and the pumpkins. Finally, Kate asked, "Did Joseph mention anything about going to supper tonight?"

"Yes, he did! Daniel said they would work until dark, and then we'll go to the Korner Bar for supper."

"Oh, good." She raised an eyebrow and leaned in. "Daniel came up with an idea to have a surprise birthday party for his dad. I don't think Joseph will suspect a thing if just Herb, Daniel, you, and I go for supper."

"That's so exciting!"

"Now, it won't be *that* big of a party — a couple of friends, a few cousins, and his sisters."

"I love that idea, it'll be nice."

Kate wiped her hands on a dish towel and turned back to her. "We all miss Joseph, not having him around all of the time." She gestured toward the kitchen table. " Leah, please sit down."

Her heart skipped a beat. *Oh, no.* She thought. *What is this going to be about?*

Kate sat down, too. "First, I would like to apologize for what happened to you over Labor Day weekend. I know all about the scene Claire made at the Cage."

Leah shook her head. "That wasn't your fault, Kate."

"Oh, I know that, but I still feel sad and sorry about it."

"Thank you. It *was* pretty upsetting."

Kate went on. "Joseph has been sad and troubled about his marriage for a long time. When Daniel came back to the farm a year

CHAPTER 24

and a half ago, Joseph started mentioning the idea of leaving for a while. I knew he didn't *want* to but he felt like he had to." Kate looked straight at Leah with glistening eyes and said, "Joseph left so he could find himself. And I believe he has. I have never seen him happier." Kate reached for Leah's hand. "I believe Joseph found himself when he found you."

Leah was dumbfounded, and couldn't bring herself to reply immediately. Finally, she rallied. "Kate, Joseph saved *me*. I haven't really done *anything* for him."

"Joseph has not been himself for a very long time. Because something was missing. Just like a bird with a broken wing who longs for the sky, Joseph needed someone to love in order to be whole."

It hadn't taken Leah long to know that Kate knew Joseph perfectly. She didn't know what to say, or what she could add to Kate's sentiments. Just like Joseph and his thoughtful answers, Kate knew how to stop her in her tracks. So, she simply said, "I love Joseph."

Kate's face warmed. "I know you do, and rest assured he loves you right back. The first time he brought you here, I knew it. He wouldn't have shared his life in such detail if he didn't want you to be a part of it. It was his way of offering it to you."

Leah's head was spinning. *How could she know all of this?* But the answer was clear, if she thought about it. Her Joseph got his deep feelings from his mother — it felt like she was having a conversation with him now.

So she started to babble, listing all of the remarkable things he had done for her. From the M&Ms down to the morning notes, she couldn't stop herself from recounting them one by one.

Both women laughed and smiled with joy, but they couldn't stop their tears. The only two people who called Joseph by his full name, who loved him the most, with wet cheeks and happy hearts, embraced in a hug. Leah had never felt more welcome in a home.

As she drove slowly back to the farm, she had tears on her mind. *Why has my time knowing Joseph been so full of tears?* She knew the answer, of course. Not all tears were out of sadness. Upon entering

Joseph's house, she sat at the kitchen table and once again picked up his note from that morning. It was short and uncomplicated, but she knew how much had gone into it, more than a few words. He put meaning into everything he did and said. As she sat there holding tight to the note, she realized she had shed more tears in the last few visits here than in the last 20 years of her life. She had become so accustomed to crying out of anger and sadness, that crying out of happiness still felt foriegn to her. She let herself cry some more, feeling fortunate for a few moments alone with her tears.

Just as planned, Joseph arrived home at dark. As he pulled down the drive, he was taken aback by his well-lit house. The lights were on, and that meant someone was home. He was happy about that — his home and life had been dark for too long. When he walked into the kitchen, he found that Leah had tidied up the house and placed two roses in a vase on the table.

He scooped her up in a big hug and kissed her forehead. "Thank you." His house had become a home again. "This is the best birthday gift that anyone could have given me." She blushed.

J.P. could have sat at the kitchen table holding hands with Leah, looking back and forth between the flowers and her eyes all night long. She probably wouldn't have minded that idea either, but she knew of the plans for the party. "It's time to go, Joseph. My stomach is going to start growling soon!"

Begrudgingly, Joseph agreed and took a quick shower. To Leah's delight, her cowboy emerged from the basement with his boots, wranglers, and black cowboy hat. She gave him a big hug and a kiss that knocked him off-balance. "Now what was that for?"

"Because you are mine, and I wanted to. And, you're looking very handsome. I simply couldn't stop myself." Leah smiled up at him, feeling dizzy. Just a few months ago she would never have dreamed that she'd be saying that to a cowboy. She'd gone from never knowing one to falling head over heels for a man in boots.

As they walked out the door, J.P. clapped his hands once, decisively. "Let's take the Chevelle.

CHAPTER 24

Leah's mouth turned up in a sly smile. "Are you sure? Remember what happened the last time we took it to Washburn?"

J.P. winked at her. "I sure do. Rodeo, street dance, and a quick stop at Mt. Zion."

He had expected Daniel and his parents at the Korner Bar for supper, but when J.P. walked in he was surprised to see his sisters, cousins, and a good handful of some of his closest friends. Everyone was delighted to have surprised him, and were happy to spend the evening together.

After a laughter-filled dinner, it was time for a few birthday gifts. The gift from J.P.'s buddy, Rich, was a T-Shirt that practically shouted *"It took me 49 years to look this good!"* To Leah's surprise, J.P. was so proud of that t-shirt, he put it on over the shirt he was already wearing. "This might not be the fanciest look, but I don't care." He grinned. "I'm the birthday boy tonight!"

The night went on pleasantly, with the group playing cards, shooting pool, and visiting. Eventually, J.P. sauntered up to the jukebox and played the only two Geroge Strait songs it had. With a twinkle in his eye, he grabbed Leah's hand and crooned, "Will you dance with the birthday boy?"

And there, on the little twelve-by-twelve foot dance floor, J.P. and Leah danced. Even though the Korner Bar was loud and full of people, for those few minutes, the couple floated in their own little world. They moved effortlessly together, comfortable and happy, anticipating one another's steps, and getting lost in the music.

The first time they danced together at the Starbrite was the night they began to fall in love. Tonight, in just two songs, they were reminded of it, more in love than ever.

As midnight came, everyone made moves to head home, but not before receiving a strong hug and heartfelt thanks from J.P. He felt happy and humbled by everyone who came to help celebrate his birthday.

Between the day's harvesting and that night's party, J.P. was overcome by a longing for "home." He hadn't realized how much he had missed it. As he looked around the bar, he had to admit to himself that, had it not been for Leah, he probably would have hated the city by now. He had searched for meaning in the city and found Leah, and he was ready to bring his treasure home. Just as foreign adventurers found precious discoveries and brought them back to their homelands, his hope was that — maybe next spring — Leah would want to make that return trip, with him.

As the party came to an end, J.P. and Leah leaned into one another. J.P. whispered to Leah, "It's midnight and I have to get home."

She looked up at him lazily. "You know, you're always concerned when it comes to midnight. Why is that?"

"Well now, you never know, I might turn into a pumpkin at the stroke of twelve."

Leah had almost spit out her iced tea, mid-drink. Not once had she and J.P. ever talked about pumpkins. She had had that secret "Country Pumpkin" nickname in her head the whole time, and there was Joseph, making wisecracks about it. She couldn't stop herself, tossed back her head and let out a long, loud laugh.

His eyes smiling, he nudged her with his elbow. "Now what's all that about?"

She calmed herself enough to respond with, "I'll tell you some other night, cowboy."

On the way home, Leah scooted a little closer to J.P, and purred, "Are we going to go to school tonight?"

"Hmm, it might be a good idea to study for a minute or two," J.P. answered.

Leah nodded dramatically. "I think we should."

So a visit to Mt. Zion was in order. That night's activities were limited to heavy petting and fogging up the windows, but Leah did manage to get the new T-Shirt off of Joseph. After a crash course at school, the Chevelle headed home. On the way, Leah decided the birthday-themed T-shirt was going to be her night gown. As her top was brazenly replaced with his, J.P. raised an eyebrow. "Well, now, I think I have an idea, but just what do you have planned over there?"

Leah blushed, "My birthday present to you is wrapped in this T-Shirt."

CHAPTER 24

J.P.'s eyes widened, and he made the Chevelle roar, in a hurry to get home.

On Sunday mornings, J.P. was usually up before dawn, but after two late nights, his routine was off-kilter. He and Leah ate breakfast quickly, and made it to St. Peter's just in time for Mass.

After the service, J.P. shook hands with Monsignor Mike, who smiled at Leah and said, "Leah! Glad to have you back."

Leah returned the smile. "It's good to *be* back."

"How have you two been?"

J.P. was happy for the small moment of conversation in the beautiful weather. "I'm back for the week to help Daniel with harvest. It's a good crop."

"Why, that is good news." He turned to Leah. "How about you? Are you here for harvest, also?"

"I am, but I'm going back tomorrow."

J.P. reached down and gently interlocked his hand with hers. "She's been helping out quite a bit. She made lunch and kept me company yesterday, hauling corn."

Leah blushed and said "Oh, I didn't do anything."

Monsignor Mike said, in a firm voice, "Don't count yourself short, Leah. At Harvest, every effort helps." His eyes crinkled with warmth. "When will you be back to visit us?"

This caught Leah off-guard — she hadn't really thought that far ahead — but J.P. jumped in without hesitation, "Thanksgiving, if not before."

They said their goodbyes and moved along so that those behind them could have their time with Monsignor Mike. As they walked away, Leah thought to herself, *"That's the first priest I've ever met in person, let alone had a friendly conversation with."* She squeezed J.P.'s hand. "There's something about him that I like. I hope I'm able to get to know him better."

They stopped at the grocery store for more supplies, things J.P. had forgotten about. They visited with Rich in the grocery store, who was eager to chat about the birthday party the night before.

Rich joked, "Why don't you have your new shirt on?" J.P. and Leah looked at each other quickly, struggling for a response. Rich added, "Well, it made it home, didn't it?" At that, both J.P. and Leah turned red in the face. Rich realized, a little too late, there was probably a story there, so he didn't push it.

On the way back to the farm, J.P. turned to Leah, who was dreamily looking out the window, watching the rows of corn fly by, fanning out repeatedly in the sun. "Daniel and I are harvesting again today. The elevator's not open, so we'll put the corn in the bin this time." He adjusted the rear view mirror. "We try not to work on Sundays, but during harvest we tend to make an exception."

When they got home, they made sandwiches together while joking and chatting casually. He packed a small cooler with the sandwiches and a few drinks. "Is this the way you always do meals?"

"Yep. We've got to eat when we have time, or when we get hungry. Not easy to plan."

They took the Dodge and stopped at Daniel's to pick him up, then headed to Doc's, where all the machinery had spent the night. They were moving to Joseph's farm to harvest corn there.

J.P. left with the tractor and grain cart, Daniel brought the combine, and Leah lead the group with the flashers on in the Dodge. Monsignor Mike's words came back to her, *"Don't count yourself short."* She *was* a part of all this. *Just look!* She was one of the drivers in the harvest parade, moving slowly down the road. She sat just a little taller in the seat.

All of the machinery had CB radios, so they could communicate with each other when needed. As they moved into the field, JP's voice crackled on. "Leah, do you want to ride in the combine?"

After a few moments of fumbling, Leah found the right button on the mic and said "Yes, I do!" Once they reached a place to stop, Daniel got out and helped her climb up into the cab of the combine. They started back up again, through the field and along the dirt road that

CHAPTER 24

she and J.P. took the first time she had visited in July, to move cattle.

At that time, in the Chevy pickup, it seemed like the corn was so tall they were driving through a tunnel. Up in the combine cab, the perspective was different; you were looking *down* at the corn stalks. Leah had thought she was sitting high in the *truck*, but today she was twice as far off the ground. She watched in awe as material fed into the combine. Daniel called it "the throat," so feeding it made sense. In the mirror she could see a bunch of different things coming out — the cobs, leaves, and shucks. Behind the seat through two windows, she could see the kernels of corn. It looked like a volcano erupting, not with hot lava, but with golden corn, hundreds, thousands, millions of kernels piling up.

Leah stared, entranced as she watched the mound turn into a hill of corn just inches from her.

Daniel smiled and said, "This is good corn." He pointed at a monitor that flashed numbers, reading *170s-180s-190s*.

Leah squinted. "What does that mean?"

"That's the number of bushels per acre."

"How big is an acre?"

"How about I just show you? Notice where we are now, and I'll tell you when another acre gets done."

She nodded. "How big is a bushel?"

"Approximately every 56 pounds of corn is a bushel." Daniel could tell by her puzzled look that his explanation hadn't been helpful. "When the bin in the combine is full, there'll be close to 350 bushels of corn, or about two acres." He pointed out the window, behind them. "Remember four minutes ago, when I said we would start an acre?"

"I do."

"Well, we just finished it." As they turned the combine around, Leah looked back to where they had come from, toward the dirt road.

"Okay. So that's an acre. That helps a little."

As the combine made its way through the field, J.P. pulled alongside them with the tractor and grain cart. Daniel pushed a small lever to extend the unloading auger, then pushed a button that caused a river of corn to run into the cart. All of this happened as they continued moving through the field. She actually was getting dizzy from all of the action. It seemed as if everything was in motion, and in truth, it was. Parts and corn were constantly moving, working together.

Leah felt like queen of the combine, sitting so high up. The lady of the farm, the helper of harvest. She grabbed the CB and called out, "Hey, Country Pumpkin! You know what you're doing over there?"

She could hear him chuckle as he answered, "Maybe I do. How about you? Is Daniel letting you drive yet?"

She scoffed. "Just about! There are only twenty or so buttons and levers, and one big steering wheel. I think I've got it down!" He shot her a wink and gave her a thumbs up.

When they got back to the end of the field, they had emptied the combine yet again. JP headed to the farmsite with the grain to unload.

As they turned the combine around and through the field again, Daniel turned to Leah. "You know, Dad and I talk almost daily."

She smiled at him. "I figured you did."

Daniel continued, "The first week Dad was at the garage, he told me, 'George and the old boys are friendly, but the gal who works there,' he said, 'I don't know about her.'"

Leah blushed with embarrassment. Her chest tightened every time she thought about the way she had acted all those months ago.

"Then every week, Dad would say he either went to a baseball game with you, or golfing, or watched a movie, went on a picnic, or went dancing. Next thing I know he's bringing you back to the farm for a visit."

Leah could tell he had more to say, so she waited, trying to focus on the rows of corn ahead of her.

"After seeing you two dance last night, I would say the 'I don't know about her,' has been long left in the past."

There was silence, or as close to it as you could get with the steady hum of the corn being harvested in the background. She wanted to tell him that was the *old* Leah. That she had spent years fitting a nice

CHAPTER 24

protective layer over herself — protection from feeling too much — and that Joseph had peeled it away, layer by layer.

Leah finally was able to find the words. "George had been through so many guys — some didn't even make it a week — so I never knew how to take them."

Daniel could tell by the tears in Leah's eyes that there was more to her answer, but he didn't push her.

She felt her eyes begin to sting. *Why does this family make me cry?*

As she wiped a rogue tear from her cheek, she knew the answer. It was the price she was paying to feel life again to its fullest.

"Daniel, your dad has become so much more than a friend."

Daniel nodded. He understood. "Dad is a person you want on your side."

"Hmm," She murmured. "That's true. I hadn't thought of it like that."

"He thinks with his head *and* his heart, and when he makes a decision he backs it up with passion."

That was right, and Leah knew it. He had perfectly summed up her Joseph in a single sentence. From baseball, to dancing, to making love... passion. Always.

As they reached the far end of the field, Leah could see Joseph once again making his way toward them.

"This is quite a three generation family, Daniel," she pronounced proudly. As she watched her love approach, she desperately hoped that, someday, she could actually be a part of it.

When they got back to the Dodge, Leah thanked Daniel. As she was climbing down from the combine cab he called out, "No, thank *you* Leah." Hearing the emotion in his voice, she simply smiled at him and hopped to the ground. She'd had enough emotional discussions for one day.

She drove the Dodge to the house, headed straight inside for a glass of water, and practically fell into the recliner. She was exhausted. Being out late two nights in a row, plus two long, emotional talks with Kate and Daniel... it had been wonderful but completely draining. Leah dozed off to sleep, her mind drifting into a dream.

She was a little girl, ten years old, playing in what seemed like a park. There were flower beds with blooming flowers, tall trees, and the grass was dark green. She was wearing her favorite dress — white with ruffled short sleeves, trimmed in pink.

"She was running happily, her shoulder length blonde hair waiving" as she ran. At the far end of the park was her mother, standing with open arms. Leah ran faster and faster, and as she got closer, she could hear her mother calling, "Come to me, Leah!"

She got so near, she could see her mother smiling with her clear, blue eyes. Leah couldn't wait to jump into her mother's arms for an embrace... but when she jumped, it was Joseph's arms that caught her.

She was suddenly a young lady of twenty. A strong youthful J.P. was spinning around and around in slow motion. She felt like she was riding a merry-go-round. As she looked at her surroundings, she realized they were in a flower garden — no, they were in the middle of the wildflower patch that was in Joseph's pasture. They continued to spin, lazily, happily staring into each other's eyes.

Leah woke up to the sound of Joseph pulling into the farmyard with the tractor and grain cart. She didn't want to move off the chair too quickly, afraid she would still be dizzy from all of the spinning. As she started to think clearly, she shook her head. *What a silly thought; it was only a dream.* She put the footrest down, stood up and, to her surprise, found that the room was, in fact, turning. She sat back down, bewildered, and took a sip of water to make sure she actually was awake.

Finally feeling steady, Leah moved quickly to the picture window to make it in time to catch Joseph driving by. Smiling, she did the "thing" and sent him a subtle wave with her finger as he and the tractor chugged out of view.

The men quit harvesting before dark. Joseph and Leah were looking forward to a long evening together. After supper, Joseph dug out a couple of photo albums, as well as his senior high school annual.

"That reminds me," Leah added, "Tomorrow, I want some pictures of us. You know... the harvest crew." She gave him a sheepish smile.

CHAPTER 24

They talked about anything and everything — their sons, school, their favorite subjects, their grades, their hopes and dreams. Even a few embarrassing moments.

As the conversation moved to bigger topics, like God and their faith, Leah brought up Mass.

"I have to admit, I was so scared to step into that church, that first time you asked me to go."

He put his hand on hers. "I know. I'm happy you went."

She gave his hand a squeeze. "You know, there's something interesting about that Monsignor Mike. I don't know what it is, but I like him."

He laughed. "Yep, he's got a gift when it comes to speaking to people's hearts, and he sure is good at making a person feel welcome." Leah agreed.

There were a few moments of silence, then Joseph decided to take a leap into the next big topic. "How about us?" he asked.

She wasn't startled by the question — they had both been waiting for this discussion for a while. Joseph continued, "If or *when* I — or we — come back to the farm, I'd like to do it by March 1st. That's when the spring calving starts. You could move all of your things, and whatever else you really needed. When my divorce is final, then we can make more decisions."

Leah sucked in a deep breath. This would be the biggest move of her life. Not only in location, but also mentality. If she were honest, though, she had been dreaming about this for weeks, since the evening they moved Nick into the dorm, actually. It was time to start thinking about moving on, with her own life.

Her face broke into a grin. "That is almost exactly what I was thinking." *Could it be that easy? So simple?* She doubted it, but if there was one thing Joseph had taught her, it was that sometimes, it really *was* that simple. Was she apprehensive about moving on from her past, and further away from Nick and George? Of course, but it was time to think about the future, too. Her future with Joseph.

That night, they went to sleep in each other's arms. There were nights of racing passion and searing heat, and then there were nights like that one — warm and intimate, a quiet, dozing promise.

Once again Leah awoke in the morning to the smell of bacon and hurried upstairs, to find Joseph at the stove. Pleased with the view, she watched him for a couple of seconds from around the corner. He was concentrating on turning the bacon so it was perfect for her — just the way she liked it, good and crispy. She swooned for a moment at his habit of always putting care and effort into the task at hand. Finally, she snuck behind him and gave him a hug. She snuggled her face between his shoulder blades and asked, "Joseph, will you keep making perfect bacon for me when we live here?" Her whole body tingled at the words "we" and "here."

"If you like. I'm sure I'll wake up before you every morning, anyway. You know me; home by midnight and up by 5:00." He pulled two plates from the cupboard. "By the way, the only meals I know *how* to make are bacon for breakfast, and cheeseburgers for all the rest."

"I know better than that," she purred, thinking back to their picnic feast, "but I guess I'll risk it and give you a try."

A chuckle at that rumbled in his chest as he plated up the bacon. "I'm going to haul corn to the elevator, you want to go?"

"Of course I do! How could you do it without me?"

Leah rode with Joseph all morning in the truck until they got back to the field at noon and stopped for sandwiches. She had brought a camera with her this time, and was excited to use it. She had Daniel take a picture of her and Joseph standing in front of the combine — easy proof to show Julie and George that she had actually been out in the field harvesting.

J.P. put his arm around Leah's shoulders. "When are you heading back for home?"

She hadn't expected the word "home" to sound so strange in that sentence. Her definition of home was changing with every hour that she spent with Joseph on the farm.

CHAPTER 24

She answered cheerfully, however. "No special time." The truth was, Leah didn't want to leave. If she left today, she wouldn't see Joseph again until sometimes Saturday. That would be the longest they'd gone without seeing each other since they had met almost six months ago. Leah chose to take a few more trips with Joseph, hauling corn to the elevator.

When it was time to get ready to leave, J.P. and Leah drove to the house so that Leah could gather her belongings. Joseph backed the Chevelle by the barn so he could wash and wipe it off for its trip to the city.

When she came out of the house, she took a moment to watch Joseph wiping down the Chevelle in front of the smiling barn. When Kate had brought pumpkins over to the farm, she had put some by the house, and had also put about half a dozen of them in the wheelbarrow in front of the barn. How fitting, her country pumpkin working side-by-side with a wheelbarrow full of cheerful, orange pumpkins. She grinned, and then ran back inside to grab her camera.

She returned breathless. "I have to have a picture of you and the Chevelle!" Joseph's eyes twinkled, actually eager for the picture. He couldn't remember ever having been separated from the Chevelle before.

So, J.P. carefully leaned against the Chevelle with a smile on his face, his arms crossed, and his cowboy hat resting nonchalantly on his head. Leah worked around and got an angle she wanted.

Joseph, the Chevelle, the wheelbarrow of pumpkins, and the smiling barn. A perfect picture.

He backed the Chevelle onto the drive next to the house, remembering the first time he gave Leah a ride in the Chevelle, smoking the tires and showing off. He carried Leah's bags out and put them in the backseat, shooting her a sneaky raised eyebrow at another shared memory. Both Leah and JP thought about the backseat but neither said a word about it.

They embraced for a long time, the warm breeze surrounding them, lightly whipping Leah's hair as she leaned into J.P. They looked into each other's eyes, flashing her back to the first time they met —

she had barely glanced at him, and now she couldn't pull her eyes away from his. Joseph thought, "My house feels like a home now."

They both wanted time to stop, simply be put on hold until they were ready to let go. The only time Leah could remember feeling like that was when she rocked her infant Nick to sleep. Perhaps those times when the music of the piano felt like making love — sweet and intoxicating. Star gazing, staring at the wildflowers with Joseph... those times could have slowed a little, too, and she wouldn't have complained.

This was saying goodbye to her past and welcoming her future. She didn't feel sadness about putting her old life behind her — simply glad to look back on what she had, and celebrate what was ahead. Another lesson learned from her country pumpkin.

"You have a nice week, Leah. I'll see you Saturday evening."

"You sure you can get along harvesting without me?"

He clucked his tongue. "Well, it'll be tough without my co-driver. See? I've helped you out at the station and you've helped me on the farm. I think we're even."

She chuckled. "I don't know how much help I've been."

"More than you will ever know."

As Leah pulled away in the Chevelle J.P. squinted into the sunset and thought, "There goes my past, and my future." He had been driving that Chevelle for 31 years, and if he had Leah for the next 31, he'd have lived a good life.

If the rest of his days were going to be anything like the last six months, he couldn't wait.

As she drove slowly out of the farmsite and onto the gravel road, she could see Daniel in the combine working toward the end of the field. She could see the truck and grain cart were peaked with mountains of golden corn, and that a hill was rising in the combine. She realized that the time Joseph had just spent with her had put him behind schedule. She smiled and shook her head. Of course he hadn't said anything — not once in the last 30 minutes had he mentioned or gave a clue that he had to get back to work.

CHAPTER 24

When Leah passed the dirt road that lead through the field, she pulled over and came to a stop. That road had taken her and Joseph to move cows for the first time. She had watched in awe as he, the animals, and the tall prairie grass had moved and worked together as one. The wildflower patch and the windmill breezed through her mind. She waved a goodbye to Daniel as they passed each other.

Caught up in all her whimsy, Leah thought, *"How could a simple dirt road have such meaning?"* She had been on streets and highways her whole life, but none had brought a smile to her face like this dirt road. She laughed at herself and put the Chevelle back in gear, and headed toward Frankton.

As she made her way through and out of town, she made sure to note all of her favorite milestones — the ancient houses, the Loup River bridge. She should have been the nervous one the first time they crossed it, but Joseph had been the one rattling away.

Leah had a safe trip back to the city. She parked the Chevelle carefully in front of her house, anxious for Julie to come over. She couldn't wait to show her the Chevelle and tell her all about the long weekend.

When Julie arrived, Leah showed off the impressive car — unable to keep the details about the backseat a secret. Giggling hysterically, they looked quickly around to see if anyone had caught them acting like a couple of teenagers.

Their customary long walk was the perfect way to end the long weekend. She replayed all of the details — harvest, the birthday party, the long talks with Joseph and his family. The two women chatted, laughed, and sighed together, thrilled to have something new and positive to add to their conversations.

When they got back from their walk, Leah decided to take the Chevelle to the staton and put it in for the night. She called George, and he met them at the station.

George was so excited about the Chevelle, he had her park it in the front show window. She was happy to tell him and Julie the story behind the car, knowing the connection to Vietnam would especially strike George, who secretly hoped the Chevelle would stay right there for a long time.

As Leah got ready for bed that night, she had never felt so elated and exhausted at the same time. As she dozed off to sleep, she once again murmured a quiet prayer, "Thank you for the beautiful harvest. Thank you for Joseph."

CHAPTER 25

At the service station, the Chevelle was the centerpiece of conversation. They were all proud of it, from Leah and George to the old boys, Fred and Pete. She got out the picture of her and Joseph standing in front of the combine and showed them all, while giving them the rundown of the whole harvesting operation. She delighted in talking about delivering the corn to the elevator, about riding in the combine, and how the grain cart drives alongside it. The boys were impressed and said that she sounded like a "Little Miss Farmer." Leah smiled from ear to ear with the thought of the farm life fresh in her mind.

Every time Leah looked up from her desk, the Chevelle was there, glinting in the sunlight. It was hard to concentrate with such a bright reminder of times spent blasting down the highway, laughing in the backseat, and the promise it meant for her future.

When Thursday came, the first thing Leah did was call Joseph and wish him a happy birthday.

"Why, thanks, Leah." She could hear his happiness through the phone.

"I wish we could be together."

"Ah, well, we already had a party."

"I know, but I can still wish for it, can't I?"

His low laugh rolled through the speaker against her ear. "I'll be back Saturday, and I promise we'll do something together."

That didn't offer Leah much comfort, so she just said, "I miss you."

"You taking care of the Chevelle?"

"I sure am. I'd even say it's the new pride and joy of the station." Her voice softened. "I always make sure to tell everyone its story." She could practically hear him smiling through the phone, pleased that Glen was getting recognition, even now. Leah added, "I have the picture of us standing in front of the combine on my desk, and you'd better believe I gave the guys a full description of being on the harvest crew.

J.P.'s sweet laugh rumbled quietly. "You're just a regular country belle aren't you?"

Her response was quick. "You give me the time, and I will be."

His response was just as fast. "I'll give you all the time in the world."

After a pause, J.P. went on, "You tell George and the guys that harvest is going great, and please let George know how much I appreciate getting the week off to go home for harvest."

"I'll do that." Her heart warmed at the word "home." With any luck, the farm would someday be her home, too. The sooner, the better.

Leah was anxious for the weekend, and excited to finally get to see Joseph. She tried to busy herself around the house, but didn't have much luck keeping her mind off of him, wishing it was last Saturday all over again; popping in at the store, making lunch for the harvest.

J.P.'s phone call at noon broke her from her thoughts, but it made her longing for him even stronger.

"It's been a good week," he said. "We actually got a lot more done than I had hoped."

"That's great!"

"We've also been moving cattle, letting them out on the stock fields."

Leah couldn't help herself, and chirped, "Did you honk the horn and call them 'Bossy?'"

"Why, yes I did."

She made herself a cup of tea, trying not to make too much noise. Stirring in some sugar, she asked, "Do any of the cows have actual names? Besides bossy?"

Knowing Leah was poking fun, he muttered "Only when they're

CHAPTER 25

naughty." His voice turning to a purr, he added, "You haven't been naughty lately, have you?"

Even miles away, she blushed. "Let me think... hmm, not since the last time I went to country school." She raised an eyebrow, "It must be something about the country, because I never broke the rules like that in *my* school."

J.P. laughed. "It must be the company you've been keeping."

Giving up the banter, Leah's voice warmed. "I'd say it is. And I love him to death."

"I love you, too, Leah. I plan on loving you until the end of time."

She didn't know what to say to that, so she simply sat there, and soaked it in.

J.P. cleared his throat. "I plan on heading back to the city at 6:00. I'll call you when I get back."

"Sounds good!"

"What should we do tonight?"

"It's up to you! You've been the birthday boy for a week now, so it's up to you."

"Okay, then, how about you see if you can find someplace that has a dance tonight?"

Her heartbeat picked up its pace. "I will do that! I can't wait. Hurry back to me, my country pumpkin."

Thinking about the evening ahead — holding each other and dancing — surprisingly made the afternoon go by quickly for both of them. Dancing had taken on a life of its own for them. From the first time they moved in time together, they both felt it. It was love in motion.

Before J.P. left the farm, he made sure to visit Daniel and tell him how proud he was of him. That this year's harvest had been such a success, between his fine job and the help of Mother Nature.

He also stopped by to say goodbye to Kate. They talked about harvest and the nice weather, but of course their conversation turned to Leah.

"She's a good lady, Joseph. And she's good for you. I can see how you two look at each other, the sound of your voices when you talk. And you two dance together beautifully."

With a tight chest, Joseph said "Thanks, Mom. It means a lot, coming from you." He ran a nervous hand through his hair. "In fact, Leah and I might be moving back to the farm this spring. Together."

Elated by the news, Kate threw her arms around J.P.'s neck in a giant, heart-filled hug.

As J.P. and the Dodge headed back to the city, thoughts of the last week — being back on the farm, Daniel's fantastic job with such a good crop, the surprise of the birthday party — swirled around in his mind. He thought about the two very important ladies in his life, and how someday soon, he would have them both close by, each and every day. He watched the farm equipment flash by as he drove, wondering if their harvest was panning out as well as his own.

As he turned east on Highway 34, J.P. was halfway back to the city. One hour left until he arrived at his little house to get ready to go dancing with Leah. The thought of going dancing had him excited. He kept changing the radio stations to find the perfect music to match his mood.

The sun was almost ready to go down directly behind J.P. and the shadows were long. He was having a hard time staying strapped in his seatbelt because he was gliding across the dance floor, listening to George Strait and dancing with Leah in his head.

As he looked to his left, he could see a John Deere combine turning around near the highway with a mountain of golden corn in its bin, dust and chewed-up stalks and shucks coming from the rear of it.

As J.P. turned his attention back to the highway, there it was. Identical to the truck he had been driving all week — fifty tons — making a wide turn onto the highway.

The driver never did see the Dodge, between looking into the sun and the dust from the combine, it had been camouflaged.

There was no hope of J.P. making it safely back to the city. Instead

CHAPTER 25

of being the last leg of his trip, it was the start of his final journey.

J.P. had seen the truck and swerved to the right. The back left corner on the truck's trailer hit the Dodge's driver side.

He was taken to the local hospital. His injuries didn't appear serious, but what was most noticeable was the bump on the left side of his head. He was in and out of consciousness for moments, mumbling that his head hurt.

The doctors agreed that J.P. had symptoms of a brain bleed with blood collecting near the temple. The immediate step was to perform a CT scan to assess the severity of his injury. After the two doctors studied the results, they concluded that the injury had caused an aneurysm, but the bleeding had stopped.

Daniel received a call from the sheriff's department, and learned that his father was at the York County Hospital. Daniel looked at his watch — 8:45 pm — and decided not to inform Grandma Kate for the time being, until he had more details. After deliberating for a few moments, he called George and asked him to tell Leah in person.

George called Julie and asked if she would go with him, and they were on their way to Leah's house in less than 20 minutes.

As the two made the short drive, Leah had just begun to wonder when she would hear from Joseph. When she answered the door to George and Julie rather than the man she loved, time slowed down all around her.

The Leah of six months ago wouldn't have been able to handle the news without shattering. At that moment, though, Leah was calm. She asked for details, but George didn't have any other than the fact that J.P. was at the hospital in York.

She barely heard him say, "Daniel's going to call as soon as possible with any news."

CHAPTER 26

In about an hour, Leah and Julie arrived at the hospital. After a long hug and introductions, Daniel filled them in.

"There's nothing new. He's in an observation room; that's all the nurse told me." As they waited, Herb, Kate, and Ranee arrived at the hospital.

At midnight, the two doctors met with all of them in a conference room near the lobby. A young, tired doctor rubbed his face with hands for a moment, and said, "The impact caused bleeding on the left side of J.P.'s brain. The result is what we call an intracranial hemorrhage. The bleeding has stopped, which is good news. That means we didn't need to perform surgery."

Leah took a deep breath to help her focus on what the doctors were saying.

The older doctor took over. "This kind of injury is severe, but, as Dr. Todd stated, the bleeding has stopped. We've given J.P. a drug called nimodipine, which is given to reduce the blood supply to the brain. The next 24 to 72 hours are critical as we watch to make sure this injury doesn't start leaking or rupture."

Leah took the moment to sit down; she felt as if the room was spinning.

"What kind of future issues and recovery are we looking at?" Daniel asked.

Dr. Todd cleared his throat. "Approximately 75% of patients with the injury do survive, but many of the survivors have lasting effects. Many patients have stroke-like symptoms, such as vision problems,

CHAPTER 26

slurred speech, and movement paralysis."

"When can we see him?" Kate asked.

"We've given J.P. a sedative, so he is sleeping now. We will keep him in the ICU to keep him under observation. When we believe he's stable enough, we'll allow you to see him."

After a polite goodbye, the doctors left the room, taking all the oxygen with them. They had presented the facts as simply and kindly as they could, but that didn't change the eerie silence, the degree of disbelief and shock that settled over them all.

Leah looked around, noting that each of them had shown such different reactions to the news. Daniel stood straight and tall, receiving strength from somewhere. He reminded her so much of his father, she had a pretty good idea of where that strength came from.

Ranee was crying into her mother's arms as Kate's lips moved silently, her fingers gripping the Rosary she always kept with her. Herb had left the room and gone outside to be by himself in the fresh air.

Leah turned to Julie, surprised to find that her friend was the one crying. Leah's cheeks were dry as she pulled her strength from her memories of Joseph; the knowledge that he had changed her for the better. From the first rose at the station to even that awful 4th of July, she could find love in every moment with him. All these racing memories flooded her mind, providing the foundation she was standing on in that moment.

At 2:00 am, they were all summoned into the same conference room as before.

"J.P.'s vitals are stable and that is good news." Dr. Todd looked considerably more tired than before. "But an injury such as this is challenging to monitor. We'll keep J.P. as still as possible and give him minimal pain relievers."

"Minimal?" asked Leah.

"Yes. Pain relievers thin the blood, and that's not what we want right now. When J.P. was admitted we gave him a sedative, but we'll begin lowering those amounts. If he stays calm we won't have to continue that part of his treatment."

This news sprouted a lightness in Leah's heart. The one thing she had desperately been hoping for was to have a conversation with her Joseph.

Her face must have betrayed her thoughts, because Dr. Todd continued cautiously. "Please understand; we don't know what effects this will have on J.P. I'm hesitant to get anyone's hopes up."

His words, combined with the look on his face — it was like someone had punched Leah in the stomach.

Dr. Todd proceeded. "The main concern for J.P. with this injury is the possibility of blood flowing in the hemorrhage. If it's a slow leak we may be able to perform surgery, but if there is a rupture, there's nothing we can do. The brain will lose its ability to function. There is also a risk of infection, which we'll watch closely. When J.P. regains consciousness and is aware of his surroundings, we'll talk to him, and do some tests to see where we stand." He gestured toward J.P.'s room. "You are welcome to be with J.P. while we wait for him to come around."

When they entered the hospital room, Leah and Kate each went to J.P.'s side. He looked as if he was peacefully sleeping, the only evidence of the accident being a small bump on the left side of his head.

As Leah's hand held J.P.'s, she felt relief flood into her. First, she took a deep breath and released it slowly — it felt like she'd been holding her breath for hours. As soon as she touched him, it was as though she received something; what she'd been getting from Joseph for months. Calm and strength.

As dawn began to show itself, J.P. started to stir. His hands fluttered, and there was a twitch in his eyes. The nurses immediately called for the on-duty doctor.

The doctor who came into the room was neither Dr. Todd nor the older doctor from the night before. He politely asked everyone to leave the room so that he and the nurses could evaluate J.P.'s injury.

Once the family had left the room, Dr Mark calmly stated his name and said, "J.P. you are at York Community Hospital, and last

CHAPTER 26

evening you were in a vehicular collision. If you understand, very carefully nod your head."

Even though J.P.'s mind was foggy, he understood, and slightly nodded. Before the doctor continued, he became aware of his headache.

Dr. Mark continued. "The blow that you received on the left side of your head caused an aneurysm." He explained the definition of an aneurysm, but J.P. already knew. His concentration turned to the people he knew who had experienced them.

Fifteen years ago, his neighbor, Mrs. Stroud, had one. He remembered the time she stayed in the hospital, how she was never able to see again. And he remembered that she passed away after only a week. On the other hand, J.P. had a cousin who'd been in the hospital for three or four weeks, and had lived a normal life since her recovery.

Dr. Mark brought J.P. back to the moment with his pen light, and asked to look into J.P.'s eyes. Until then, J.P. hadn't focused on his vision. When the short examination was complete, the doctor asked J.P. to look up to the ceiling, then toward the door. J.P. realized how blurry his vision was.

"Okay, J.P. Please move your left hand."

J.P.'s hand lifted slowly off the bed.

"And now the right."

J.P. tried. There was no lift, but his fingers did move.

Dr. Mark gave the nurses a concerned glance. Paralysis.

"Thank you, J.P. Next, can you tell me your full name?"

J.P. opened his mouth, and something like a *J* sound emerged. J.P. tried to clear his throat, and tried again. This time, something like *"Jo-eff"* came out.

Dr. Mark began speaking again, but J.P. was paying very little attention. He was thinking about the work ahead of him, what he'd need to do to have a hopeful, normal life. He quietly slipped back into unconsciousness.

For the third time in less than 12 hours, Leah and J.P.'s family were being updated in the small conference room.

Dr. Mark told them that while J.P.'s vitals were good, the damage done by the aneurysm had left J.P. with some physical concerns. "I believe the vision in his right eye is affected, but at this point I don't know how bad it is. J.P. can move his left arm and leg, and his right fingers do move slightly. His speech, unfortunately, was not clear."

"Do you have any idea what his recovery will look like? How long it will take?" Daniel asked what they were all wondering.

"The testing I performed is just the beginning. In cases like this there is a wide range of recovery. Some patients recover to a normal life relatively quickly, while others' progress is slow." He paused, took a breath. "Some simply do not recoup. We are in the early stages of this situation. I know this is difficult to hear, but time will be the deciding factor. While we wait, however, you are welcome to sit with him."

It was near noon on Sunday when J.P. started to stir. Time was immeasurable; he couldn't tell if minutes were flying by or standing still.

The next reality to register was Kate's voice, and at the same instant he felt someone holding his left hand. He knew it was Leah, her hands were always warm.

In normal life, many humans believe speaking — and the understanding of speech — is one of the most treasured things our senses afford us. For J.P. in that moment, however, touch was the lifeline holding him afloat. He could feel Leah's hand, and that was all that mattered to him. Smell and taste were irrelevant, and he could only vaguely hear his mother's sweet voice.

As J.P.'s mind came out of the fog, his sight became focused. He could see Daniel, Kate, and Leah surrounding him. To his ultimate surprise, however, hovering at the end of his bed was Claire.

When she could see that J.P. was coherent, she stepped alongside him and whispered, "J.P., I'm so sorry. I never hated you. I hated the farm. I just didn't love it like you did." She stopped for a moment to take a few deep breaths. "It wore me down. When I started working off the farm, I felt so free! I had independence from the awful spell

CHAPTER 26

that the farm had on me, and... I'm sorry I let it tear us apart." Claire bit her lip as she let her eyes rest on his. Her confession wasn't quite complete, but it was close. She leaned down to give him a soft kiss on the cheek and stood up without telling him her secret — that deep down, she still loved him.

She gave Daniel and Kate tearful hugs, then gave Leah's hand a firm squeeze. Claire left the room without another word.

J.P. looked at each of his loved ones in that cold, quiet room. He wanted to speak to each of them, but he knew his words wouldn't come out the way he wanted. He was thinking clearly about each of them, however, and what he wanted to say.

To Daniel, J.P. would have said how proud of him he was. For his work this year on the farm and for the young man that he had become. His will granted everything on the farm to him, and included an insurance policy. J.P. couldn't think of a better person to carry on the family tradition.

To Kate, J.P. would simply say, "Thank you." For being a fine mother to him, and for passing down her kind ways, and the values he holds so dear.

Finally, J.P. looked at Leah and thanked God that he found her. The last six months had been the best his life had ever seen. He found the romance he had always dreamed of. To give and to receive that kind of love was a blessing. He gave Leah's hand a squeeze, and was able to give her a slight smile.

With that last smile, he found a quiet peace, and there was an absence of light.

A loud beeping sound blared from the monitor. The nurse called "Code blue!" over the intercom.

As the doctors rushed into the room, the nurse asked Leah and J.P.'s family to wait in the conference room.

As Dr. Todd and Dr. Mark entered the room, Leah tore her eyes from the checkered tile floor to look at their faces.

As if the load they were carrying was heavy, both doctors' shoulders were slumped and sagging.

"We're so sorry. J.P. experienced another hemorrhage." Dr. Todd swallowed. "We tried emergency surgery, but the damage was already done."

Leah could have sworn the air in the room suddenly weighed a ton. She felt like she was suffocating.

Daniel stood tall and straight, even though it was taking the last of his strength to do so.

Kate's lips were quivering as she continued to pray.

Dr. Todd proceeded with the tough job at hand. "Whenever we have a patient with a very serious injury, it's procedure to see if they are an organ donor. J.P.'s driver's license indicated that he is. We will transfer J.P. to Lincoln East hospital, as that location is an organ transplant location." His eyes creased with sadness, he said, "You may go spend time with J.P."

The only sound in the room was the hum of the monitor. They knew that J.P. was free and no longer in pain.

CHAPTER 27

They knew J.P. was free, and no longer in pain. The only sound in the room, the ventilator sighed heavily.

Daniel's was running the last week through his mind. It had been the best week they ever had together. They worked together so smoothly, and on the most impressive harvest they ever had. He thought of watching his dad hustle from the tractor with the auger wagon and smiled, just a bit. His dad had been so happy at his birthday party, happier than he'd ever seen him.

Kate's tears were for the plans Joseph had made — he and Leah coming back to the farm next spring — and for their final, big hug the night before. Their last one.

Leah softly touched his left cheek, undeservedly slapped by women who didn't understand. She laid her hand on his chest, and wondered who would receive his heart. Would they feel life as Joseph does? She studied his face. Would the person who regained sight because of him see beauty in everything? From ants to wildflowers to giant, lumbering cows? She shook the thoughts out of her head.

Daniel and Leah were already holding Joseph's hands. Kate moved forward and connected them all with hers. Quietly, they recited the Lord's Prayer together, knowing J.P. wouldn't have wanted it any other way. Daniel's lips parted, and his deep voice filled the room. "May the angels lead you on this journey, and may our Heavenly Father receive you with open arms."

Julie had stayed at the hospital for the duration and now she drove Leah home. Leah was exhausted physically and emotionally. Julie tucked her into bed, and went to sleep on the couch in the living room. After such a terrible weekend Leah was grateful that she fell asleep immediately.

Exhausted, Leah crashed into sleep, landing in a shimmering, vivid dream.

She found herself walking down the dirt road on Joseph's farm. She was walking west and the sun was getting low in the western sky. The corn was tall, just as it had been the first time Joseph had taken her to the farm. She looked ahead on the road and could see two people, standing tall and casting a long shadow in her direction. She continued walking toward them, the soft dirt sliding beneath her shoes. As she approached them in the dimming light, she knew within her heart that it was her mother and Joseph.

Her mother was wearing a pink pantsuit that Leah could remember her wearing on special occasions. Joseph was dressed to go dancing, sporting his black cowboy hat, favorite Wranglers, and his grandfather's cowboy boots.

When she got close enough, she could see that both of them were smiling. She reached desperately for their hands, and when they touched, she marveled as her mother transformed into an eight year old little girl, wearing a pink sundress. Joseph and Leah held hands, and started to move in a circle, like they were playing a child's game. Leah's mother giggled and clapped her hands as they turned slowly, around and around. Joseph had a smile on his face as he looked into Leah's eyes.

The only words that floated through the shimmering dream were Joseph's, as he held her gaze and whispered, "Everything is fine."

Leah awoke in the morning with a start — the dream still vivid and clinging to her mind, despite the fog from such a heavy sleep. Leah had never been a sentimental person, but she believed with all of her heart that the dream was a message from Joseph. *Everything would be fine.* When things were going well, Joseph would always

CHAPTER 27

sigh and say, "Isn't that heavenly?" He believed that, in heaven, we would be full of joy — like the happiest moments we've had here on earth. She chose to believe that Joseph had just sent her a little preview of what was to come.

When Leah shuffled into the kitchen, she found Julie and Nick were sitting at the table, chatting over cups of coffee. They both stood and enveloped her in a hug before grabbing another mug from the cupboard and filling it to the top. They sat around the table and visited, sharing memories of Joseph and how he changed their lives.

Finally, at noon Leah got dressed and suggested to Nick and Julie, "Let's go to the garage." Determined to find some structure and stick to a semblance of her routine, she knew the garage would provide some welcome distraction.

When George saw them park, he met them at the office door. George's cracked voice was muffled by their long hug, but she knew what he was saying. "I'm sorry, Leah."

He stepped back and adjusted his cap. He turned toward the shop window. "This morning I was sitting in the Chevelle, trying to feel better, and I..." He jammed his hands into his pockets and looked away. "Well, I looked into the console and I found an envelope. I put it in there so you'd have some privacy." He gestured to her office.

Leah sat down at her desk to find the envelope, the word *Leah* written in Joseph's careful, looping handwriting, and opened it.

In late afternoon when comes the losing of daylight,
  I think of our first date at the Starbrite.
  When the twinkle of stars come out at night,
  It reminds me of when I look into your eyes, knowing everything is alright,
  When I see the shining grin of the moon,
  It reminds me of your smile, and I stare at it like a loon.

I hope from now on, when you see a dove,
It reminds you, as it does me, of our love.
— J.P.

Her hand flew to her heart, sitting in the very place she had read the first poem he had ever written her. *How did he know?*

She shook her head — of course he hadn't known this would be the last note he'd write for her — but the promise in his words felt prophetic. With her eyes full of tears, Leah handed the note to Julie, who took a quick glance at it.

"You mind if I read this to George and the guys? I think they'd like it."

Leah nodded, and followed her out into the garage. Listening to the poem, telling stories about Joseph — it felt like a small memorial service, among the tireless cars and ancient oil stains. George cleared his throat.

"He once said to me, 'We all have a story,' and I'll never forget it. I knew right then and there he was something special."

Nick put an arm around Leah and said, "J.P. showed me more about baseball in five minutes than I had learned in years of being on the team." He told them about filling in divots on the infield, choking up on the bat, and stepping out of the batter's box to control the pitcher.

Leah leaned her head on her son's shoulder. "We were going to move back to the farm together. I was going to keep doing the books for the garage from Frankton, and do my best to be helpful."

She was grateful for George and the old boys, giving her something to smile at with jokes about being "Queen of the Farm."

When Julie offered to stay the night again, Leah surprised them both with a "No, thanks. I'd like to be alone." It seemed strange to say it, but she *was* alone now, truly alone. Nick had moved on to college, and she felt drawn toward moving forward on that journey by herself, at least for the night.

After Julie left, Leah took a short nap. Upon awakening, she felt

CHAPTER 27

like leaving the house, although she had no place in particular to go. So she simply drove. She rolled the windows down and shut the radio off, filling her mind with the sound of the wind and her thoughts. She couldn't remember what she was thinking about when she realized she'd stopped her vehicle in the parking lot of Nick's baseball field.

She stepped out of the Blazer and leaned against it, looking up to the bleachers, the top row, the far right. The exact spot that she and Joseph had claimed during Nick's baseball games. They had learned so much about each other up in those bleachers. As a tear slid down her cheek, she shook her head in disbelief. Who knew her son's baseball games would be such an important part of a romantic summer? She couldn't bring herself to actually *sit* in the bleachers; that would have been too much.

Leah headed her Blazer west on O Street. In minutes, she was at her destination, the Starbrite. She drove one slow trip around the parking lot, then finally came to a stop in the same spot that Joseph had parked that first night of dancing. As the memories flowed over her, she settled her forehead on the steering wheel. She remembered all the details of the evening — that cool, drizzly night was the first time in her life that a date had brought her flowers. How nervous she was when they started to dance! She knew that night while their feet floated together on the dance floor that she was in love with him. Joseph calmed her, and taught her how to follow his lead. Like he did in so many ways.

With that thought, she knew she had one more stop to make, and headed east back toward the city.

As Leah entered the cathedral, she could feel a disconnect between two worlds — warm and noisy outside and cool and quiet inside. At the holy water font, Leah dipped her right index finger into the water and touched her forehead. She had never made the sign of the cross before, so she did what felt comfortable, just a dip and touch

For a few seconds Leah wondered what she was doing there, in that unfamiliar pew, but her uncertainty didn't last long. Joseph had led Leah into church other times, and she was certain that it was Joseph who led her there today.

It had been seven days since she had helped Joseph harvest; seven days that felt like a lifetime. *"That's right,"* she thought. *"I did have a life before Joseph."* The last six months felt like a lifetime of their own — a Cinderella story. Joseph was both her country pumpkin and her prince, and as sure as she was sitting in church, she knew he was sent to her from heaven.

Leah opened her eyes, and they centered first on a statue of Mother Mary — a figure who could certainly understand the pain of loss — and then to a large wooden crucifix suspended from the ceiling. She realized the metal crucifix that Joseph wore was a small replica of this one, hanging in the cathedral.

Joseph believed and lived his faith — not only in the pew, but every day in the life he led — and Leah knew, with tear-filled eyes, that Joseph was with God.

When Leah wiped her eyes, and her vision became clear, she gasped. Directly below the cross, painted carefully on mahogany wood, were two mirrored doves.

Joseph's rumbling, kind voice emerged from her memories, and he whispered in her mind,

"I hope from now on, when you see a dove,
　It reminds you, as it does me, of our love."

Her footsteps echoed through the cathedral as she made her way to the main doors. Before she left, however, she stopped at the font, looked backward, and murmured, "Thank you."

CHAPTER 28

Leah arrived at Herb and Kate's farm later that week. Kate had called her earlier with the funeral arrangements, and the announcement that Joseph would be cremated.

It made sense, of course, but it was a shock nonetheless. She wouldn't be seeing Joseph again, not in his earthly body.

She had been greeted by Kate's arms, her tears, and a heartbroken whisper of, "Our Joseph!" They held each other tightly for a moment.

Kate pulled back a little, and looked her in the eye. "Before Joseph left on Saturday, he stopped by here to say goodbye. He told me of your plans to move back to the farm next spring." She swallowed down a sob. "He was beaming with excitement. Joseph had told everyone he was going to the city in search of work, but I knew he was in search of *someone*. He had me and Daniel, but he wanted more. Joseph became whole by loving you."

Taken aback, Leah stared open-mouthed at the woman before her. Joseph was so kind, so thoughtful, so loyal. He was vibrant and observant, compassionate and never pushy. His small question — *"Do you want to go to church with me?"* — had changed her entire life. How could she have made *him* whole?

With a squeeze, Kate added, "I hope you get some rest. It's going to be a difficult week."

The week was difficult, but Leah also found it to be beautiful. There was visitation and there were scripture readings, and a seemingly endless parade of the people who knew and loved Joseph, all eager to express their gratitude for her country pumpkin.

Following the scripture reading, many people came forward to share their stories, but the one that struck her most was a young man — his friend Rich's son — who stepped up to the small church microphone.

"J.P. has been my friend my whole life. Honestly, I can't remember *not* knowing him. Even in my youngest memories, one thing never changed — J.P. *always* had candy." The entire congregation laughed knowingly, and Leah's heart soared. "It didn't matter if I was 5, 10, or 15, JP always talked to me one-on-one. I don't know if he felt like a kid, or if he made me feel older, but he always made me feel important."

As the stories went on, Leah delighted in hearing new stories about the man she loved. While each memory was unique, they all had the same theme: J.P. was a kind and humble friend who saw the beauty in everything, and, above all, he knew how to love.

The next morning Leah met George, Julie, and Nick early in the St. Peter's parking lot. She appreciated Kate and Daniel's offer to let her sit with them, but she was going to sit with her family today.

As Leah entered the church she felt different; her mind was aware, but her body was numb. Her heart was heavy, but the Holy Spirit was giving her the gift of faith and hope, even if she didn't realize that's what it was.

Leah led her family to the pew she had shared with Joseph. They were surprised when she knelt down. She had never given church a second thought, but it was recently becoming second nature to her. As the church filled to over-capacity, Leah realized they were only four of four hundred people there to say goodbye. In awe, she settled in for the service, which ended up being comforting and uplifting; exactly what she needed.

When Monsignor Mike was finished with the gospel reading, he came down and stood next to the urn and near the family. At the sight of the urn, and the tribute that had been lovingly placed next to it, her heart stopped and her breath whooshed from her lips.

CHAPTER 28

There, on an end table was Joseph's dancing cowboy boots with his black cowboy hat tipped on top of them. Tears welled up in her eyes. These were the boots and hat that Joseph would have worn to their next night of dancing. As Leah cleared her eyes, she refocused on the chain with its crucifix, draped gently over the boots.

"Monsignor Mike's voice filled the sanctuary. He started by saying, "Joseph learned the lessons of life, and he loved them well." The people who spoke last evening testified to that. How could there be a more important task, than making a child feel important? Joseph did that. Jesus did that when he told the women, 'Let the children come to me, for they will be saved.'

As a baseball coach, Joseph believed you did the small things right to become better. As it was said last night, 'We were winners who won, but never bragged about it. You just gave it your best.' In his faith, he believed that as well. For many years, he opened the doors for people and welcomed them into this church as an usher. He was welcoming them to know God. That is Joseph down to his boots — in life, love, and faith.

"He was a generous, humble friend; a servant to not only our Heavenly Father, but to anyone who was in need. That was Joseph." Monsignor Mike took a moment, then continued. "Joseph had considered many places home. Certainly his farm was home. The community was home. St. Peter's was also home. He had a long family history here in this church. In fact, he was the 4th generation of his family to celebrate here at St. Peter's. But now, Joseph has a new home with our Heavenly Father." He held out his hands and smiled to the packed church. "We can all picture how comfortable Joseph is in his new home.

"All of us here today know how comfortable Joseph was in his homes. On the farm with his hat and boots on, with his animals and crops. Around the community, it was not unusual to see Joseph at as many sporting events as he could get to. He was an example for all of us — how to live and love life. We may miss him, but let us remember Joseph and give honor and glory to God, by not forgetting him. Joseph indeed lived up to the meaning of his name: 'Joseph - May God Add.'"

At Monsignor Mike's last words, there was total silence. Everyone present knew that he had said it all perfectly. Calm and comfort were beginning to overtake the sadness and suffering among everyone.

Before Communion, Monsignor Mike announced, "We cannot share Communion with those who are not of our faith. We do invite those who cannot to come forward and receive a blessing. When you get near, please fold your arms across your chest so I know the difference."

Leah went forward for the Blessing. He said, "May God be with you, may you receive his Blessings. May you turn to him in time of difficulty for his healing." With a touch on her forehead, Monsignor Mike finished with, "In the name of the Father and of the Son and of the Holy Spirit. Amen."

After the services and luncheon, Leah and her family set out for a tour of Frankton. She rattled on what she could remember about each milestone, trying to replicate the stories Joseph had told her. They all tried earnestly to absorb the history lesson, and before they realized it, they were headed into the countryside.

Finally Leah quieted down, and they took in the scenic area.

To everyone's surprise they came to a stop on the dirt road. The gate was closed and cattle were grazing on the corn stalks. Leah opened the door slowly and got out. George, Julie, and Nick did the same. Leah pointed, "Right there is where the picture of us and the combine was taken." She told them how Joseph could call the cows by honking the horn and calling them "Bossy," laughing at the memory. And, with shining eyes, she told them about the wildflower patch back in the pasture.

They stood there for almost half an hour, taking in the beauty that Joseph had loved so much. They had *known* him, but Leah had helped them *feel* his presence, giving them a glimpse into his world.

As they got back into the Blazer, Leah said, "I want to show you one more thing." They drove slowly, coming up on the mailbox, proudly

CHAPTER 28

displaying the name, Joseph P. Dreuel, R. 1 Box 32. They stopped at the mailbox, and looked toward the barn. Leah whispered, "This was going to be 'home.'" She did not say anything about the smile on the barn — she kept that for herself.

CHAPTER 29

George did not hire another guy at the station. He simply did what he could and let that be good enough.

Leah got back into the routine of her life. She made it a point to spend more time with Julie, even more aware now of what a true friend is: someone who feels what you are experiencing and is willing to share it with you.

Leah and Kate kept in touch, talking about once a month. Their talks never got too serious. They talked about the weeks of Thanksgiving and Christmas, and of course Kate talked about the weather. She could talk for hours about the cold and snow in the winter, and her hopes for an early spring.

Leah talked mostly about Nick and how school was going for him, that some Saturdays he would help George at the station.

Sometimes talking to Kate was joyous for Leah, and other times it was almost more pain than she could bear.

Leah didn't know what the holidays would have been with Joseph. She *did* know that there would have been Joseph's faith and church involved. He had told Monsignor Mike, without a second thought, that he would see Leah Thanksgiving or before.

Christmas, of course, was when everyone became more friendly and generous — more like her Joseph.

On Valentine's Day, Leah brought two red roses into work and put

CHAPTER 29

them on her desk. Throughout the day, she looked at the flowers, letting them lift her spirits. She had never received flowers on a regular basis before Joseph. Leah could only imagine how important a day Valentine's Day was to him.

With summer came the smell of freshly-cut grass — another reminder of Joseph.

Leah drove by the golf course and actually pulled into the golf course parking lot. She walked by as people were using the driving range, thinking about how Joseph could hit the golf balls so well.

Nick was not playing baseball that summer. Leah and Julie did go to a game because one of Nick's friends still played. That was only an excuse to go; Leah wanted to try to get a better sense of the game by Joseph's standards.

One long, sunny day in July, Leah asked Kate if she could visit. It would be one year since she first visited the farm, and Kate knew as much. "Of course. We would love to have you visit," she had said, warmly.

As the day drew near she became excited and anxious. The day of, she put her hair in a ponytail and put her Yankee's cap on. The drive was full of memories; all good, about the small, beautiful part of her life she had spent with Joseph.

As she crossed the Loup River bridge, her anxiety was replaced with a feeling of happiness that brought peace and comfort.

Kate's flowers were as plentiful and beautiful as last year. She met Leah at the door with another of her warm, welcoming hugs. After a short, pleasant visit, she instinctively headed in the direction toward Joseph's farm. There it was: *The Dirt Road*. She pulled into a field a short distance away and parked, getting out of the vehicle and walking just a little ways. As she stood and looked around, she noted that the corn looked even taller than last year's crop. It was beautiful, the tall dark green stalks. The ears of corn were looking back at her eye level. It looked like a good crop to her, she thought. And then she laughed. How could she tell? She only had a few days of harvest experience. She didn't laugh at herself for long, though, as Monsignor Mike's words came back to her. *"Don't count yourself short, at harvest every effort helps."* Leah smiled and thought, maybe she could help Daniel with harvest again that fall. She decided she didn't need to go see the smiling barn — she was already smiling here.

The visit's timing worked out perfectly for Leah to attend Saturday evening Mass at St. Peter's. As Leah entered the church, she dipped her right hand into the font. She made the sign of the Cross saying, "In the name of the Father and of the Son and of the Holy Spirit Amen."

She walked down the center aisle, three fourths the way up on the left side and genuflected. When she entered their pew, Leah knelt. Her first prayer as she glanced at the crucifix was the prayer that Jesus had taught when he was a man here on earth "Our Father."

Next, Leah looked at the statue of Mother Mary. As she had noticed before, a hand was extended forward. Leah looked at her face, and felt the peace in the expression; not an actual smile, but not a frown either. Leah said "Hail Mary full of grace."

In silence, Leah recited "Angel of God." When she finished, she glanced to her left, then to her right. She felt as if she was speaking to Joseph. She knew, physically, that he was not there, but spiritually she could feel his presence.

When it was time for Communion, she stood up and got in line. As she approached Monsignor Mike, she did not cross her arms on her chest. She put one hand forward. Monsignor Mike held up the Host and said "The Body of Christ."

Leah responded "Amen - I believe."

After Mass had ended, just like the times before, many of the congregation gathered in front of the church. Leah made an effort to speak to Monsignor Mike, who genuinely smiled and said, "It is nice to see you again Leah."

"Thank you."

He looked at her with a raised eyebrow. ""I couldn't help but notice that you received Communion."

CHAPTER 29

Leah broke into a grin. "I started convert classes last November."
"Well, congratulations, Leah. I'm very happy for you."
"Thank you. I am, too."
"Are you here for the weekend?"
"No, just for the day. I visited Kate this afternoon, and drove around for awhile, enjoying the countryside." She went on, "A year ago this weekend was the first time that I ever came out here."

Monsignor's comforting smile warmed her heart. "Please come back anytime, you are always welcome."

As Leah drove back to the city that evening, she let her feelings sweep over her. The past few months, she had felt a mix of confusing emotions — sadness, anger, sometimes happiness. That night, though, she wasn't feeling any of those things — she had finally understood what it was to be content.

ONE YEAR LATER

Nick graduated with a degree in Vehicle Repair and Paint Design. George had all but given the service station to Leah when Nick graduated, so they could have a place for their business.

With Nick's youth and enthusiasm, he was ready to take on any repair job.

Leah was excited and proud to have him in the business. This was a new chapter in her life. It had always been her and Nick — parent and child — now they were both adults, working together.

There were reminders of a past chapter in Leah's life all around. On the counter was a single red rose in a vase. On the break table was a tupperware container of M&Ms. On the wall behind Leah's desk in a frame was a poem titled *It All Reminds Me of You*. On Leah's desk was the picture of her and Joseph, standing in front of the combine during that wonderful, fleeting fall.

Sitting in the showroom of the shop was the first project that Nick finished in his new garage. Nick and Leah had taken it to some car shows for fun and to advertise the station.

The car was a 1969 Chevrolet Chevelle Super Sport car. It had an orange extension and a black interior. For originality, there were two senior keys hanging from the rear view mirror. On the passenger side was a carrier box, complete with well-worn eight track cassettes. In the back seat were two throw pillows, orange and black to match the car.

There were always three signs sitting in front of the Chevelle, whether it was at the shop or at shows. The first sign read:

1969 Chevelle Sport
Refinished at Nick's Repair
Lincoln, NE

The second sign read:
The Car's Nickname:
Country Pumpkin

The third sign read:
Previous Owner
Joseph Paul Dreul

On a particular Sunday evening in August at the City Collectors Car Show, Leah, Nick and George sat in the shade of a large tree. They were all smiles after just receiving the second place trophy for a Chevrolet car.

Also happy on that cool evening in his playpen among their lawn chairs, was a one-year-old, giggling, red-haired boy. Everyone called him by his nickname, "Little Joe." Everyone, that is, but his mother.

Leah always preferred his given name, Joseph.

ABOUT THE AUTHOR

Ron Dubas is a fourth generation farmer-rancher whose heart lives in the fields of the Great Plains, as well as on his sleeve. With a lifelong interest in local history and his family's stories, he shouldn't have been surprised when the seeds of a Nebraska romance began to blossom in his head. After 13 years of writing, wondering, and waiting, Ron is thrilled to be able to share *Wildflowers Beyond the Road* with his family, friends, and the friends he has yet to meet. Ron lives in Nance County — the place his family has called home since 1894 — with his beloved wife of 46 years. He's grateful for the land, this life, and the Lord that guides his way.